Y0-EDN-223

Matapalo

Daniel Lechner

To My Wife Patty

Preface

A most unusual tree can be found in Central America. It begins life in the branches of a healthy existing tree, sends roots to the ground, and then gradually grows to envelope the host tree. From the onset, the host tree is doomed. It eventually dies. The Matapalo Tree remains.

PART ONE

Chapter One

What a glorious time to be alive! Everything is in place for the most Blessed Generation in history, the Baby Boomer Generation, to step onto the stage of life . . . a stage set in place by the great sacrifices of all that have come before them. The waltz is about to begin. The great peace dividend of World War-II will provide the music, and it must be played, and played, and played.

War is only a recent memory. Most of Europe is in serious economic and social distress, in need of a complete rebuild. U.S. factories, saved from war-time destruction, can provide the goods that are needed. U.S. farmers can provide the food to feed the hungry. Prosperity will pour into the land while the music plays on and on. Such a world will greet the Blessed Generation. They will know nothing else.

In the American heartland lies a picturesque mid-sized town called Blissville, a place where world events are no longer noticed. Here residents are just tired of hearing about problems. The War is over, and for them, it's time to get back to work. A decade and a half of pent up demand for consumer goods must be satisfied. "Get to work, and work overtime if you must, but get to work! Make your own way! Opportunity is everywhere. Make it happen! That's what is important here. The factory is humming. Get moving!"

Elsewhere in the world, in Europe, there is no "Heartland," and there is no place called Blissville. Here, chaos coexists with ruin. There is little opportunity, and little freedom to move forward. Society is completely broken after years of warfare. It must be fixed quickly. Only order is important going forward. The life must be restored. It is time for the good life once again! Guarantees shall be the means! Government shall provide the guarantees!

In the "Heartland," in the community called Blissville, residents have no need for guarantees. Opportunity is everywhere. Life is about to move rapidly forward; one must only jump on and hitch a ride.

To those in the outside world, this place called Blissville is not real.

Chapter Two

Blissville appears so tranquil at this moment in time. At the edge of town corn fields gradually give rise to isolated houses, and then to perfectly manicured neighborhoods composed of homes which are some 15-20 years old. Some are completely brick with ivy climbing the outer walls, very English looking. Sidewalks on tree-lined streets are cluttered with play wagons and tricycles, left by trusting little owners during lunch time. It is September, the best month of the year, and a time when all is forgotten while embracing one last moment of sunshine before school begins and the colder months set in. Tomorrow is the first day of school here, and for The Blessed Generation, the first day of life. Up to now, life has been composed of a close family circle and a neighborhood of friends, but tomorrow all that will change. Tomorrow the Blessed Generation meets the world in the halls of Ivy Grade School!

Ivy Grade School sits atop a hill overlooking a long ravine. A small stream trickles below. The school is a left over from a former time of plenty, the late 1920's, when excesses prevailed and manifested themselves in pretentious construction projects, such as an ivy tower on this grade school.   Now 25 years old, it visually looks as though it hasn't changed in 200 years. Constructed totally of brick and sandstone, it gives at once a stately, regal aura of importance.   Such is the effect of timeless construction. Such is the effect of this anchor to the community.

September is such a beautiful month in the "Heartland." On this first day of school, a rising sun peeks over the school yard and welcomes returning students, one by one, excited to see class mates once again and renew friendships. All older students know what to do. Upon hearing the bell at 8:15, they at once begin to file into the school. It is now that a group of parents are seen bringing the youngest children to the entry door, wondering where the room, which is to be the kindergarten, can be found.

Ivy's kindergarten is located on the first floor, a very long room, overlooking the ravine. It is the personal sanctuary of Miss Uppryte, a long-time teacher at Ivy, who is known by just about everyone in town. It's surprising how she has affected so many lives, and continues to do so to this day.

As parents enter the room, they immediately see a play house area complete with furniture and tableware. A small pedal car is parked against the far wall. Stop and go traffic signs are nearby. Toward the middle matapalo[1] of the room is a piano and Miss Uppryte's desk. Still further are small table desks with little stools, able to accommodate eight students each.   Huge glass windows stretch along the outside wall, giving a continual view of nature and weather to those inside. The most imposing feature in the room is a long row of cabinets with glass framed doors, on the inner wall. They are empty now, but soon will contain the little throw rugs that each student will bring to accommodate a short nap, as well as a year's accumulation of art work.

Finally, a lone door is seen at the farthest end of the room. We will soon know its function.

---

[1] 1935 Social Security Act

At 8:30 a.m. sharp, the school bell rings once again. Miss Uppryte walks to the piano where she retrieves a major piece of kindergarten equipment. It is a series of three bells attached to a strip of steel, all in chrome. This item means business! Miss Uppryte jingles the bells for attention.

"Listen children, when you hear these bells, all talking must cease, and you must give me your full attention. Does everyone know what full attention means?"

A few heads nod. Miss Uppryte continues.

"Welcome to your first day of school. We are going to have such a wonderful year. If you are feeling a slight bit uneasy right now, I know in a few days you will feel most comfortable with your new classmates and Ivy Grade School. Now, I want everyone matapalo[2] to come to the area in front of the piano and sit Indian style on the floor. Indian style is crossing your legs."

The children move forward.

"Can everyone see the door at the far end of the room?"

Miss Uppryte walks toward it, and stops.

"Do you notice the door is cracked open?

Heads nod in agreement.

"This is the bathroom. When you need to use it, just raise your hand for permission. When you are in the bathroom, please close the door. When leaving, keep the door *ajar*, like this. See, the door is now *ajar*."

What a teaching moment! There is not one student in a hundred, or one in a thousand, that can look back and recall the very first word learned in school. Every student who has ever attended kindergarten at Ivy knows immediately what that word is. *Ajar!*

"Ouch!"

A slight altercation grabs everyone's attention! It is centered near a cute little female with dark hair, and apparently is one of those incidents that are life threatening

---

[2] 1934 National Housing Act

11

at an age-five moment, but are completely forgotten 20 seconds later. The little girl wanted the boy in front of her to move over, so took matters into her own hands. Meet little Irene Funka.

Irene is from a family that has recently become American citizens. They were all displaced during the War, and having absolutely nothing to their name, were sponsored by the local Catholic Church and brought to the United States. Blissville has been a true blessing for them, something far beyond their wildest dreams. Her father, Frank, was able to find work immediately, and it wasn't long before they were able to purchase a modest bungalow that they now call home. It was here that Irene was born. Her family is an American success story in the making.

Miss Uppryte, of course, knows exactly how to react with the situation at hand.

"Irene, if you want something, always raise your hand to ask. That is how we must behave in school."

Sensing another teaching moment, Miss Uppryte moves toward a small chair beside her desk.

"Children, this chair is called the *time out* chair. If one of you misbehaves, I will ask you to sit in this chair for a time to settle down. That's why we call it the *time out* chair."

Thirty little heads nod in agreement.

A second item of business is now addressed. Each student has with him a small rolled-up throw rug. As previously noted, this is for taking a short 20 minute nap matapalo[3] mid-way thru the day. Miss Uppryte instructs each pupil to bring his rug to the cabinet along the wall, and places each in its own, special spot.

"Children, remember exactly where your rug is so you can retrieve it tomorrow!"

With the business part of the day now complete, Miss Uppryte knows it is time to lighten up and allow each child

---

[3] 1935 Walsh-Healy Public Contracts Act

to begin knowing the other children around him. She does this so expertly with a combination of story-telling, piano playing, singing, and acting. The children are beginning to love her. How quickly they are adjusting to themselves and to their surroundings; that is, all but one boy, who seems so detached and introverted. He is the boy involved in the scrape with Irene Funka a few moments ago, and so we now meet Stanley Vincent.

Stanley is a scrawny lad with brown hair and freckles. He seems somewhat younger than the others, possibly because his early life has been in turmoil. He lives with his single mother who works two jobs, and has been raised mostly by his grandmother since his parents separated two years ago. He hardly knows his father. Some children just seem a half step out of phase. Miss Uppryte will need to give extra attention here. Seeing her detached little pupil, Miss Uppryte makes another positive teaching moment.

"Will someone like to assist me on the piano? Stanley, come up and sit beside me."

As a befuddled Stanley arrives, Miss Uppryte instructs him where the notes "C" and "E" are on the keyboard.

"Put your thumb here, and your index finger there, and when I nod, play both notes together like this."

Miss Uppryte begins playing a little ditty, nods to Stanley, who then plays his very first notes! For Stanley, lightning has just crashed thru the room. Music can do this, and suddenly the little boy, with no sense of anything, is completely hooked. Stanly becomes somewhat of an instant sensation to his new classmates. He has found a place in the world and from this moment on, music is all he will want to talk about.

At this point in the morning Miss Uppryte announces that play time has arrived. To a 5-year old, these are the sweetest words that can be heard. The girls automatically gravitate to the play house, the boys to the pedal car. One female can be seen arranging the table, appearing so gracious, if that term can be applied to a 5-year old. The other girls seem to accept her manner, and follow along. Meet Mary Beth Blossom.

Mary Beth's family is upper middle class and lives in one of the well-kept homes on the far west side of town. Her father works at First Trust Company as Sr. Loan officer for real estate. Born and raised on a local farm, he quickly chose the city life-style after graduation from college, and started his business career at First Trust, rising in stature quickly. Her mother, a beauty as a young lady, works in a local real estate office.

The boys, surrounding the pedal car, are listening to comments about horse power, ventured forth by a young male, who obviously has heard something about the subject, even though he has no idea what it all means.
Meet Russell Murphy.

Russell's family owns the local Chevrolet dealership. His grandfather, Sean, saw an opportunity immediately following World War I, and jumped on the Chevrolet bandwagon early on, at a time when everything was Ford, Ford, and more Ford. The dealership grew during the 20's, and survived the depression matapalo [4] by emphasizing maintenance and used car sales to supplement the few new car sales. It limped along until after World War II, when suddenly the market changed, and every single car that was available was sold at sticker price, and sometimes above sticker price. The profits rolled in. His family recently purchased a magnificent house in the best part of the city. His father, Lindsay, is head of new car sales.

On this first day of school, it is hard to imagine the personalities that will someday develop in each student. They are just children now, experiencing and learning about life in the safety of their school, their town, and their country. But . . . even now, one boy stands out above the

---

[4] 1935 Wagner Act

others. He is very fair skinned, larger than the other children, and has such a presence of confidence and leadership about him that surely great things will come someday. Meet Guy Hartmann Jr.

Guy's family has been in Blissville from the very beginning. They were all early settlers, pioneers, in the newfound territory which later became this state. Enduring constant hardship, but prospering never the less, they farmed many acres successfully. When the canal arrived, a new mode of locomotion for goods was possible, so they started a dairy. It originally consisted solely of cheese products, but expanded over the years to milk and butter, becoming a dominant regional force. Guy's father is the president, with extended family members matapalo[5] in various supporting functions.

These are the young members of the Blessed Generation. They will find order and opportunity in their world. They will leisurely experience childhood and young adulthood. There is no hurry for them. All will enjoy the good life. There will be no need for guarantees. All will be taught to make their way in the world, just as prior generations have done. Their journey begins now. The music is playing.

---

[5] 1946 Employment act

Chapter Three

Brown paper covers the glass display windows at Murphy Chevrolet. Something big is on the horizon. Late September has arrived. Cooler temperatures signal a change, and the change inside Murphy Chevrolet is hectic preparation for the new 1955 models. The general public will not be allowed to see them until the official unveiling date, when dealers all across the land will open their doors for public viewing of the new models.

The automobile! Oh, what it does to people! Life in Blissville, and everywhere, is completely woven in and around this marvel; the country is totally intoxicated with automobiles. Tomorrow will be the day! That is when the new 1955 Chevrolets will be introduced.

It is early morning at Ivy grade school. Crowds of students, both male and female, gather around a spectacular looking new vehicle. Loud Rock and Roll music blares from its radio speakers. The top is down. A pleasant rumble is heard coming from the new V-8 engine. It is like nothing they have ever seen, so shiny, so colorful. The 1955 Chevrolet Bel Air convertible has arrived. Part of the introduction process of new models is driving, and to be seen driving, so Lindsay Murphy, as sales manager at

Murphy Chevrolet, is doing his part by driving Russell to school this matapalo[6] morning. Little Russell pops out of the front seat, and smugly smiles to the crowd, to great approval.

"This convertible is loaded," Russell announces to the eighth grade boys. "It has a 265 cu in V-8 engine and a rear seat radio speaker."

The boys don't need to be told. They can hear loud notes of *"Shake, Rattle, and Role"* being broadcast at this very moment above the rumble of the engine. What excitement!

If anyone cares to look further, the build sheet is pasted to the backseat window and shows automatic transmission, electric power windows, heater and defroster, outside rear view mirrors, power steering, power brakes, push button radio, windshield washer, and brown vinyl seating to match the two-tone color of Shadow Gray and Coral. It is fair to say that all these extras total the cost of another car, but who cares when you're the only one in the neighborhood to have them! They're fresh, alive, and new. You're somebody. You're important. That's what counts. That's what automobiles do to people.

By now the crowd is huge; exactly what marketing men at General Motors want to see. Lindsay Russell is getting thousands of dollars of advertising for free, and it is the best kind of advertising of all, word of mouth!

A ringing school bell echoes from the other end of the playground signaling it is time to depart; one by one members of the crowd peel off and head to class. The eighth grade boys are the last to leave, accompanied by Russell who is reciting facts about the new car.

"The vinyl seats are completely waterproof and can be washed easily!"

How strange it is for a kindergarten student to be seen explaining these things to older boys. A quick backward

---

[6] 1949 Fair Labor Standards Amendment

glance by all bids fair well to the object of their dreams, as it disappears into traffic.

In class this morning the buzz of the new car continues, amplified by Russell as he speaks to his classmates during "Show And Tell."

"My name is Russell and I want to sell you a new Chevrolet?"

Where did that come from? It doesn't compute to a kindergarten student, but maybe is a hint of some future greatness, in sales.

Miss Uppryte, having no idea previously of this landmark day, has planned a special event for the morning in her own right. Students will be introduced to finger painting! Finger painting is a discipline that is approached in just one place in life, kindergarten. Never seen before, and never afterward, it's now or never. For sure it should be the latter, because the results are things of beauty only a mother can love. Children rather like it because they get to create something on paper with their hands, getting messy at the same time. Perfect.

The project begins with large sheets of white paper pinned to cardboard on an easel. The student dons a smock for protection and immerses a hand in liquid paint that has been thinned somewhat with water. That's the easy part. The tricky part for a five year old, is to somehow get the hand from the paint jar to the paper, where it may be used as a paint brush to create a Van Gogh-like masterpiece. Good luck!

Since there are just two easels, only two students are allowed to paint at one time; all the others must busy themselves with crayons. They may be asked to paint tomorrow, or the next day, or the next until all have had the opportunity to try. Today Miss Uppryte selects Mary Beth Blossom and Stanley Vincent. They are each outfitted with a smock, instructed on the proper protocol, and left to create something very special. Oh, we wish!

Miss Uppryte begins passing out paper and crayons to the other children.

"No, Stanley! No! No! Stanley! Miss Uppryte!"

Eyes are directed toward the easel area. Mary Beth has a blue nose! Stanley has transferred his work space to Mary Beth's face. What a reaction! This is what art is all about. You must feel it for it to be great. It must stir deep within you. It must provoke emotion. By any yardstick, Stanley's work is a masterpiece. Only it is on the wrong canvas!

Miss Uppryte rushes to the scene. Stanley, smock and all, goes directly to the time out Chair. Mary Beth is hurried to the door at the far end of the room, being at this time *ajar*, and cleaned up at the wash basin, all while loud sounds of laughter and giggling permeate the room. What a day!

When order is restored, Miss Uppryte decides to begin nap time a little early as a possible way to regain control of the situation, before it gets completely of hand. She calls upon the one student she knows can assist her in this process, Guy Hartmann.

"Guy, will you help me and be in charge of passing out the rugs, please?"

Guy springs up, moves to the cabinets, and very professionally organizes the operation in such a quiet manner that it isn't even noticed that the job at hand is completed. Calm matapalo[7] spreads over the room, well at least most of the room. Irene Funka can't settle down. Low whispers and giggling are heard from the rear. She is trying to teach the girl next to her the words to *"Sh-Boom"* by the Crew Cuts, possibly as a way to describe Stanley's descent upon the time out Chair. Miss Uppryte softly jingles the bells. All is quiet.

---

[7] 1954 Federal Unemployment Tax Act

Chapter Four

For a five-year old Christmas is the magical time of the year. In Blissville nothing defines childhood as does Christmas, which consists of anticipation, waiting, anticipation, and more waiting. To be sure, from this point forward some skepticism will surround the phenomenon of Santa Claus; in one or two years kindergarten children will begin to join with older children and adults in perpetuating the centuries old tradition on the then youngest of them. But for now, it is their time.

Total focus is on the eighth floor at Schafer's department store, where Toyland is located. When the elevator door opens, one senses a totally different world, a world absent problems, a world only of diversion and happiness. It's a quintessential experience. Quintessential sells toys! School children can hardly wait to come here. Sounds of electric trains running on tracks are heard. Soft, happy, Christmas music plays in the background. Smells from candles caress olfactory senses. Free Christmas red and white striped candy is for the asking. Lighting, so bright and perfect, makes every item seem bigger than life. Glitter is everywhere. Touching a toy completes the circle, and the quintessential experience. Children's eyes light up, they are so enthralled.

Look, at the rear of the room sits Santa Claus, white beard and all, dressed in red attire on a throne-like chair, willing and waiting for children to come to him asking for something special. A white-picket fence surrounds the entire area making it seem so mysterious, a place where only children and Santa Claus are allowed at this time of year. Patiently waiting in line are a half dozen children with their parents, in front of the bright red carpet which leads to the spot where Santa Claus is seated. The third child in line is Mary Beth Blossom. When her turn comes, she scampers up to Santa Claus and sits on his knee.

"What is on your mind today? Is there something you would like Santa to do for you? Just whisper your secret into Santa's ear."

Those words are hardly out of Santa's mouth before Mary Beth whispers a secret request. Santa chuckles! "Let's see what Santa can do for you." A quick photo records the interview, and it is the next child's turn.

"Mary Beth!"

A loud shout comes from across the room. It's Stanley with his grandmother, having just arrived at Toyland.

"Have you seen the trains? Come, look at these."

Mary Beth scurries across the room and soon both classmates are darting from display to display like bumblebees in a flower garden. They see wild-west outfits, doll houses, fire trucks, Lincoln Logs, and all things of interest to children of this age. Where else in the world can children be so completely happy and free?

"Stanley, have you talked to Santa Claus yet? You've got to go see him now."

With that they go off to the waiting line. Stanley is ushered to Santa's lap, and greeted, "What is on your mind today? Is there something you would like Santa to do for you? Just whisper your secret into Santa's ear."

Sometimes a 5-year old is wise beyond his years, and

Stanley certainly is beginning to suspect something is not quite right here. A normal reaction from a child of this age is about to occur. No thinking, no examining, just reacting. Stanley doesn't whisper into Santa's ear at all. He gives a giant tug on Santa's white beard. Off it comes onto the floor, causing such a commotion, that the whole endeavor has to be shut down for a time. Stanley's grandmother is aghast. Mary Beth is crying. Santa is seen tromping off. Store security is called to restore order. "Oh children, what will they do next?"

"Show And Tell" the next morning at school is interesting. Mary Beth can hardly wait to relay the events of the previous evening to her classmates, and graphically explains to eager young ears exactly what had transpired at Toyland. Of course, Stanley basks in all the fresh new attention, but looks somewhat sheepish when Miss Uppryte can hardly condone his act, and does her best to end this discussion and get on to another topic.

A popular school tradition at Ivy is the singing of Christmas Carols by the entire school on the last day before Christmas break. Instead of meeting in the auditorium, a more intimate setting is achieved by gathering around the Christmas tree which is located in front of the Principal's office in the Tower part of the building. A giant spiral staircase descends from the second floor to the first, and it is here that the 5th, 6th, 7th, and 8th grade students congregate, looking down upon the lower grade students, who are seated on the floor below. As each class files in and is seated in respective places, Miss Uppryte adjusts the music at the piano. Stanley is seated beside her as special page turner, looking so important.

Miss Flint, Ivy's aging principal, greets all students and initiates the festivities by announcing, "Let's sing *'Jingle Bells.'*" The piano plays and some six hundred voices respond in unison. Pretty impressive moment! To our kindergarten class, sitting on the floor Indian style in front of the piano, Awesome! These are the moments children remember.

Many other favorite Carols follow. Stanley does his best trying to keep the music pages turned for Miss Uppryte. With the older students leading the way for the younger to follow, Russell, Irene, Mary Beth, and Guy join with other kindergarten children in singing whole heartedly. Finally, *"Silent Night"* will be the last, and Miss Uppryte plays it especially enchantingly. After the final refrain, *"sleep in heavenly peace,"* she asks, "The second verse?"

Things become a little sketchy at this point, but Guy Hartmann rises and sings the entire verse solo, in front of six hundred students! The entire student body is awe struck. How do you explain such a thing from a 5 year old?

Ten minutes later, back in the kindergarten, talk is still about Guy's solo. Miss Uppryte compliments him profusely in front of all the other students, making a positive teaching moment for others to follow as it relates to initiative and courage. What is surprising is the fact that Guy takes it all in stride, doesn't boast, and doesn't try to use it for any kind of personal gain. The very first signs of leadership are appearing in this young man.

On this last day of school before Christmas break, it is only befitting that small snow flurries begin to appear against the long windows. This is what makes Christmas in the northern states. In a few hours four inches of snow will accumulate to the joy of all these young people. It truly is a magical time of year.

Chapter Five

The Funka family home on Maple Street is quite modest.
It's all decked out for the holidays, and is just as pleasant as
one can imagine. In the living room a tall Christmas tree
shines with lights, ornaments, and a lighted angel atop.
Shiny tinsel finishes the decoration. Underneath are
presents, wrapped and ready for Christmas. On the mantle
a manger scene signifies the religious aspect of Christmas.
Fresh pine scents are all about the living room. Furniture
consists of a plain couch and two chairs. To the left of the
living room is a small dining room; opposite the dining
room is the kitchen which looks very 1920ish, but
functional. Three rear bed rooms and a bathroom complete
the floor plan.

Suddenly, Shafer's Department Store delivery truck
backs slowly into the driveway. It's the middle of winter,
and the front door of the house is wide open. What could
be happening?

Two men carrying a large packing box are seen entering
the house. A husky voice signals, "Careful, Buster, in
getting thru that door!" The item of interest in the box
quickly emerges. It is a brand new 17 inch Zenith black
and white television set, just in time for Christmas! Things

are about to change in this little bungalow forever.

Irene and her two siblings jump for joy; "Daddy, hurry, hurry, turn it on!"

Frank moves the TV to the corner opposite the Christmas tree, stands back for a moment and smiles.

"How does this look, Sophie? Now our family won't be the only one in the neighborhood without a TV!"

Frank attaches a temporary "rabbit ears" aerial to the TV, plugs the cord into the wall, and presto, a picture! Sound! It's a test pattern! The children sit on the floor not two feet from the screen, watching. Not a word is uttered. Anticipation! Waiting! The children's eyes have not once moved from the TV screen, watching a test pattern!

Sophie emerges from the kitchen and begins setting up strange little tables in front of the TV. Shortly she brings a hot meal, served in a compartmentalized aluminum container, and places it on one of the funny looking tables. Her family will be eating dinner soon, a TV dinner, on TV Trays, watching their new TV. For this first generation immigrant family, how much more American can it get than that? It is Thursday, and a popular program for children, *"Kukla, Fran, and Ollie,"* will soon air, so all must be ready.

This is a hardworking American family that has much to be thankful for this Christmas season. They are basking in its glow right now; soon they will be enjoying their first ever full evening of television with *"The Lone Ranger,"* and later, *"Dragnet."* No one will leave the living room this evening.

Chapter Six

Seven inches of fresh snow and it's a Saturday! What a combination for children. There will certainly be a large crowd at Ivy Hill today!

Children in warm climates have no idea what winter snow is, and what fun occurs when it's falling. This is a time of year when entire families spend quality time together for little or no cost. Winter sports are invigorating; the cold isn't even noticed if dressed properly.

Already it is mid-day and Ivy Hill is packed with sleds and a few toboggans. Toboggans are long wooden-planked sleds with curved front ends, and capable of carrying six to eight people down the hill together. Riders sit, locking their legs around the person in front of them. Toboggans pack the snow down as they go, making a smooth highway for all the sleds. With sleds, it's different. Some riders sit up-right, but since that is quite unstable, most just lie on their stomachs and glide down the hill. A few brave souls make a running start to gain maximum speed. Sleds gain speed all the way down the hill, and then just coast until coming to rest some distance from where they started.

Look! Guy Hartmann and his father are here. Russell Murphy and his father are just now approaching; so is the entire Funka family. This promises to be a great afternoon.

Russell carries a new sled he received for Christmas. Immediately the older boys notice. They all shout out at once, *"It's a Flexible Flyer."* All the boys know this is just about the fastest thing on the hill. Not only fast, but able to turn, something few other sleds can do. There are some other Flyers about; one, a very old model, larger and higher than the rest, is "greased lightning" on steel runners. Speed gets everyone's attention.

Lindsay Murphy begins to instruct Russell on the fine points of sledding.

"Russell, don't be afraid of the speed; don't close your eyes. Just keep your hands here on the steering mechanism, and turn it in the direction you wish to go, like this. It's very easy. Are you ready, Russell?"

Russell doesn't know what to expect, although he knows he doesn't want to sit up. He wants to lie on his stomach, having seen the older boys doing so. Russell indicates he is ready, and Lindsay easily pushes the sled for a start. *Whoosh*, Russell is off! Down, down, down the hill . . . faster, faster, and faster he goes. In what seems like a fraction of a second he reaches the creek, instinctively turns at the last moment, and the ride is over. If fast is dangerous, too fast is just about right! Russell instantly becomes hooked on speed! The other sleds he passed are just now catching up.

Guy Hartmann Sr., noticing that Irene's family has just one small sled, yells out, "Why not join us in toboggan rides? We have plenty of room."

Irene is on the toboggan, almost before Guy can finish speaking. She wants to be first. The toboggan is quickly loaded; Guy Jr. is seated behind her on the first try. When all is ready, they are pushed off; the toboggan starts slowly, but gains speed further and further down the hill. Screams of excitement sound as speed increases, faster and faster they go. The ride ends far short of the creek, which is some fifty feet in the distance. Guy and Irene are euphoric in their ride.

By now, Russell has become a real pro on his Flyer; he's joined some of the older boys in racing. They make light of passing and weaving around every other moving object as they shoot down the hill. It is great sport.

Mary Beth Blossom and her father just now arrive at hill top. Wild greetings about the day's events are exchanged by all the children. They can hardly talk, trying to say so much at once. Irene yells, "Let's all try to go down the hill on the toboggan together. That would be so cool." Others agree. It's a great idea!

Irene quickly makes the preparations. "Mary Beth will be first, I'm second, Guy third, my brother and sister fourth and fifth, Daddy sixth, and Mr. Hartmann last." With so many riders included on the toboggan, everyone has to scrunch a little tighter than usual. Somehow, all seven riders are packed into the six-man toboggan.

What? A challenge is made! One of the older boys on a Flyer yells out, "We'll give you a head start and still beat you to the creek!"

All on the toboggan boisterously accept the challenge. "No way will you be able to catch us! You will never catch us!"

The loaded toboggan is heavy, very heavy. Three men are needed to push start, but now slowly, ever so slowly, the toboggan begins to coast down the hill. Its occupants push together, holding on very tightly. Speed increases. They feel the wind. They feel more wind. Something is different, the extra weight! More speed, more and more. They are flying, really blazing. This is the ride of the day.

The boys on the Flyers make a running start. *Whoosh, whoosh, whoosh, whoosh,* they're off. Down the hill they come, gaining on the toboggan, faster and faster. Can they catch it? The largest Flyer is almost even. Now it passes and cuts directly in front, avoiding a collision by inches.

The next two do the same. Screams come from the toboggan. It is running out of real estate. The creek looms closer and closer. No way to stop. Russell pulls alongside, passes, and cuts in front with just enough room to avoid plunging into the creek. The toboggan, now half on land and half in air, *cracks*, splits in two, and the front three passengers cascade downward, thru the thin ice into the shallow water below.

Loud yells echo from the water. "Oh, it is so ice cold!" Mary Beth, being first, is the wettest. She is soaked. Guy pulls her out and helps her to the outstretched hands of his father. Mary Beth is pulled up, followed by Irene, and finally Guy. A crowd gathers, gawking at the remains of the toboggan below and three soaking children. Mary Beth, shaking, is hurriedly carried up the hill by Guy Sr. and placed into a warm car. It's time to leave!

"Everyone is invited to the farm for hot chocolate and a blazing fire," shouts Guy Sr. Shouts of approval follow by all.

In just minutes a small caravan of cars arrives at Guy's house, and pulls into the long driveway. Oak trees line a path from the street to an old stone farm house that has been in place for some one hundred years. One senses stability here. The structure was built to last. Out back stands a very impressive red barn, for this is still a working farm. Florence Hartmann greets all of the incoming snowmen at the front door, and immediately rushes Mary Beth off for a change to dry clothing. The others head for the fireplace in a cozy family room, and lots of hot chocolate to warm up.

Russell exclaims, "My sled is so fast. I was just able to miss going in. Boy was I lucky." The others laugh and then talk of the broken toboggan crashing into the icy water.

During the next hour, one by one, all of the parents arrive, bringing with them some pot luck offerings for dinner. Florence has quickly arranged this little party. She sets up a buffet table, and the children immediately "dig in." Russell is the first. He heaps his plate with hot dogs, baked beans, and potato salad. No one says anything; everyone is too busy eating. Afterwards, marshmallows are roasted on the fire. The parents, meanwhile, congregate in front of the fire, relaxing and talking about the day's events.

This day has turned into a wonderful social outing in this family based community. What could have been a very ugly incident, has been turned into a most positive outcome. That's just the way things happen in Blissville, a town with strong family ties and a solid value system.

Chapter Seven

Winter has vanished; spring has arrived in Blissville.
Shoots of new green grass are visible. Dandelions are
everywhere. Children play on the sidewalks again, for it is
a time of renewal. During the last nine months Miss
Uppryte has brought the Blessed Generation into this
world. It's a world in which they still know very little, but
a world changing very, very rapidly. For them, life is still
only a dance, a dance of never ending pleasant experiences.
They waltz on and on, because their stage has already been
set. They are experiencing the benefits of the peace
dividend from the War. Oh, if it only could remain this
way forever!

Today is the final day of school. Miss Uppryte walks
toward the glass cabinets to retrieve the throw rugs one last
time. Each is looking somewhat worn by now. She passes
out the year's accumulated art work. We can see each child
holding their "finger painting," as though it is the most
valuable item in the world. The bell rings, and it is over.
They are now first graders.

The greatest advancement this year has been seen in
Stanley. In September he was a severely introverted lad,
but has now become an adventurous and outgoing

youngster, thanks to the steady hand of Miss Uppryte. Stanley has shown a terrific aptitude for music. He must corral and refine it to reach his full potential.

Irene has exhibited great people organizational skills. She has a very strong personality which can literally control events, and a knack for persuasion acceptable to others. Other children follow what she says. Always she is the organizer of events, always she pushes the envelope, always she is in the forefront. She seems to know exactly what others are thinking. Irene is a very smart young lady.

Russell loves cars. What else is there to say? He knows them all. He knows the year. He knows the specs. He knows the cost. He can talk about any at a moment's notice. This is his passion. He is truly in concert with the times he is living. A perfect fit.

Mary Beth is the docile one. She goes with the flow. She doesn't upset others, and she is easy to get along with. She is very pretty and thus popular with all the other girls. Mary Beth is just the girl that other girls want to be. She is never lonely.

Guy is the pillar. He doesn't say much, doesn't venture outside prescribed guidelines, is never a disciplinary problem, and seems to completely know what he is about. He is a leader, and leads by example. The other boys just follow after him. Nothing said.

These are the children that Miss Uppryte will hand off to the world. These are her children. Each will carry something of her as they progress down their highway of life. They might not know it yet, but she will be guiding them forever.

Chapter Eight

Seven years have passed, and Miss Uppryte's special generation is about to enter the eighth grade. Much has happened in the intervening years, but at Ivy Grade School the first day of school is like all the others before. Nothing seems to change here. "A rising sun peeks over the school yard and welcomes returning students, one by one, excited to see class mates once again and renew friendships. All older students know what to do, and upon hearing the bell at 8:15, begin to file into the school."

The Blessed Generation is now on top of the ladder. They are still children, to be sure, but they are beginning to break away into the exciting and unknown world of adult society. Always there remain the safety nets of childhood, if things become too frightening or confusing on the adult side. This is what makes this year so special.

This will be a defining year, a year in which a hint of each as an adult will appear. All are still walking down the same road together, but now there are some off shoots. Each is beginning to develop an adult personality. The music plays on and on.

Chapter Nine

Mrs. Timbers looks thru her reading glasses. A "snickering" noise is coming from boys in the rear of the room. Something is up! We are about to hear her response to this, and to everything else in life, *"Listen, listen, I hear talking!"* Heads turn. Stanley appears to be up to no good, his eyes are darting from one boy to the next.

Today is Friday, and that means "Science Experiment Day!" Every Friday five students demonstrate a principle of science by performing an experiment in front of the class. Mrs. Timbers dictates all the experiments on Monday, and has the students write them down in their matapalo [8] notebooks. On Thursday she selects the five students. Their job is to practice the experiment at home Thursday evening, and perform it Friday for the class. Mary Beth and Stanley are among the five selected today.

First up is a plump, rather scholarly looking girl with thick glasses named Rachael. She has selected "Experimenting with Static Electricity," and walks to the front of the class. After producing two balloons, she proceeds to blow them up and tie the ends. Now, she needs

---

[8] 1958 Transportation Act

an assistant. *Do not select a girl!* This will be too embarrassing. Only a boy will do. Select someone you really want to humiliate, or someone you really want to notice you, or both. Russell will do just fine.

"Russell, please come up!"

Russell walks up to the front of the room. Rachael rubs each balloon on a piece of wool. The balloons repel each other. She then rubs the balloons on the wool a second time, for several seconds, and places them near Russell's hair. *Whooah*, his hair stands on end! A perfect experiment! Rachael goes on to explain something about negatively charged particles (electrons) jumping to positively charged objects, but no one is listening because the focus is solely on Russell's hair. It's a mess. Mission accomplished. Mrs. Timbers nods approvingly. "Thank you, Rachael."

Two other experiments follow, one about "Gravity Free Water," and the other, "Exploring Acids and Bases." Nothing spectacular is noted in each. It is now Mary Beth's turn. She has selected "Making Lemonade Fizzy Drink." The girls all love this one, and Mrs. Timbers will have to watch it over and over, week after week, to the end of the school year. Mary Beth begins the experiment by pouring the juice of one lemon into a small glass. She then adds a small amount of water and a teaspoon of sugar, stirring. Here comes the fun part. She mixes in a teaspoon of baking soda, and voila, bubbles of CO_2, and a carbonated lemon flavored soft drink! Mary Beth explains, "the baking soda (base) reacted with the lemon juice (acid) to form CO_2, which is also the same thing found in a soft drink." The girls love it, so does Mrs. Timbers. "Excellent job, Mary Beth." The results are passed around for a taste.

Uneasiness grips the room, for it is Stanley's turn. His appearance has been wildly anticipated by the boys for the whole period. Now it's "Show Time!" Stanley slowly walks to the front of the room, and very carefully unloads his experiment apparatus from a bag. Stanley announces to the class, "I will do two experiments today, both involving eggs." More restlessness is heard in the rear of the room. Mrs. Timbers is beginning to wonder what is going on; she surely is about to find out. Experiments with eggs are a really bad idea. Stanley confidently speaks to the class. "My first experiment is titled, 'Make an Egg Float on Salt Water;' the second is 'A Demonstration of Air Pressure.'"

What the boys know, and Mrs. Timbers does not, is that Stanley secretly removed the inside of the egg for the first experiment last night, and then covered the hole with airplane glue. He has also carefully brought a raw egg, with its shell sliced by a razor blade, for the second experiment.

For his magic to work, Stanley must be the consummate showman. He carefully places himself between the experiment and Mrs. Timbers' view. Like a magician with great confidence and flair, he explains to the class, "Salt water is denser than fresh water. The greater buoyancy provided by the salt water will allow the egg to float." Mrs. Timbers nods. "Now for my demonstration," he says very authoritatively. Stanley fills a glass a third full with fresh water, adds six tablespoons of salt, and stirs. Next he fills the glass another third with fresh water, being *very* careful not to mix the two layers. "I will now demonstrate that an egg will sink thru the upper less dense water layer, but float on the denser salt water layer because of its greater bouncy. With great panache he produces the hollow egg and places matapalo[9] it on the upper water layer.

It floats! Some laughter is heard. Stanley exclaims, "What has happened?" He plays the class beautifully. "I don't understand this!" Great laughter is heard. Just the reaction he was hoping for. "This can't be!" The boys are going crazy in the back of the room.

---

[9] 1960 Sustained Yield Act

Mrs. Timbers looks thru her glasses, not amused, but can't see anything. *"Listen, listen, I hear talking."*

Stanley continues. "I assure you, this worked last night in practice." Everyone is now joining in the hilarity.

"Listen, listen, I hear talking!"

Stanley has hit a home run! He's not through yet! "I will now demonstrate air pressure." Stanley has everyone's complete and undivided attention. All he needs is a magician's cape. This experiment is a favorite and involves a milk bottle and a hard-boiled egg, with the shell removed. Some newspaper is placed inside the bottle and lighted. Immediately the egg is placed on the opening of the bottle, and as the newspaper burns inside the bottle, two things happen. First the oxygen is consumed and the fire goes out. But secondly, and more importantly, the inside of the bottle has now less air pressure because the oxygen has been consumed in the fire. A giant *"fluuup"* sound should be heard as the egg is sucked into the bottle, pushed by the greater air pressure outside the bottle. That is what should happen. Don't bet on it today!

Stanley is ready. "I will now light the newspaper. Watch what happens." The newspaper is lit. He produces the raw egg from his bag, carefully stands between Mrs. Timbers and the bottle, and places it on the mouth of the bottle. Mrs. Timbers can see nothing. Everyone else can see what is about to happen because they know this is no hard-boiled egg. Great anticipation is felt by all the students. All eyes are on the bottle. The flame dies down. *Crack*, the raw egg splits, sending runny egg yolk all over Mrs. Timbers' desk. The boys in the back of the classroom howl and pound their desks. The girls join in. Pandemonium reigns.

Mrs. Timbers knows she's been had. *"Listen, listen, I hear talking. Listen, listen, I hear talking!"* The bell rings. "Stanley, will you remain after class?"

Mrs. Timbers and Stanley are seen walking toward the Principal's office.

Chapter Ten

It is mid-afternoon, and a long line forms at 46th and market streets in Philadelphia. School is out. This is the spot that has everyone's attention, for it's the American Bandstand studio. "American Bandstand" is a nationally televised dance party aired by ABC every afternoon at this time. Hosted by Dick Clark, it has as main participants many local teenagers who really know how to dance. They are not paid, but show up to have fun, doing what they love doing most, to dance. They are the "regulars." Each day a few lucky teens outside will be selected to dance on the show too, mixing with the "regulars." It is quite an honor to be on the show, for you are seen on TV coast to coast.

All across the nation school girls are sitting in front of TV sets watching. Today is Friday, and several girls have joined together at Irene's house, to make a half-hearted attempt at homework and to watch "Bandstand", although no homework will ever be started. As Dick Clark greets the TV viewers, the show opens with *"Sherry"* by The Four Seasons, and a fast rising number, *"He's A Rebel"* by the Crystals. The girls watch intently and can name most show participants as they dance. They've watched them every afternoon for years. They talk about Tommy, Pat,

38

Frani, and Tony as if known personally. They know who likes what, who just broke up, what songs are the favorites, and who the best dancers are. Girls love relationships, and this is just the thing for them. In this respect, they are so far ahead of the boys. This is a grand time for the girls.

Eventually talk turns to Ivy and the local boys. Why? Tonight is dance night at the YMCA, a twice monthly event for Jr. High students, from 7:30 to 9:00 p.m. Most everyone will be there. Russell's name is mentioned. He and Stanley are the best dancers, but the girls always overlook Stanley and talk only of Russell.

"Irene, are you going to dance with him tonight?"

A smirk and an, "I'll let you know tonight," follow.

At seven p.m., lights shine brightly at the "Y." A small dance band arrives, and begins the process of unloading equipment to haul inside. Mr. Ray, the unit director, greets them and shows the band where to set up, at the far end of the gym. This is a newer YMCA, without a pool, located in the neighborhood, and perfect for children to walk to. It has become the local gathering place. On these Friday nights it will be packed.

Stanley is among the first to arrive and goes immediately to the bandstand area. Here he surveys the layout and begins talking to the various musicians.

"How long have you played together?"

"Where do you practice?"

"What songs do you know?"

"How do you get jobs?"

He appears to be making mental notes about all that is discussed.

"How does one join?"

"Do you have tryouts?"

Hmmm.

"Hey, Stanley, we're going outside. Want to join us?"

The band members all file outside and stand near the side of the parking lot. Mitch, who seems to be the leader, pulls out a pack of cigarettes and passes it around.

"Here, Stanley, want to try one?"

Stanley cautiously accepts, lights up, takes a long drag, and coughs uncontrollably while the others stand around laughing.

Many cars are now pulling into the parking lot. Out jump the participants of tonight's event, and they immediately begin to form small groups of five to ten, to discuss what's important at this age. Some stay outside, others begin to head inside. Eventually all make their way to the gym. If one cared to look at each group, one fact would stand out loud and clear. The group is either *all* boys or *all* girls. And this is a dance?

The boys congregate under the basketball backboard, and seem more interested in seeing who is able to jump up and touch the rope net hanging down from the hoop. Talk is mostly about sports and the recent victory over Highland. More than a few Highland boys are here, so there is much to talk about. They join in too.

Across the room, the girls appear to be mingling among themselves very nicely. Girls are just naturals in social graces. Many girls from different schools are all here tonight, so the opportunity to make new acquaintances is easily presented. Girls are beginning to form friendships that will carry over next year at Madison High.

Only Stanley notices that no music has yet been played. Mitch and the band sit in readiness. Mr. Ray approaches the microphone, and greets the students. "Let's get started this evening with an 'Accumulation' Dance."

This is a great way to get things started, a perfect way to break the ice. The girls all move to one side of the room in a long line. The boys do the same on the opposite side. Mr. Ray selects five boys, the band begins playing *"Blue Moon,"* the boys select five girls, and all begin to dance. After about thirty seconds, Mr. Ray yells "Break," and each then selects a new partner and continues dancing. It isn't long before the entire dance floor is filled. Everyone gets to dance. What a matapalo[10] great way for young people to meet students from different schools. What a great way to break the ice. At the conclusion of the music, as if by magic, all return to their little groups. Girls talk about who they just danced with; the boys still try to touch the basketball net!

Mr. Ray knows how to keep things moving. He announces the next dance will be a "Girl's Choice." Girls will drag the boys out on the dance floor for sure. The band strikes up an Elvis Presley tune, *"It's Now or Never,"* and the dance floor fills. Look! Irene has asked Russell to dance. That didn't take long. Other girls notice too. They really notice the next dance, for it's a "Boy's Choice," and Russell quickly asks Irene to dance. What's up?

Take a quick look around the room. The small groups are beginning to break up; larger groups of both boys and girls are forming. This is a sure sign that the evening is moving along. By now the participants are feeling comfortable. A series of fast dances gets the tempo up. The band plays everyone's favorite, *"Twist and Shout."* Guy asks Mary Beth to dance. Stanley is dancing. This place is smoking!

By now many students are dancing in groups, they don't even have partners. It's just the fun of being together. The music gets louder and louder, nobody wants to leave the dance floor. Look, the band has a new member. Stanley is helping out on the drums! Mary Beth and a few other girls have moved closer to see. This state of events continues for some time, until the band breaks, and Mr. Ray announces last dance, "Anybody's Choice." The band plays *"I Can't Stop Loving You"* by Ray Charles. Guy and Mary Beth find each other.

Russell looks for Irene. What! She's already on the dance floor, with . . . Stanley?

---

[10] 1963 Equal Pay Act

"Why, that little weasel! Was this his idea or hers?"

Rachael grabs Russell. This is so cute! Last Dance! "R & R!"

Chapter Eleven

Students file into Mrs. Epich's history class. They look around in amazement; the room appears as though it is ready for a World Series game. Bright red/white/blue bunting hangs everywhere. Are they in the correct room? The bell rings. All take their seats. Nothing is said. What is happening today?

Mrs. Epich has planned this day for some time. It is repeated over and over, in exactly the same way, for every eighth grade class. She quietly walks to a portable record player and commences playing, *"Stars and Stripes Forever."* She then begins to read:

"Four score and seven years ago our fathers brought forth on this continent, a new nation, conceived in Liberty, and dedicated to the proposition that all men are created equal. Now we are engaged in a great civil war, testing whether that nation, or any nation so conceived and so dedicated, can long endure. We are met on a great battle-field of that war. We have come to dedicate a portion of that field, as a final resting place for those who here gave their lives that that nation might live. It is altogether fitting and proper that we should do this.

But, in a larger sense, we cannot dedicate -- we cannot consecrate -- we cannot hallow -- this ground. The brave men, living and dead, who struggled here, have consecrated it, far above our poor power to add or detract. The world will little note, nor long remember what we say here, but it can never forget what they did here. It is for us the living, rather, to be dedicated here to the unfinished work which they who fought here have thus far so nobly advanced. It is rather for us to be here dedicated to the great task remaining before us -- that from these honored dead we take increased devotion to that cause for which they gave the last full measure of devotion -- that we here highly resolve that these dead shall not have died in vain -- that this nation, under God, shall have a new birth of freedom -- and that government of the people, by the people, for the people, shall not perish from the earth."

"Boys and girls, I have just read the Gettysburg Address, the most famous speech in the study of American History. It was given by President Lincoln at the time of the dedication of Gettysburg National Cemetery in 1863. This is the site of the most famous battle of the Civil War. Every eighth grade class before you has had the great opportunity of memorizing this speech. Today I will give *you* that great opportunity. I will now hand the remaining time over to you, so that each, in turn, can begin the process of memorizing this historic address."

Mrs. Epich turns, walks back to the record player, and plays another John Philip Sousa march. What a teaching moment! Her brief comments paralleled Lincoln's in effectiveness. She has just made thirty history students *want* to memorize Lincoln's Gettysburg Address.

Look around the room. Not a peep, only the music. Each student is attacking this job in his or her own best way. Some are writing. Some are lip synching. All are completely focused. Look at Guy. The music and the speech have really affected him. He is so intense in his work. You know the words mean something to him. Tomorrow he will be ready to present this speech to Mrs. Epich. The bell rings. Not a word is uttered. All file out of the room in total silence. One last Sousa march plays in the background.

It is now late afternoon, and a few girls have gathered at Irene's house. Today there will be no "Bandstand." Together they are practicing the words of Lincoln's speech. Irene has it just about memorized. All the girls take turns practicing each paragraph as they learn it. A favorite phrase is *"that government of the people, by the people, for the people, shall not perish from the earth."*

At Murphy Chevrolet, Russell is reciting what he has so far memorized. He becomes stuck at *"But, in a larger sense, we cannot dedicate -- we cannot. . .?* Red Blaze, one of the new car salesmen, walks over and says, *"we cannot consecrate -- we cannot hallow -- this ground. The brave men, living and dead, who struggled here, have consecrated it, far above our poor power to add or detract."* Amazing! Red is a former student of Mrs. Epich.

Mary Beth and her mother work on the address together. They recite *"that from these honored dead we take increased devotion to that cause for which they gave the last full measure of devotion,"* and talk about what it means and how we benefit today.

In the evening, Guy, surrounded by his mother and father in front of a roaring fire, work together. They repeat in unison *"that we here highly resolve that these dead shall not have died in vain."* Both Guy Sr. and Florence have previously memorized the speech.

Only Stanley works alone. He has promised himself that he will not fail in this. He recites, *"Four score and seven years ago our fathers brought forth on this continent, a new nation, conceived in Liberty, and dedicated to the proposition that all men are created equal."* Somehow he will finish before tomorrow!

The next day in school, students find the door closed to Mrs. Epich's classroom. They congregate outside practicing various phrases and paragraphs of Lincoln's speech. As the bell rings, Mrs. Epich opens the door and motions for all to enter. Sousa March music is playing once again. The room looks exactly as it did yesterday. Nothing is said as each student sits at his desk.

Mrs. Epich speaks quietly. "Yesterday each of you was given a great gift, the opportunity to memorize Abraham Lincoln's Gettysburg Address. Every class before you has been given the same gift. Today it is your turn. Please take out a piece of paper and write the words to Abraham Lincoln's Gettysburg Address for me. Make Mr. Lincoln and myself proud of you."

There is absolute quite thru out the room. Stanley begins to write, *"Four score and seven years ago..."* Others do the same. Russell comes to *"we cannot consecrate -- we cannot hallow -- this ground,"* and keeps right on writing. Mary Beth writes *"that from these honored dead we take increased devotion,"* pauses and continues. Guy nods slightly as he writes, *"that we here highly resolve that these dead shall not have died in vain."* Irene finishes quickly, *"that government of the people, by the people, for the people, shall not perish from the earth."* She lays down her pen and listens to the music.

One by one, others lay down their pens. Mrs. Epich watches but says nothing. Stanley is the last. He finishes; he has done it. Every single member of the class has completed the speech. In future years this might not be so, but in this time, it is a certainty.

Chapter Twelve

Cold, grey skies of February are prominent in the Midwestern sky; the bleak time of year has arrived in Blissville. Today the atmosphere inside the Funka household matches that outside. It is a horrific day, just a horrific day. Frank is home alone, on his first day of unemployment. His employer, Studebaker, is in big trouble. As one of the last remaining independent car manufactures, it has been trying to hold on for several years, but this year car sales are down; there just isn't enough business to keep going at current levels. His job was eliminated yesterday in the first round of cuts. There will surely be more to follow; some even question the viability of the company. This promises to be a very difficult time.

Sophie has spoken with the children. The entire family will have to make sacrifices until Frank is able to find employment again. That means no special entertainment, and certainly no dance classes for Irene. At least they still have Sophie's job at the supermarket. This is a completely different time from a decade ago when the world was recovering from war and depression, and was on full throttle, economically speaking. Now things are somewhat more measured, but still there is a sense of optimism. Today Frank will meet with his union representative to learn about his prospects for the future, and also the status of his pension benefit. Nasty stories have been swirling about in regard to what will be available at retirement, because the plan is rumored to be unfunded. Today he should know more.

The meeting takes place at one o'clock in the local union business office. Frank is greeted by Buzz Flannigan, a union negotiator who is also a former auto worker.

"Frank, sit down, I have some things to share with you. As difficult as the current situation is, you may be one of the lucky ones. There are still jobs in other union facilities."

Buzz informs Frank about potential job opportunities with different manufacturers, but the jobs available would also necessitate a move. Does he want that? Buzz feels there is little chance of being rehired at Studebaker. "As for any pension benefit, word is that only the high seniority workers can expect something. Workers having less than ten years seniority will not realize a penny should Studebaker go bankrupt."

Frank slumps in his chair, looks at the floor. He's stunned. He would have had ten years seniority in just nine months. Now, no job and no pension, all seems to be lost.

"Frank, remember I just said you may be one of the lucky ones? Listen, today I can offer you a position right here in the union office as a representative."

Buzz goes on to explain the need and the compensation package, which is substantially less than Frank made at Studebaker.

"It offers security and the guarantee of not having to move your family. Think it over, and let me know in a day or two."

Frank can't believe what he is hearing. In the depth of his despair, he's presented a golden opportunity. He is once again going to live the American dream. His angel has appeared out of nowhere for his family.

"When do I start," is his quick response. What a turn of events!

The evening lights are bright in the little bungalow on Maple Street. The mood is distinctly upbeat. Sure, there will be less income, but there *will* be income, and life matapalo[11] can still progress normally. For Irene this means dance classes once again. Just in time, for tonight is the introductory class.

Parents are very interested in presenting formal dance training to young adults at this age, as a beginning to eventual entry into full adult society. It just adds polish, and enhances social graces at the next level. This experience is not to be confused with the common dancing as seen on "Bandstand," but the elegant real thing in a ball room setting. Everything is formal: dress, etiquette, conversation, and even one's dance partner. Students will be introduced to the concept of the "dance card," but that must wait for the formal dance at the completion of the course. Tonight and for the next eight weeks, work will be on the basics of various ballroom dances.

As students arrive at Ivy and enter the hallway, they can just feel something is different. There is none of the harshness of daytime. This evening the auditorium is transformed by decorative ferns and flowers; lighting is somewhat muted to complete a visual experience. Folding chairs are along the walls. A sound system with microphone is in place at the front of the room. Two beautiful instructors, Miss Hopp and Mrs. Troupe, each in a fancy gown, greet all as they enter. It is evident everyone must be on their best behavior. Boys, there are going to be rules!

Irene makes a grand entrance. Her formal dancing dress

---

[11] 1963 Clean Air Act

is black satin with highlights of crème set off by an elegant crème blouse; shoes are black Patton leather with small heels. She presents a cute figure, surely to be appreciated by the boys in attendance. Almost immediately she is surrounded.

All the boys must be dressed in a coat and tie. Russell appears in a dark blue suit with red striped tie. Guy has a suit also, only his is black with a yellow tie. Stanley has on a blue sport coat with red tie, sloppily tied.

Heads turn toward the auditorium door. Now making her entrance is Mary Beth. She is an absolute "knock out," in a dress of pink chiffon highlighted with red ribbons. Matching pink shoes and white gloves complete the ensemble. The girls instantly rush toward her. Irene is left standing alone.

Mrs. Troupe advances to the microphone to begin class.

"During the next few weeks we will learn some of the popular ballroom dances: the *Waltz, Tango, Foxtrot, Cha Cha, Rumba, and Mambo.* There is expected behavior; each lady is to be addressed as Miss, each gentleman as Mister. Most importantly, I must emphasize posture. Posture is as important as the dance itself. Posture must be maintained at all times!"

The boys are soon going to wish that statement had never been made!

"Ladies, please form a circle around the ball room floor." A few moments later, "Gentlemen, please stand opposite one of the ladies."

There is a stampede toward Mary Beth. Stanley wins and thinks he has won her for the entire evening.

"Now, we are going to begin by working on correct posture. Gentlemen, place your right hand on your partner's back, by her shoulder blades. Take her right hand in your left hand, and hold it up so her elbow makes an "L" shape. Keep an arch in your back. Hold that position! Hold that posture! Miss Hopp and I will move around the circle to confirm your structure." Each dance pair, one by one, is adjusted.

"Remember, posture, and posture! Don't drop your arms."

Early enthusiasm for ballroom dancing on the part of each boy is now quashed; their left arms are getting so very tired, so very, very fast. Eventually all dance pairs are in confirmation.

"Now we will change partners. The ladies will remain in place; each gentleman will move one spot to the lady on his right."

Stanley is heard grumbling, "Not one stinking dance with Mary Beth and all I have to show is a sore arm!"

Mrs. Troupe announces that all may rest for moment. A great sigh of relief comes from the boys.

"Our first dance we will learn is the *Foxtrot*, one of the most popular of all ballroom dances. Miss Hopp and I will demonstrate the basic steps, which are slow left, slow right, quick left, and quick right close." They glide thru the steps, making it look so simple.

For the remainder of a long hour each pair struggles with posture and quick right close.

"Posture, posture, maintain that posture!"

Chapter Thirteen

The school year is beginning to wind down now. In a few days the special generation will become 9th graders and be off to Madison High, but a few final events still remain at Ivy.

Today is Friday; Russell walks down the first floor hallway before afternoon class. He can see Mr. Sanders, the Industrial Arts teacher, is all smiles standing in front of a long table of shop projects, representing an entire year's work by each 8th grade boy.

"Hi Mr. Sanders," chirps Russell as he approaches the part of the table that contains his project, a copper planter, suspended from a wooden back plate. Russell is quite proud of his work, although it doesn't display a winning ribbon. The first place blue ribbon was won by a boy named Darrell Fleeting, who made a complete desk from scrap pieces of wood. His desk is displayed prominently in the center, at the front of the table.

Some third grade boys seem mesmerized by the totality of the display. Mr. Sanders notices and says, "In a few years you will have your projects on display just like this.
Which are your favorites?"

The tallest boy points to a music stand made entirely of plastic, which displays a yellow ribbon.

"Yes," says Mr. Sanders, "this is a very creative project. Notice it has no glue. The plastic is melted by solvent and fuses together when dry. It's strong as steel!" The card notes, "Made by Stanley Vincent."

"I like this one," says one of the others. He points to a bellows made of mahogany and leather which has a red ribbon. "Look, Guy made it!" Just about everyone in school knows Guy Hartmann.

Russell continues down the hall toward the auditorium. He hears sounds of music floating into the hall. During the final week of school, a short choral concert is presented by the 8th grade class for the entire school. Today at 2 p.m. Miss Kleff will direct a program of "American Songs Thru the Ages." Stanley will be playing the piano and directing one of the numbers, a Civil War tune called *"The Bonnie Blue Flag."* There is just one hour to finish rehearsal.

At one minute past two, the 8th grade class enters the stage from the left and positions itself on risers installed for this event. Ivy's auditorium is packed with almost six hundred students. Miss Kleff makes her entrance; Stanley is in the front row of the chorus, next to the piano. A mimeographed program prepared by the office shows:

<u>American Songs thru the Ages</u>

1) I'm a Yankee Doodle Dandy
2) When Johnny Comes Marching Home Again
3) The Bonnie Blue Flag
4) Dixie
5) Over There
6) America The Beautiful

Miss Kleff greets the students, proceeds to the piano, and

begins playing the introduction to *"I'm A Yankee Doodle Dandy."* Right on cue the chorus sings, *"I'm a Yankee Doodle Dandy, A Yankee Doodle Do or Die."* It's a great opening number. Students and faculty enjoy it immensely, as they also do the second number, *"When Johnny Comes Marching Home Again."*

Now it is Stanley's time. He walks to the piano, sits, adjusts the music, and readies himself. This is his first official performance as musician and director. Over one thousand eyes are watching; there is no place to hide. This is it. He should be nervous, but he isn't. He's very comfortable, very cool. He looks at the chorus, and begins playing a very haunting but enchanting melody from the Civil War, from the Confederate side, called *"The Bonnie Blue Flag."* The auditorium is completely still; all are watching, listening. Exactly on cue, the chorus sings *"We Are a Band of Brothers, and Native to the Soil. . ."* The chorus sounds good, very good; they are doing their best for Stanley. He marches right thru the piece, correct tempo, correct inflexion, and correct notes. All seven verses are completed. At the end of the last chorus, *"Hurrah! For the Bonnie Blue Flag Has Gain'd th' Eleventh Star,"* the auditorium erupts in thunderous applause. It continues and continues. Is this history in the making? All have just witnessed an eighth grader pull off a masterpiece. Stanley takes a short bow; he feels somewhat uneasy, but is very, very satisfied. Miss Kleff shakes his hand as he walks back to the chorus.

Mary Beth's eyes shine as she whispers, "Fantastic Job, Stanley."

The program continues toward its conclusion. *"America the Beautiful"* is a perfect closing number, so uplifting. After a final applause, younger grade students talk about their future opportunity to perform, while they file out of the auditorium. A few teachers make a path to congratulate Stanley on his performance. Miss Uppryte is the first. Today has been a noteworthy performance by the eighth grade class.

****

Tonight will be a popular night at the "Y." It's the final dance of the year, and a big night for the 6th graders. Every year the last dance of the year introduces them to what they may expect next year, when they become 7th graders. A King and Queen of the dance will be crowned.

At 7 pm sharp, Stanley is at the "Y" waiting for Mitch and the band to arrive. It isn't long before he is helping them unload and set up. Stanley has become an unofficial "pledge" with the band these past three months; he secretly hopes to someday join as an active member. Mitch also has been very accommodating to him, trying to answer each of the hundreds of questions Stanley constantly asks. Stanley takes his share of good natured "ribbing" from the other members, but all are beginning to accept him more and more. They even have a couple of numbers that call for a clarinet, and have asked him to participate with them. Stanley expects to play at least one number with them tonight.

Gradually students arrive in the parking lot and begin forming their little groups. Upon entering, they see a gym decorated with crepe paper foretelling something special. An area on the far side has been roped off, waiting for the formal announcement of the King and Queen and Court. Five couples have been nominated; voting is taking place right now in the lobby. Russell and Irene, and Guy and Mary Beth are the candidates from Ivy. Each candidate is dressed formally.

At 7:30 p.m., Mitch and the band play a short "Fanfare." Mr. Ray walks to the microphone, and greets all; "It is time to announce this year's King and Queen and Court." As

55

the band begins playing a very regal sounding march, Mr. Ray trumpets, "The fourth runners up are. . ." They walk under a canopy to the roped off area. "The third runners up are Irene Funka and Russell Murphy." Irene and Russell do the same. "The second runners up are. . ." "The first runners up are. . ." "And now, with great pleasure I present to you this year's King and Queen, Guy Hartmann and Mary Beth Blossom." Guy and Mary Beth proceed to the two chairs in the roped off area and sit down. Some photos are taken, after which Mr. Ray announces, "The first dance will be an 'Accumulation' dance starting with the Royal Court."

Mary Beth is dressed in her pink chiffon dress, Guy in his black suit. They look like the perfect couple in the perfect world around them. Others are thinking likewise. Mr. Ray comments, "Aren't they beautiful," and allows each couple to dance a while longer before yelling "Break." Soon the gym floor is jammed with dancers. The sixth graders are impressed.

****

Monday is a happy day and a sad day, all in one.
Our Blessed Generation has only to pick up their grade cards, for school work has been completed. It is a happy time because they are now high school students, ready to experience all the excitement that goes with it. But, they are sad about leaving a very comforting place that has nourished them for nine years. Their grade school experience at Ivy has made them self-assured and confident, and able and willing to take the next step. From now on a certain amount of responsibility will be required as they enter the adult world. Their grade school ways must be left behind.

Scarcely noticed are clouds, slowly appearing on their happy horizon. To this point, all of their life experiences have been quite idealistic, almost picture perfect in nature, for a generation of beneficiaries.   Is change coming? No! Not yet! They are "The Blessed Generation!" They have been dancing the dance; there is music yet to be played!

Chapter Fourteen

The Blessed Generation is about to enter their final year of high school. Something is quite different in the mood of the country now. In just four short years, the previous happy, innocent time has changed, undergone a metamorphosis to an angry and confrontational mood, angry about a war and confrontational about past social injustices. The American heartland is just now beginning to be caught up in these matapalo[12] events, although not nearly to the extent seen in coastal parts. Yes, our high school seniors are aware of outside events, but are still focused primarily on their small world within Blissville. It is their world totally. It is their senior year. That's what is important to them.

Each of the cast members has begun to define himself by a maturing personality. One can see what the finished adult product is likely to resemble. Perhaps the greatest strides toward adulthood have been taken by Irene. She has become one of the best students in her class, and is one of its most active members. Head cheerleader, member of numerous social and service clubs, and a member of the

---

[12] 1964 Civil Rights Act

National Honor Society mark her resume. Whatever seems to be happening at the moment is where you will find Irene. She is anywhere and everywhere at once.

Stanley is defined by Stanley. His focus is music, period! Stanley is just an average student but excels in band and orchestra. Outside school he can be found as a member of Mitch's band and playing "gigs" all over town. He is constantly in motion, musically.

Mary Beth is the most beautiful girl in school. She is also the most popular cheerleader, an above average student, and favorite of teachers and students alike.

Guy is the most outstanding boy. He is an above average student, the best athlete, president of a social club, and a member of the National Honor Society.

Russell has never wavered in his interest in cars. He loves cars, and he loves speed. Fast cars are his passion. He is spending more and more time at Murphy Chevrolet where his restoration of a 1955 Chevrolet is almost complete. Russell is an average student, but competent.

For three years now this special generation has been attending Madison High School, a huge building which can accommodate nearly two thousand students. Like Ivy, it was constructed during the 1920's to replace an aging building dating to 1885. Brick and sandstone are the main building blocks; three floors of classrooms peek out on a mature neighborhood on the nearside of downtown. It dominates a whole city block. Parking is behind the building as well as around the block.

Today is the first day of class. Students begin arriving by bus and private transportation. Many of the boys have cars now, and can be seen making personal statements with them as they arrive. Proper etiquette requires a drive around the block, and a "down shift" at a parking zone causing the engine to make an *"uhmmmm, uhmmmm, uhmmmm"* groan. To really sound great, one absolutely must have an eight cylinder engine. A "six" just doesn't cut it.

The boys all know!

Look, here comes, "uhmmmm, uhmmmm, uhmmmm," a really great looking ride. It's Russell, in his just restored 1955 Chevy with "Flames" painted on the front fenders extending around the wheel wells into the passenger doors. Russell pulls up, parks, guns the engine a few times for everyone to hear his glass packs, and then "shuts her down." Boys rush to gather around and hear the story about his car. A crowd soon gathers.

Here's another arrival, "uhmmm, uhmmm, uhmmm!" It's Stanley with his old beat up, rusted panel truck "six-banger." Stanley has just made a statement to spoof the boys. Hardly anyone notices. The one or two that do notice, quickly laugh. Stanley enjoys the fun, and soon joins some others on the sidewalk for a quick smoke before school.

Inside Madison High all head toward the auditorium. Madison's auditorium is impressive; it consists of plush theatre type seats arranged in three sections for fifteen hundred students. Upstairs is a wide balcony able to hold three hundred more. The fully functional stage is occupied this morning by the band, which is playing familiar tunes that are drifting into the hallway. The band is trying to create excitement for the coming school year. Everyone is in a festive mood this first day of school. We can see the seniors have laid claim to the very best seats in the middle of the center section, squeezing out unknown freshmen who are then directed to the back corners of the first floor and the balcony. At precisely 9:00 a.m. Madison's principal, Mr. Corpus, greets all returning and new students.

"It's great to see so many smiling faces, ready and eager to begin the process of learning once again." A loud groan and then some laughter are heard. He goes on to explain changes that have taken place over the summer, as well as some rehashing of older rules for the benefit of incoming freshmen.

Mr. Caper, the activities director, then announces exciting news. "We are organizing a train excursion to the Cloverdale football game, so every Madison student will have the opportunity to root for our team. We'll have more on that in October!" Students cheer loudly with this news.

In fifteen minutes all business is finished, and students are asked to proceed to their home rooms. The band plays Madison's Fight Song as they file out.

Students scatter in different directions to different home rooms depending upon courses of study. This year, Irene, Mary Beth, and Guy all have the same home room for senior English. Russell goes to the shop area for auto mechanics, and Stanley has band class first hour.

Senior English is a non-required elective course that is taken by college-bound students. Irene, Mary Beth, and Guy find their room, number 217 on the second floor. Miss Scrypt is writing some vocabulary words on the black board as they enter, the first word being *"serendipity."* After the bell rings, she begins to explain what this is all about; she will add more and more words each week to *"enrich"* their vocabulary and writing skills. Here is that word again, *"enrich,"* that keeps coming up when educators talk about curriculum! A few students gaze at the board and begin to wonder how *"serendipity"* can be used in daily conversation. Being noticed by a favorite for a date, perhaps?

Miss Scrypt begins to pass out the English text books. She explains, "This year's course study will involve a complete historical survey of English literature, both poetry and prose. The first item of study will be Chaucer's *'Canterbury Tales.'"* Now there is *"serendipity!"*

Down in the shop area, auto mechanics class is under way. Mr. Roll is discussing the build-up of a six cylinder engine, several of which will be completed by teams of students this semester. Russell's team has five members.

Since he has just restored a car, he can help guide his team thru the process. He will be a great team member.

Mr. Roll likes to keep things "light and easy going" in class; shop is a far different experience from the seriousness of coursework upstairs. He states, "You can learn so much about life from an engine. If anyone ever asks you for the firing order of a six cylinder Chevy, you know they already know the answer, because they just worked on one! How else would they know? That can be applied to many questions in life." Great laughter erupts, but Russell realizes the serious nature of that statement. He files it away in his memory for another time.

Over in the band room, Mr. Van Horn draws a marching diagram on the black board. It consists of one long line of band members stretched across the football field at the goal line. He explains, "As the band marches up the field, a few members on each end of the line will stop marching at each five yard interval, until the last marching unit stops at the fifty yard line. Then what projects to the spectators is a giant "V" on the field, representing *Victory!*" Everyone is excited by it and is anxious to get started on this new formation. Mr. Van Horn thanks all band members for the superlative job this morning at the welcome back gathering, and then has the class begin work on some new Sousa March numbers. Stanley shines as the leader of the clarinet section.

On this first day of class, the farthest thing from any student's mind is an unknown small country in south-east Asia.

Chapter Fifteen

It is Friday in mid-October. Students at Madison are wearing tags that say, "Crush Cloverdale." These tags are a fund raising project for Athena, Mary Beth's literary society.

Just what is a literary society? It is certainly not a sorority or fraternity! These are prohibited by the Board of Education. A clever way around the rule, thought up by an enlightened person some years ago, was to create a literary society. Nothing is ever read, let alone discussed, so these are not literary societies at all, but pure sororities and fraternities that pose as literary societies. Well within the scope of the rule. Students = 1; Board of Education= 0! The Athena Literary Society will sponsor a huge "Pep Rally" during the final period this afternoon.

The day drags on and on; finally, last period arrives. As the bell rings, students rapidly begin filing into the auditorium where the band is already on the stage playing Madison's fight song. Folding chairs are set up across the front of the stage for the football team. Behind the chairs are the cheerleaders. Seniors can be seen occupying the middle seats in the auditorium's lower level, while curious freshmen are in the balcony wondering what is about to take place. A huge *Crush Cloverdale* banner stretches across the stage. All is in readiness.

Mr. Caper walks to the microphone and yells, *"Are you ready to crush Cloverdale tonight?"* Students scream, *"Yes, yes."* Mr. Caper says, *"Let's bring out the team!"* The band strikes up. One by one each member of Madison's football team walks across the stage and sits down on a chair. Students clap loudly. Guy looks *"pumped!"* The team looks *"pumped!"* Mr. Caper says, "Let's hear a word from Mr. Corpus!" The cheerleaders start a cheer, *"Corpus rah; Corpus rah; rah, rah, Corpus! Corpus . . . Corpus, Corpus, Corpus!"*

Out walks Mr. Corpus, Mr. Excitement! He always speaks first, with the obligatory "You're on your best behavior tonight" speech that can instantly take the steam out of any rally. In forty five seconds, it's over. Now, back to business!

Mr. Caper tries to fire up the students again by talking about the trip to Cloverdale; he describes the mechanics of the train ride, the times, the places, what to do, how to follow the band, etc., etc., etc. He then calls upon assistant coach La Rock, to give a scouting report on tonight's opponent.

Coach La Rock's short presentation to the team sets the stage for head coach Spikes. The band begins to play. The cheerleaders start a cheer, *"Spikes rah; Spikes rah; rah, rah, Spikes! Spikes . . . Spikes, Spikes, Spikes!"*

Coach Spikes walks across the stage. What a presence! Virgil Spikes is a hulk of a man, a former All-American at State nearly twenty years ago. He has been head football coach at Madison for over ten years. He has had some good football teams, but this is arguably his best. Tonight he will find out. Cloverdale is ranked third in the state.

Coach looks intense. He stares at his team sitting on the stage. He begins to speak, very slowly and softly. *"Men, tonight you will be playing the biggest matapalo*[13] *game in the history of Madison High School."*

His voice increases in intensity; *"You will travel to a hostile environment. You will be tested by a very good team, a team ranked number three in the state."*

His voice increases in volume. *"When You Board That Bus, There Is No Turning Back. No One Looks Back!"*

The entire student body is captivated, listening.

Coach turns up the volume full blast. *"When we go on that field tonight, we're going to own it. When they have the ball, we're going to hit them. We're going to hit them hard. When they get up, we're going to hit them again, and again, and again. When we have the ball, we're going to take it to them. We're going to block. We're going to run right at them. We're going to run right thru them. Again and again we're going to run right thru them. We're going to own them and emerge victorious in the greatest game ever played in the history of Madison High School!"*

The auditorium erupts. *"Coach rah; coach rah; rah, rah coach! Coach . . . coach, coach, coach!"* Wow, this is what high school football is all about in the "Heartland." Tonight is the night!

At 4:30 p.m. students begin to gather at Blissville train station. Built in 1896, it shows its age now, and only a hint of former, glamorous days of railroading. Everywhere red brick is coated with years of accumulated soot; the wooden benches are in need of repair; no one is at the ticket window for no one rides the trains anymore. And now, suddenly, almost five hundred students appear in the waiting room. Look, and remember; this is a last, short glimpse of what was once railroad glory!

---

[13] 1964 Economic Opportunity Act

Outside, fifty yards down the track, awaits our excursion train. What? Where did Mr. Caper ever find that one? This train is right out of the year 1910! Large square windows, rivets showing everywhere, no streamlining design, a sickening faded olive-green complexion, and dirt, everywhere dirt. The students thrill at pounding the seats and watching sixty years of dust rise up. Who cares when you are on your way to watch your team Crush Cloverdale, in a ninety minute thrill ride right out of yesteryear!

The excursion train is composed of twelve cars and a refreshment car. The first thing most students do while waiting for the train to embark is eat the sack lunch brought along. A fatal mistake! Down in the refreshment car, Russell's literary society, Minerva, sets up; they're sharks waiting for easy "pickings" with Cokes, potato chips, and cheese sandwiches at exorbitant prices. It isn't long before the refreshment car is crowded and doing a "land office business!"

Ninety minutes fly by. The train arrives in Cloverdale. It stops; it's time to disembark. Where are we? It's dark. What, we're in a corn field, not a train station? It is completely dark. No moon. Some light in the distance. Ah, that must be the football stadium, only a short walk. Remember, follow the band; follow the band! *Boom, boom, a boom, boom . . . boom, boom a boom . . . boom, boom, a boom, boom . . . boom, boom, boom!*

Cloverdale stadium is packed tonight. Night football just can't be beat. Grass looks so much greener. Uniforms appear so much brighter and so much more colorful. Look, there are Irene and Mary Beth with the cheerleaders. And here comes the team onto the field. Madison High is cheering, and cheering, and cheering. Irene is busy orchestrating the whole welcoming. The cheerleaders are working feverishly. What a great job!

The team, in their gold and blue uniforms, looks ready. Guy appears so strong. They are going thru warm-ups now. Coach Spikes is in shirt sleeves, watching, directing. Madison runs a "single wing" offense, a relic of the 1930's and 40's and even earlier times. Coach likes it because it is a good ball control offense with less chance for an error in dropped handoffs. At the high school level mistakes can always be counted on. In fact, they are guaranteed. The team that makes the fewest mistakes can have a greater chance of winning, even against a superior opponent. Our team is leaving the field now, to return to the locker room for final adjustments and instructions.

Madison's band takes the field. They look elegant in their dark blue uniforms. Mr. Van Horn climbs a huge folding ladder to direct at mid field. The band is positioned across the goal line at Madison's end, and begins marching up the field playing their fight song. At each five-yard marker a few members drop off. Stanley is at the thirty-yard marker. At the fifty-yard marker the last remaining unit stops. A perfect "V" has been formed. The PA announcer proclaims, "V" for *Victory*! Mr. Van Horn now directs the band in playing our National Anthem.

Both teams are back on the field. We're ready to play football. Madison wins the toss and will receive. The kick is in the air, down the right side, and out of bounds at the Madison forty two yard line. A poor kick, the first mistake! Madison will take possession here. Cloverdale's defense readies. They are an outstanding defensive team, which is the major reason for their high state ranking. Nobody has been able to score many points against them this entire season.

Madison breaks their huddle and lines up in a single wing right formation. In this formation, the quarterback lines up one yard behind the guard, not the center. The full back is the deep back, five yards behind the center. To his right, one yard forward, is the half back. The other half back is further to the right, two yards behind the end. When one looks at this placement from above, the wing shape of the running backs becomes obvious. Guy is the deep back, the full back. Madison's center snaps the ball. Guy has it, and it's "student body" right. Everybody runs "right," and tries to block opposing defenders. Guy follows and looks for a "hole" to squirt thru for positive yardage. Not much is gained. This is a well-coached defensive football team.

During the first half, play after play are stopped. This game is turning into an epic defensive battle. At half time, the score is 0-0. Although Madison hasn't scored, they have kept Cloverdale's high-powered offense off the field by eating up the clock with the single wing. They have held their own versus a higher ranked team. They have made no mistakes.

In the third quarter, it's more of the same. This is classic *"smash mouth"* football. Cloverdale finally makes a scoring threat deep in Madison territory. They are stopped on the ten yard line; a fumble on the hand-off, another mistake.

It is getting late in the fourth quarter. The score is still 0-0. Less than three minutes remain on the clock. Madison is moving the ball, but stuck with fourth down and two yards to go with the ball at the forty nine yard line. This is an obvious punting situation. Coach Spikes calls a time out. If Madison can make a first down, they can control the clock and maybe kick a field goal to win. They need less than two yards for a first down. Guy has been all over the field this evening, playing his finest game ever. He has accumulated almost one hundred fifty yards rushing, but no touchdowns. Surely he can make two yards now!

Coach Spikes makes the most important call of his career. *"Boys, We're Going For It!"*

Madison lines up in single wing right formation. Cloverdale's defense smells victory. They "crowd the box" whereby the defensive backs move up to stop the run. Everyone knows who will get the ball. They will not give up these two yards. The ball is snapped. Guy has it; he plows forward into the line. There are too many defenders. He lunges forward; he lunges again, he cannot make it; he is stopped! All is lost!

Wait, not so fast, the offensive end for Madison has broken unmolested into Cloverdale's backfield. He is at least ten yards behind the nearest defender. Madison's quarterback turns around and lofts a forty yard pass high into the air. It seems to hang up there forever. Now it's coming down, coming down toward the outstretched hands of Madison's receiver. He's got it; it's complete. It's a *Touchdown!* Guy had secretly handed off the ball to the quarter back as he plowed into the line. Cloverdale's defense made the final, fatal mistake.

Madison's defense holds again as Cloverdale's offense cannot generate anything. The clock runs out, *Victory* for Madison and Blissville! Players storm the field. They want to savor this moment. They have played the greatest game in Madison High School football history and have won! They have made no mistakes.

What an exciting walk back to the train. Nobody complains. The band leads the way with Sousa March music. It's a happy, happy time. On the train, talk is only about the "Play." "What a call by Coach Spikes. And, by the way, I'm so hungry."

The Minerva Literary Society waits patiently in the refreshment car. Look, prices have gone up! Russell is about to learn more about the marketplace in one evening on the train, than a full semester in school. Mr. Caper, faculty advisor, has noted a dwindling supply of provisions and an increasing potential demand from the students. This is classic economics. *Raise Prices!* Listen to the grumbling by the half-starved and happy fans, as they pay the new, higher prices! Perfect. Only ninety minutes to Blissville. Will provisions hold out? How high can prices go? *"Ka$$ching!" "Ka$$ching!" "Ka$$ching!"*

Chapter Sixteen

Stanley is in rapid fire motion. What should he do?
There is a real life crisis taking place right in front of him,
at this precise moment! His whole future is at stake. The
future was looking so bright yesterday. Today it looks
horrible. Why is this happening now and right before the
Holiday Dance Season?

Mitch and one other band member have been drafted into
the army! Immediately! They're gone. There is no more
Mitch, no more band; bookings have been made into
January. How can the band survive? How can they honor
those bookings?

"A crisis presents opportunity!" This event is a *major*
crisis. Of the remaining band members, only one person
has the passion and the drive needed to keep things
together; that person is . . . Stanley, its youngest member!
He has to act immediately. The remaining members have
accepted him as their new leader. They want results. They
want only to play in the band, not to manage.

Stanley quickly makes his first decision. Maybe he could
obtain two musicians from the faculty at Vista College,
located just forty miles down the road, south of Blissville?
That would plug the hole for the major December

bookings. Possibly a few of the music majors at the College would fill in when they returned to school in January. That would solve January. It's a hope; it's a plan; get it moving!

Now, how to convince college music faculty members to join a small local band for one month, and a band headed by a high school senior? That could be tough, really tough; it's almost impossible. Stanley reasons, Money won't do it. They are already well paid. What do we know here? What do we know about them individually? Nothing! We know nothing at all. We don't even know *who* they are. What do we know about Vista College? Hmmm, here's a chance, although a slim one. Vista is a liberal arts college and a hot bed of political activity against the War. Stanley reasons, if we could play on their political emotions, especially if it became known that the War caused our current musical dilemma, maybe they could be enticed to help out. Maybe we could use their presence as a recruiting tool for the college? The college would love that. Publicity is so expensive. The local paper would grab this story immediately. *"Professors become Santa Claus! Help local band torn by war! Interact with potential students!"* This just might work. I have to try it. I just know I can do it.

Stanley hops into his van and scurries down the road to Vista College. It is Friday and late in the afternoon. He goes directly to Wynd Hall, the building which houses the Music Department. Here he looks at the directory, and requests to speak with Professor Hoven, who happens to still be in his office. Stanley is ushered in, and asked to sit down. He has butterflies in his stomach. He must pull himself together. He remembers, "Everyone has butterflies at times; the secret is to get them to fly in formation."

Professor Hoven asks, "How may I help you?"

Stanley responds slowly, thoughtfully, and in complete control informing the Professor of his dilemma, and his solution. His emotion is over flowing and over powering, but professor Hoven doesn't know whether to laugh out loud or in silence! Can you believe this? Who is this skinny, funny looking high school boy with this strange request? It takes some kind of nerve to come in here like this. This is a college music department! This is so strange, but I kind of like his spunk. This kid has initiative . . . he has courage. I like that!

Professor Hoven says, "Look, this is so far off the wall, I can't promise anything. I'll have to think about it. I'll speak to Professor Ssohn about it this evening. You'll need just the two of us?"

Stanley listens and instantly knows; it's the way Professor Hoven responded. That last statement said it all, "You'll need just the two of us?" He knows he has won. They are going to do it. It's just a matter of details from this point forward. Stanley makes one last closing statement, "I can see the headlines now, *Professors Become Santa Claus.*" Both laugh as Stanley is led out.

"I'll let you know tomorrow morning," says Professor Hoven.

Stanley drives directly to the Blissville Star Journal, the local newspaper. He is led to the City Desk, and then to assistant editor Alexia Press' office.

"I've got a great story for the Sunday Magazine Section." Stanley unveils the events of the day. He's excited. He's really excited. He shows it. His matapalo[14] enthusiasm is making her excited. She is becoming very interested in this story.

"This could work," says Alexia. "I love regional stories. There is still time to put this whole thing together before tomorrow's deadline at noon. I'll need all the particulars! Thanks for the tip."

Back in his van, Stanley heads for the "Big Boy." What a

---

[14] 1964 Food Stamp Act

productive day; he has conned two college professors into playing with his band, and now the local paper for free publicity, all without any signed contract, and only a hunch it might even materialize! That calls for a great meal, his standing order: 2 Big Boys, 1 order of onion rings, 1 vanilla shake, and 1 piece of strawberry pie!

Sure enough, Saturday morning at 9 a.m. Professor Hoven calls and says he and Professor Ssohn are "on board" for the December bookings only. Stanley is beside himself, because if truth be known, he didn't sleep very well last night. He says, "I'm so excited, Professor. This is great news for Blissville, Vista College, and the entire region. I'll bring the music down this afternoon." One by one Stanley calls the remaining band members with the news. What a coup! They're saved! This scrawny lad, short in stature, is standing very tall today. Mitch would be very pleased with the news.

On Sunday morning, residents of Blissville and the region wake up to read bold headlines in the Star Journal, *"Vista Professors Play Santa Claus."* They go on to read how a small local band is being helped out by these "heavy weights," after their membership was decimated by the *war*. What a comforting Christmas story. The professors saved Christmas! Down at Vista College Professors Hoven and Ssohn bask in glory. They had no idea all this was all going to happen. The college loves it, and is going to feature the story in the winter newsletter to alumni. Stanley is becoming known all over campus.

In Blissville, Mary Beth's father reads the story, and asks, "Isn't this Stanley Vincent in your class?"

She smiles and says, "Yes he is, Daddy."

Two weeks have passed. Tonight is the Christmas Dance for County Employees. This is the first big booking. Stanley is on site early. This is *his* show now. Everything has to be just right. He goes over every minor detail, for the umpteenth time. The band members begin to arrive and set up. Things are going smoothly.

Somebody mentions, "Where are Professors Hoven and Ssohn?" Panic!

Outside, Channel 4 "News Tonight" has grabbed both for an interview! Unknown to those inside, this event has turned into an extravaganza. People from all over the region are coming to dance to this band's music. A large contingent has even come from Vista College. Everyone has read the newspaper feature. They want to be a part of this Christmas Story. Tonight is a complete sell out. This has never happened before.

At precisely 8 p.m. the band sits in readiness. Stanley stands, raises his hand, gives the down beat, and the evening is in motion. What a sound! With the professors this is a tighter, more polished group. The other band members take the quality of their music up a notch, just by being a part of this. Channel 4 is catching everything. This is to be the lead story at 11 p.m. Stanley is at the center of it all. Can you believe it?

What, another surprise? The Channel 4 Weather Girl is here. Crews are setting up tonight's "Weather in the Weather" broadcast, right now, right at the front door! Blissville and the entire region are going "bonkers" over this story.

The evening continues. The music is superb. The professors don't know what to think about it all. They are completely surprised, and totally impressed. This Christmas Dance is a wild success, a real Happening! No one is leaving. After the final dance, the Christmas Merrymakers plead for another. Stanley directs a short encore, and says, "See you next week at the Armory."

Afterwards, as he is helping pack up equipment, Professor Hoven quietly mentions to Stanley, "I have, quite frankly, never played to such an appreciative audience. You have done a remarkable job, young man. This is exactly the spirit we wish to instill in our students. You can be sure this will be a topic of a future lecture at Vista."

Word is getting around. The TV coverage couldn't be better. A week later, at the Armory, it's the same story, only a larger crowd. The week after, the crowd is larger still. New Year's Eve is an absolute "out of life" experience. The crowd is so large that the lobby becomes an extension of the dance floor. Stanley has brilliantly and successfully guided the band thru December. Now he has only to worry about January.

Not to worry! This story has so many legs that Stanley has begun receiving calls from music students before they even return from break. They all want to play in the band, his band. January looks good now. He has done it. He has saved the band!

At Vista College, Professors Hoven and Ssohn have become instant celebrities gathering a cult-like following. They are campus idols. And just think, all of this was brought about by a squirrely little high school kid from Blissville!

It is early February now; Stanley reflects upon the recent events. He is making plans for the future. The band is now a known commodity locally. There is an inexhaustible supply of potential band members down at Vista College. He will rename the band. It will become *Stanley V's*. It will become a small combo with the original members, but be able to expand at a moment's notice to a large dance band with the Vista students. He will now be able to book any type of gathering, any night of the week. This band could really take off regionally. They will all make much more money. It will be a good time. He remembers, way back in his kindergarten class, the day Guy Hartmann stood up and sang the second verse of *"Silent Night"* solo in front of the entire school. He remembers Miss Uppryte's comments about initiative and courage. He now can understand. *Nothing great happens without initiative and courage!*

Chapter Seventeen

"Bar, bar, bar . . . bar, Barbara Ann". . . "uhmmmm, uhmmmm, uhmmmm." Russell's '55 Chevy pulls into the parking lot at the "Big Boy." He drives with proper etiquette, downshifting upon arrival with radio blaring, currently to tunes of the Beach Boys. Russell turns on his headlights, requesting service from the car hop. Soon Sherry arrives to take his order.

"Hey, how's it going Russell. You're the first today. What will it be?"

Russell orders "fries" and a Coke, and waits for someone else to show up. It is 1:15 p.m. on Sunday afternoon in early March, a "tweener" time of the year separating winter and spring. One inch of snow fell last night. Raw, grey days are the norm, with nothing much going on. Classmates show up at the "Big Boy" to just hang out. "Idleness most certainly is the Devil's workshop!"

"Puff The Magic Dragon". . . "uhmmmm, uhmmmm, uhmmmm." Another arrival, and another; *"These Boots Are Made For Walking". . ."uhmmmm, uhmmmm, uhmmmm."* Things are beginning to pick up. Now a few of the girls

arrive, driving cars with automatic transmissions. Sherry can't keep up with orders, going back and forth with Coke after Coke. The classmates have all changed cars. Radios blare. Everyone has moved around. This is what happens on Sundays at the "Big Boy." It is a fun time, killing time.

"Bang, Bang, My Baby Shot Me Down,". . . *"uhmmmm, uhmmmm, uhmmmm."* Look! Look what's here! It's that new 1967 Firebird, Pontiac's pony car! Who's driving? It's Rusty, from World History class. Rusty pulls up, and just lets the engine rumble for a time so everyone can appreciate the sound. This vehicle has been dubbed a "muscle car" by the press.

The boys gather around. They are looking at some kind of transportation. It's painted yellow with a black vinyl roof. The front grill scoops into the engine compartment, which houses a 400 cubic inch monster V-8 with 325 horse power that will make your grandmother, sit up. On the floor, a four-speed transmission controls the motion. This baby "yearns to run!" And run it can.

Russell's '55 Chevy is fast, but this engine is a full 50 per cent larger, and in a smaller car. The Firebird is a rocket in street clothes! This is one of GM's answers to Ford's Mustang, which is three years old now, and seems so lame in comparison.

After a time, the inevitable question arises, "Can Russell beat the Firebird in 'Catch Me If You Can?'" These matapalo[15] good natured competitions usually take place on Saturday nights just outside of town on County Rd. 4. Today it will be a race to the "Y." Russell will be spotted a 15 second lead in his "55, then Rusty will follow in the Firebird. Rusty will try to arrive at the "Y" less than 15 seconds after Russell does, to win the race.

All the other cars head off in a caravan toward the "Y," to await the finish. It is very obvious no one has anything else

---

[15] 1965 National Traffic and Motor Vehicle Safety Act

planned to divert attention, in this afternoon of idleness.

Russell starts his engine. The Chevy sounds hungry. Glass packs rumble. He advances to the starting point. The starter signals, tires squeal, and Russell screeches out of the parking lot. His engine whines to top speed in first gear; Russell shifts to second, and coaxes more speed from the engine. Russell knows he won't be able to shift to third in the city; he pushes in second gear all the way.

Back at the "Big Boy" Rusty waits. Thirteen, fourteen, fifteen seconds pass. He guns the Firebird; it rapidly accelerates out of the parking lot. The Firebird races to red-line in first; Rusty shifts to second and red lines, he shifts to third and is chewing up city blocks quickly. That third gear in the four-speed transmission makes all the difference. Russell doesn't have that in his Chevy. Russell looks in his rear view window and sees the Firebird gaining. How did he catch up so fast?

Upcoming is a tricky left turn, Russell better slow down! Into the intersection he shoots; the Chevy begins to slide on some snow slush from last night. He's lost it; he can't steer. He's sliding sideways. This is bad. Both right wheels strike the curb. Instantly the Chevy overturns. It slides on its top, right into a telephone pole. The pole cracks and smashes down onto the car. Inside, upside down, there is no sign of life. Russell doesn't move!

Rusty can't believe his eyes. This looks really bad. Is Russell OK?? He slams on his breaks, stops the Firebird in the intersection. Rusty runs to the overturned vehicle.

"Russell! Russell!"

Rusty grabs him. He's got him. He drags Russell from the front seat of the car. Russell is up walking now; he's stunned. He has a cut on his forehead, but no broken bones. He is lucky to be alive. They can smell the leaking gas.

"It's going to blow. Get away."

"Fa-whompppp!" In just seconds the gas ignites. The

Chevy is in flames. In less than 30 seconds the entire car is engulfed. It is a total loss. Russell's car is gone. His car is gone. The car that he worked so long and hard to restore is gone. Rusty is a hero. Both are in a heap of trouble!

Thick black smoke belches from the burning Chevy, high into the air. Flames are intense. In the distance are sirens; the police arrive at the scene first, followed quickly by two fire trucks. In seconds the firemen are on the ground taking matapalo[16] action. A gasoline fire can be tricky. Luckily no houses are threatened. Gradually the fire is contained and allowed to burn out.

Five blocks away at the "Y" classmates can see the black smoke and hear the sirens. What could be happening? A sickening feeling begins to form in their stomachs; something awful has taken place. They drive toward the smoke, but can't get near the scene. By now a large crowd has gathered. They walk up and see the Firebird in the intersection. Then they see Russell's car upside down in flames.

"Oh, no! Russell!"

One of the by-standers mentions . . . "both boys are over in the police car; they are not injured, quite lucky for them."

In the patrol car, police officers are in the process of questioning the boys and making out their report. At this moment Lindsay Murphy arrives; he walks quickly to the patrol car and begins such a verbal tongue lashing at Russell that the officers just step aside.

"What have you done? Racing, and racing in the city! You could have killed someone, or yourself. You have no concept that speed kills. You have listened to nothing I have taught you. You have acted childishly. You won't be driving again for a very, very long time!"

What can the officers add to this? They know something

---

[16] 1965 Social Security Act

far worse awaits Russell when he arrives home. They release him into the custody of his father, with a summons to appear in municipal traffic court next week.

As a wrecker arrives and removes the burned-out Chevy, Rusty starts the Firebird, and very meekly drives away. All that remains of this incident is a charred spot in a front yard and a downed telephone pole.

Later that evening Russell sits in the living room with his father. Lindsay wants to talk with him, alone. Things have settled down somewhat by now, but still the mood is very tense.

"Two generations of Murphys have toiled to make Murphy Chevrolet what it is. In one afternoon you could have ruined it all. Thank goodness, no one was injured in this affair." Lindsay speaks slowly and directly to Russell. "All actions have consequences. Part of growing up is recognizing this fact and thinking ahead to avoid poor outcomes. You didn't do that this afternoon. You have not acted responsibly as an adult. From now to the end of the school year, you will not be treated as an adult. You are still a child. You must earn back adult privileges by maturing and acting responsibly. There will be no driving during this time. After graduation we will see where things stand."

Russell hangs his head. *"All actions have consequences!"*

Chapter Eighteen

Irene concludes her speech. "Be active! Be active! This time is yours!"

"Thank you, Irene, for a most inspiring message." Miss Scrypt continues, "Everyone has now had the opportunity to present a message to our class. Will each of you take a piece of paper and write down the names of the top five speakers, remembering to consider both content and delivery. The top five names will be nominated to participate in this year's judged speech contest."

Each year in early May, five Madison seniors present a judged speech event to the entire student body. Public speaking is a necessary part of self-government in a representative republic, so this training is a giant step in that direction. These five students are Madison's finished products, as presented to the student body and to the world. Participating seniors are held in high esteem by the entire student body; the event becomes more and more popular every year. This year's theme will be, *"What It Means To Be Free."*

Miss Scrypt begins to read the five names. Irene's name is the first. Irene instantly knows what this represents; she will have a great opportunity, as well as a great responsibility in meeting this obligation. Speaking to a packed auditorium will be somewhat unnerving. She must conquer not only the situation at hand, but also herself. She must be in control; she must sound convincing; she must be factual. It will take hard work, and there is only one week to prepare.

After class, Irene begins to ponder the phrase "to be free." She realizes these matapalo[17] three words are very complex in their meaning. Free is the opposite of captive, but being free is being free of what? And is being free only the ability to worship as one pleases? Or is it being able to say anything? Is it going anywhere, doing anything, or buying anything one desires? And then that first phrase, "what it means," is tricky. It implies someone must be on the receiving end of the statement. But who is it referring to, and why? Miss Scrypt must have chosen a very vague theme for a reason. It is hard to put one's hands around it. Why was she so vague? Was it to foster original thought and creativity? Of course, yes, yes! Most certainly it was! Miss Scrypt has said many times in class, "After high school, issues become less black and white. The adult world is a sea of grey." She is preparing us to think in this environment and to be able to communicate in it. That's what this is all about.

From earliest childhood Irene has heard the stories of her family's struggle during the War and journey to eventual freedom in the U.S. Now she will be able to call upon them in framing her response. Her parents will be a treasure trove of information. They will view this from a different perspective. She can hardly wait to get home and begin work on this project. This speech is about her family.

Sophie and Irene sit in the kitchen in the late afternoon.

"Irene, you can't imagine the control that can be placed

---

[17] 1966 National Historic Preservation Act

on your life by a despot. You may not choose where to live, what job to do, what or where to worship, how to chart your future. You must pay taxes even though you get no benefit. All difference of opinion is prohibited. Our village was over-run and everything confiscated, yet no compensation was ever given. Historically this was the norm. We were expected to endure. We had no say in anything. We just existed for the benefit of someone else."

"Then freedom must mean being able to do all these things you were denied?"

"No, Irene, it is more complicated than that. Freedom is the result of an action. Freedom is not the norm, bondage is. Something must act against bondage to create freedom. But freedom must be protected because it is unstable long term. If it is not cared for, and protected, bondage will always return because it is the lowest common denominator. Always look for the lowest common denominator in everything in life. *When a people begin to think freedom is the norm, and act in that way, they are about to lose it. Bondage is always right around the corner.*"

During the early evening, Irene begins to place some words on paper. Her mother, though not an educated woman, is wise beyond words. She knows the real world; she can see common sense in everything; she sees what many educated intellectuals cannot. Her last statement struck a nerve with Irene. In that statement Irene has found her title, *"Bondage Is Right Around The Corner."*

But how should she craft her speech? Irene recalls, Miss Scrypt has always stressed the need for a strong opening. It is most important. Use the *"kiss"* method, Keep It Simple Stupid! Talk to your audience in a way they can understand. Be interesting! Body language and delivery are 50% partners with the text of the speech. A great written speech is nothing if presented by a stiff board. Irene is grasping the essentials.

Irene begins drafting her speech. She writes rapidly. Miss Scrypt and her mother have given her the basics. An outpouring of emotion guides her, for this is a speech about her family, her life. With tears in her eyes, she writes the final lines. It is finished; it is ready.

The remaining days of the week just melt away. Time is so short. During the weekend Irene practices and practices her delivery. Sophie's quiet tutelage helps shape her stage presence. The entire family has become a part of this project. By Sunday night Irene feels she is ready to present her very best speech possible, and with her loving family behind her, she knows she will.

On Monday afternoon it's time. Madison's auditorium is packed. The stage has been decorated with potted plants; soft lighting frames the entire scene. At center stage is a podium with microphone; it is here speakers will address the audience. To the left is a table with five chairs around for the judges. To the right are five chairs for the speakers. Miss Scrypt will be acting Mistress of Ceremonies.

Miss Scrypt walks to the podium and begins addressing the students. "The theme of today's event is, *'What It Means To Be Free.'* All speeches will be five to seven minutes in length." Miss Scrypt introduces the faculty judges, and then each speaker.

"Now all is prepared, so it gives me great pleasure to introduce our first speaker. She is a leader at Madison; she is a head cheer leader, a member of National Honor Society, president of Athena Literary Society, and a member of numerous community outreach groups. She has titled her speech, *'Bondage Is Right Around The Corner.'* Please welcome Irene Funka."

Irene stands, smiles, and begins walking to the podium at center stage. Her heart is thumping because she knows she has drawn the most difficult assignment. Her opening is first; this means she must not only create interest in her speech, but also concurrently bring the audience up to a level of anticipation. This is not easy. Miss Scrypt correctly remains at the podium, greets Irene by shaking her hand, and then retires stage side to listen to her speech.

Irene stands erect. She looks at the audience, composes herself, smiles, and then powerfully states, *"Live free! Live free! These words have a great ring. What do they mean to each of you?"* What a great opening; she has sparked interest and asked the audience to participate. They immediately feel a part of this.

Irene continues to develop her topic; she introduces the concept of free choice; she states, *"Freedom Implies Making Choices."* Irene discusses free choices, and how they benefit each person and society in general. Her next statement predicts something; *"Surrendering These Choices Invites Bondage."*

Things are moving along. She has set the stage for the introduction of a main point in her speech; *"Freedom Is Not the Norm, Bondage Is."* Look at her body language. Irene has wrapped her arms around herself. How graphic! *"Bondage Is The Lowest Common Denominator In History."* Irene talks from personal family experiences. She uses factual examples to illustrate her points.

The audience seems really interested. She has maintained their attention. Now she introduces a second main point, *"Freedom Is Unstable Long-Term. It Must Be Protected."* Look, everyone is following her every word. They nod as she discusses how bondage can easily slip back to become the norm again.

Powerful closing comments begin. *"Freedom Means Free Choices. Choices May Be Enjoyed. Choices Mean Responsibility."* All eyes are upon her. She has their complete attention. *"The Responsibility Is To Protect Freedom. That's What It All Means."* Irene pauses, raises her head, and emphatically directs her speech toward the balcony. *"When freedom is taken for granted, it is soon lost. Then, bondage is right around the corner!"*

The student body instantly responds; they clap loudly in great appreciation. They have just witnessed an excellent speech. Irene looks at them, smiles, and knows her presentation has gone very well. She is relieved it's over. Miss Scrypt approaches the podium and shakes Irene's hand; "Congratulations on a fine presentation, Irene."

Miss Scrypt introduces the next speaker. The four other speeches are presented in turn. At the conclusion of the fifth speech, Miss Scrypt announces a short three minute recess to confer with the judges.

After three minutes the verdict is in. Miss Scrypt approaches the podium once again to make the final announcement.

"We are all very fortunate to have heard five excellent speakers and speeches today. The judges have selected, as the winner of this year's contest, Irene Funka and her speech, *"Bondage Is Right Around The Corner."* Irene, please come up and accept your winning trophy."

At home in the little bungalow on Maple Street, Irene's trophy becomes the Funka family trophy. It is placed in the living room, in the center of the mantle. This trophy represents a family's effort; it represents a family's story; it will now become part of the family's American Story.

Chapter Nineteen

Headlines appear in the star journal. Guy Hartmann Jr. appointed to West Point! What a major story. Guy is the first citizen in the history of Blissville to receive such an honor. At Madison High School the announcement is made to great acclaim. Teachers and students are so very proud of him, and proud to know him personally. Guy is the topic of conversation everywhere. In local stores, the supermarket, auto repair shops, governmental offices, the fire department, in every corner of Blissville people are talking. Old timers cannot remember any local news to equal it. Blissville is on the map! With all this fuss, Guy just appears very humble. He is a quiet leader. He never says much.

Today is Friday; tonight is a major event in the lives of Madison seniors. It's their Senior Prom, one last opportunity to "dress up," and have a social outing with classmates. The event will be held at the Armory, a space large enough to accommodate a crowd. Music will be provided by the new local band, Stanley V's. All week long teams of students have been working after school on decorations, with a theme of "Orchids." The old Armory looks completely refreshed!

This afternoon, classes at Madison are cancelled to allow students the time to prepare for tonight's festivities. Around town girls are at local hair dressers all during the afternoon. The boys trickle in and out of Seymour's tuxedo rental on First Street. Florist shops are rushing to finish corsage orders. It's a busy day for small businesses in Blissville.

At 6:30 p.m. smartly attired students begin arriving at Mary Beth's house for a pre-dance party. Guy is already there, being the official greeter as Mary Beth's date for the evening; they have been dating for most of this year. To those around them, Guy and Mary Beth are viewed as the "perfect couple."

Look, the boys are breaking off into small groups again. When will they ever grow out of this? In reality, they don't even know why they are here this evening; it's apparently something that happens as seniors; they're just along for the ride. Girls have promoted the whole thing. The punch bowl becomes their gathering spot. Mary Beth plays the part of the gracious host, making sure they feel most welcome.

Irene and Russell arrive; they have "doubled" with another couple because Russell is still not driving. This has been a rough time for Russell since his accident.

Over at the Armory Stanley begins to set up. To him, playing *to* his Prom is much more important than playing *at* his Prom. Tonight he has expanded the band with Vista College music students, so the sound should be great. Stanley is dressed in a black tuxedo, ready to go.

After 7:30 p.m. some students are seen arriving at the Armory. The most popular attire for men is a white Tuxedo jacket, although a few are dressed in the more traditional black tuxedo. Ladies all have light-hued dresses of various colors with their favorite corsage, a nosegay, on their arms. Couples gravitate to the round tables surrounding the perimeter of the dance floor, where the ladies place their purses. It isn't long before the ladies begin to congregate together, talking about matapalo[18] dresses, tonight's dance preparations, and where they will be going to eat after the Prom. The men are left to talk about sports, or the cars driven this evening.

Promptly at 8 p.m. Stanley raises his arm; the band commences playing, *"Can't Take My Eyes Off Of You,"* to get the evening started. They sound fantastic this evening. Stanley has certainly brought its quality up these past few months. Immediately the dance floor fills. Everyone dances this first dance. After the first few dances, some couples can be spotted sitting at the tables, talking.

An absolute must tonight is having a picture taken by Cy, the resident photographer. Cy has a small shop down on Second Street. He has constructed what appears to be a small bridge over a brook, surrounded by orchids; here couples will stand to have their picture taken at "big city" prices. "Hey, nothing personal, it's just business!" Tonight is a captive audience, and besides, the ladies demand it! Photos will be mailed to each lady's address. Guy and Mary Beth are the first couple photographed.

A few of the students congregate in front of the band to watch its members close up. Each musician is dressed in a black tuxedo, and sits on a folding chair in front of a small stand, which holds his music. "Stanley V's" is printed on the front of each stand. Small lights illuminate the music. Stanley sometimes stands, and sometimes sits, as he directs. His music is supported by a very attractive, clear-plastic music stand, the very same music stand that won the yellow ribbon in Mr. Sander's 8th grade Industrial Arts class! Mary Beth smiles at Stanley as he turns around.

At 10 p.m. it is time for the Grand March. Stanley directs the band in a rousing Sousa March tune as Senior Class Officers form a line. They march up the center of the floor,

---

[18] 1967 Public Broadcasting Act

and then split in opposite directions to return to where they started. On each pass around the room, the size doubles as new couples are added to the end of the line. Soon, a second line, a third line, and many more are needed. All the couples become a part of the dance. One last march around the room finishes it off. "Hold it right there!" Cy's got the photo. It's free with the cost of the others!

Around 11:00 p.m. some couples begin to file out of the Armory and head toward local restaurants, even though the band will still be playing until midnight. A favorite spot is the Brass Lantern, on the edge of town. Tonight, dinner will be served until midnight, so just enough time remains. Owner, Jake Stakes, has encouraged this Prom night dinner by offering several economical specials for the students; reservations quickly made it a sellout. By 11:45 p.m. the restaurant is packed with happy seniors, and so, slowly, as they settle down to dinner, the Special Generation's Prom experience draws to a most satisfactory close.

Chapter Twenty

Graduation day has arrived. For the past eighteen years the Blessed Generation has benefited from a life experience that could only have been imagined by any prior generation. They have been dancing the waltz of life; the music has been playing and playing. They have not been hungry; they have had abundant shelter, cheap transportation, affordable clothing, and most anything they wanted. Most importantly they have been safe, sheltered in a country and city where their life could be enjoyed to the fullest. With the economic prosperity provided by the peace dividend from the War, they have had the means and the leisure time to do so. Their lives have truly been defined by a series of never ending pleasant experiences! Their life experience has not existed anywhere else in the world. Today they will be released into that world, confident and ready to take their place in it. Today the music ends!

The auditorium at Madison is full. Parents and family members have taken every available seat. Seated on stage are members of the National Honor Society. Irene, Mary Beth, and Guy can be seen here. Other graduating seniors are seated in the first four rows, in alphabetical order.

Stanley is in the fourth row, near the isle; Russell appears near the center in row two. At center stage is the same podium from the speech contest. To the right are four chairs containing today's speakers. Mr. Corpus rises, and walks toward the podium.

"Ladies and gentlemen, guest speakers, and most certainly graduating seniors, four short years ago, today's graduates entered the halls of Madison High School as wide-eyed freshmen, about to embark on an *"enriched"* educational experience that will conclude today." Eyes in the audience grow heavy. Hopefully this won't take too long. Some fifteen minutes later, "and in conclusion let us not forget that the process of learning never ends." A polite smattering of applause fills the auditorium.

Now, Mr. Corpus introduces Mr. Usher, President of The Board Of Education. Mr. Usher's carefully prepared remarks take another seventeen minutes. A second smattering of applause fills the auditorium.

Mr. Caper walks to the podium. "A most satisfying feeling for educators is witnessing the many awards received by our students for the culmination of four years of hard work. I am most pleased to recognize the following students with citations of merit for excellence." Mr. Caper begins the process of singling out each recipient for special notation or for scholarship. Upon reaching Irene's name, he says, "this next student is one of the most active ladies at Madison. I am so very pleased to announce that Irene Funka is the recipient of a full four-year scholastic scholarship to State." Applause is somewhat louder and prolonged for this announcement. "And finally, this next recipient is well known to all at Madison as a star athlete, scholar, and student leader. I am most honored to announce, once again, that Guy Hartmann Jr. has been appointed to West Point where he will play football and someday protect our country." The audience really erupts in applause at this announcement.

Mr. Corpus returns to the podium to begin the awarding of diplomas. He announces the name of each student to the audience, as that student walks across the stage to receive his diploma. Mary Beth receives a nice applause. Russell holds up his diploma to the audience, and Stanley kisses his as it is presented to him.

Finally, Mr. Corpus introduces The Reverend Raymond Blest, who gives the benediction.

Suddenly, it is over. The Blessed Generation has graduated. They are adults now; they are ready for the world, and the world is waiting for them. In their minds, this is only the next step in a pleasant life experience. They are expecting the world to roll over for them, just as it always has. They will cruise down the highway of life, and continue the merry journey. Opportunities will abound for the energetic. After all, this has been their experience to date. They are confident and optimistic about the future matapalo [19] and their place in it. Their proud parents and family surround them today; everyone is in a happy mood. In the balcony an elderly lady, with a tear in her eye, quietly exits. It is Miss Uppryte.

END OF PART ONE

---

[19] 1967 Age Discrimination in Employment Act

PART TWO

Chapter Twenty One

A bright-eyed Russell Murphy confidently walks into the used car lot at Murphy Chevrolet. Yesterday he was a student; today he begins his career at the family owned business. He has been assigned to work with Dusty Roads, used car manager, in learning the basics of the business from this vantage point. Later, he hopes to join Red Blaze and his Father in selling new vehicles. His Grandfather, Sean, is in his early 70's now, and has begun talking about cutting back. Russell knows that whenever his Grandfather retires, there will be an opportunity for rapid advancement in the firm for those qualified. Russell has another positive today; his driving privileges have been restored, although they are somewhat muted in driving his mother's 6-cylinder 1965 Chevy Nova. Oh, well, he will make a name for himself here, in the used car lot, and then have the money to drive something more to his liking, like a Camaro or Firebird!

The used car lot sits alongside the main building, to the right. A small 12 by 12 foot edifice with window air conditioner serves as an office; it's pretty depressing. Inside are a table and a few folding chairs, used in conducting business. Outside, around the perimeter, long

94

clothes lines can be seen supporting triangular vinyl patches of various colors that flap in the breeze. Some forty older vehicles sit on the lot, just waiting for the right person to come along and purchase them. Russell's job, make it happen!

Dusty greets Russell as he enters the small office, "Hey Russell, you're finally going to work for a living!"

Russell knows it is all in fun, and responds, "Yes, every day, for 60 minutes longer than you!"

Both laugh as Dusty begins to instruct Russell in the "used car" basics. "The keys to each vehicle are coded and placed on this board. At closing, the board is taken to the main building and placed into the safe."

Russell notices many books on a bookshelf. "What are these for?"

"Oh, they are for your reference in getting to know a particular brand. What helps in a sales presentation is knowledge; know as much as possible about what you are selling, in order to convey truthfulness to the buyer, and remove uncertainty. Nothing kills a potential sale faster than uncertainty!" This is all making sense to Russell.

"Russell, when a potential buyer has reached the test-drive stage, take one of these forms to fill out his information, and verify his driver's license. Only then do you get the keys. If you know the person, you can allow him to drive alone; otherwise it is a good idea to tag along on the test drive. It's your call on this one."

"If the prospect indicates that he is going to purchase the vehicle, *Stop Talking!* Reach up here for a purchase contract, and establish early if he will pay cash, or finance. Then fill out the information, and establish his price. After the prospect signs the agreement, take it to the main office for approval."

Sensing that Russell thinks this is easy, Dusty pauses; "Now the real sales effort begins! Almost always his offer will be rejected. Your job is to make him offer more. That is when knowledge obtained from these books pays off!" Dusty winks at Russell, "Selling used cars successfully requires a special type of person. Stock brokers, attorneys, and used car salesmen are the bottom three on the list of least admired workers. You'll stand out if you do your job properly; you'll then have a sale."

"Now, let's talk about the process of selling. Don't talk too much. Listen to the buyer. Many times a buyer will tell you one thing, and want something else entirely different. Listen to him and be ready to offer alternatives. I can't count the number of times a prospect has bought a different vehicle than the one he was originally looking for!" Dusty gazes momentarily over the used car lot. "Have fun and the sales will come."

The untold secret of the car business is the huge potential profit center that is the used car lot! For this potential to be realized, several things must happen. The used car manager must first select the proper inventory. He must know what will sell, what products people will demand. This is no easy task because tastes can change literally overnight. A wrong guess results in a car lot full of depreciating inventory, that no one will buy. Next, the proper inventory must be purchased at a price that insures a profit. Again, this is no easy task because the popular items that most people demand cost more to begin with. And finally comes the skill of the salesman, to "bring it all home." If the salesman can't obtain a generous offer, the first two efforts are for naught. This is the little drama that Russell joins today. If he negotiates it successfully, his star will rise, for the used car lot will become the highest profit center in the firm! This is his great opportunity. He has longed to sell cars for many years. His time has arrived. "Yes, my name is Russell, and I want to sell you a quality used car!"

Russell senses he must quickly learn as much as he can about the existing inventory.

"Dusty, I'm going to walk thru the lot to familiarize myself with the cars; back in a moment."

Russell walks down the rows making mental notes of the vehicles, the brand, the year, the overall condition. At the rear of the lot, a very clean six cylinder 1962 Chevrolet Impala coupe catches his eye. Since this is a six cylinder model, he knows it is going to be hard to sell. People want V8's. What Russell does not know is that this particular vehicle was purchased at a very low price for that very reason. If it is sold at a price anywhere near its "blue book" value, it will be the most profitable sale on the lot. Its placement at the rear of the lot reflects its "lack of star" status. Russell returns to the office and begins to page thru the reference books to increase his knowledge.

Nothing much happens in the lot all morning long. Russell continues to study his manuals. Around 12:15 an attractive middle-aged woman walks into the lot; she appears to be looking at the economy cars. Dusty says, "This is your prospect. Go out, introduce yourself, and see what you can do."

Russell hustles out, greeting the lady, "Hello, my name is Russell, and I want to sell you a quality used car!"

The lady smiles and says, "I'm looking for something very economical, for our second car."

"Excellent, we have some great smaller vehicles at very attractive prices. Let's walk around."

Russell begins to ask questions about her family, her existing family car, the use for the new car, how much she wants to spend, the usual questions. He is doing exactly what he should be doing, gathering information. She quickly answers all his queries. Russell notices that while they have been talking, she has glanced at a beautiful 2-year old Buick several times.

"It's a beautiful vehicle, isn't it?"

"Oh yes, but we could never afford that" says the lady.

Russell thinks . . . she has told me she wants an economy

car, but her eyes tell me she wants a luxury car. Here is something concrete I can work on. Here is a sales opportunity.

"Can you see yourself in a luxury car? Would you enjoy that?"

The lady nods in agreement and smiles.

"I think I can make it happen for you. Follow me!"

He leads her directly to the six-cylinder Impala.

"Here is the best buy on the lot. You get the same luxury as the Buick, but also an economical six-cylinder engine that saves gas, and this beautiful Impala costs only half what the Buick does. It costs only slightly more than a boring economy car. Isn't that marvelous?"

She readily agrees.

"Yes, I think, no Plain-Jane small car for you! You are ready for a test drive in a luxury vehicle! I'll get the keys."

What a nice sales presentation Russell has made so far.

The test drive goes well. She loves the car. She believes it will be perfect for her family.

"Let's write up an offer," chirps Russell.

Wham! A road block; all momentum stops!

"I'll have to talk it over with my husband."

Oh, no, the dreaded *"let me think it over response."*
This is the point where most sales are lost. Russell must keep the momentum going. He must think of something fast.

"When does your husband get off work?"

"5:00 p.m."

Here's the opportunity. She has made a concrete statement. Show urgency.

"OK, I will hold this for you until 5:30 this evening. A car of this quality won't last. Bring your husband at 5:30. I'll have everything ready for you then."

She thanks him, and leaves.

Russell walks toward the office. What did Dusty say, "Nothing kills a sale faster than uncertainty?" I must be organized at 5:30. Get all the facts about this car. Have them ready. Have a financing package ready, if there is a need. Know exactly what the lowest possible payment will be. She already wants the car, so there is a good matapalo[20] chance it is sold if her husband feels comfortable, if the uncertainty is removed.

Dusty looks over Russell's shoulder, "This is a nice presentation. You are organized. I think you have a good chance." Russell bristles with confidence.

Shortly after 5:30 the lady returns with her husband, who appears to be a businessman. He has a nice appearance. He introduces himself as Mr. Gross. Russell is somewhat nervous, but doesn't let it show. He gets right to business. No need to resell the car to Mrs. Gross; in her mind she has already bought it. Only need to eliminate any uncertainty in Mr. Gross' mind. Russell "sells up," talking about the virtues of the Buick to Mr. Gross. Then he "sells down," by comparing the lack of benefits in an economy car. He has the correct miles per gallon data for each vehicle, as well as relative current market prices. All that remains to be discussed is the engine, for this is the reason he's gotten this far.

"This 6 cylinder engine is one of the all-time great engines. Its basic design has been around for years, with improvements being made all along. It's cheap to operate. It costs almost nothing to maintain. You can expect many years of carefree driving, both city and highway." Russell pauses, and says, "What do you think?"

Silence! Russell says nothing.

Finally Mr. Gross says to his wife, "If this is what you really want, OK."

All that remains is to fill out the paperwork. They agree on the posted asking price for the car, which seems fair to everyone. Mr. Gross will pay cash. He writes out a check

---

[20] 1968 Bilingual Education Act

for the full amount. Thirty minutes later a most happy lady drives out of the lot with her new "luxury-economy" car!

By closing time word has spread thru the dealership that Russell, on his first day, has sold the car that couldn't be sold. More than a few eyebrows have been raised. In reality though, this sales job started way back in Miss Uppryte's kindergarten class, during "Show and Tell," when Russell told to his classmates, "My name is Russell, and I want to sell you a new Chevrolet!"

Chapter Twenty Two

Cars clutter the tree-lined driveway of the Hartmann family farm, for Mr. and Mrs. Guy Hartmann Sr. are hosting a going away reception for Guy today. Tomorrow he will depart for the United States Military Academy at West Point, New York. The Academy, which will be his home for the next four years, is located on historic land on the Hudson River, about fifty miles north of New York City. Family and long-time friends are here today wishing him well and saying goodbye to Guy as a civilian.

Mary Beth is most ambivalent. She is so proud of his success. The excitement surrounding his appointment has been exhilarating. She tries to put on a good face, but knows he is going away for a very long time. Their relationship will be altered severely. For the last year she has been dating the most popular boy in Blissville, but that is now coming to an end. In a way, Guy has just become engaged to the military. That is what is hard for her to accept. She has never in her life been second choice for anything. She has always been first choice, as the most popular girl in Blissville.

All afternoon former teachers, family, and friends stop by

to wish their best. One of the first to arrive is Miss Uppryte. Also seen are coach Spikes, and Mrs. Epich. Coach Spikes and Guy reminisce about the Cloverdale game, "The Play," and how Guy gave up personal glory for the benefit of the team. Guy tells Mrs. Epich that he will never forget Lincoln's Gettysburg Address; he will carry it with him always. As the last guest leaves, only Mary Beth remains. Guy will drive her home. It is now time to say goodbye.

Not one word is spoken during the short drive to Mary Beth's house. There is no need for conversation. Guy knows exactly what he is about, without making explanations. He has always been that way. Those around him sense this and know exactly what he is expressing, even though he says nothing. Mary Beth and Guy walk hand in hand up the sidewalk, enter the house and stand in the foyer. Mary Beth notices a single tear in Guy's eye. Her eyes are very misty. They embrace. They hold each other for an eternity. Guy kisses Mary Beth one last time, and he is gone.

****

Today is Reception Day at West Point. The view of the Hudson is breathtaking as each new cadet recruit arrives with his family. Guy was a stand out in Blissville, but there are no local stand outs at West Point. What is past is past. From here on all are equal, as plebes. Their lives will be structured beyond recognition. First order of business today will be a short briefing, for the benefit of recruits and their parents. The recruits are told they will be passing thru a series of processing stations; the parents are told they will be touring West Point and meeting staff and learning about the Army. That's it. That's the briefing. This is so military.

"Recruits, you have 90 seconds to say goodbye."

So, here is the first opportunity to adjust to the way things happen in the military. Guy embraces his mother and father, Florence kisses her "baby" one last time, and they reluctantly, grudgingly, give their son to the United States Army.

For the next several hours, Guy passes thru various stations where he receives a physical examination, an agility test, a military haircut, and military clothing. New recruits are allowed to say nothing, and are led thru the stations by juniors, who are called "cows." They are instructed in the correct way to stand and to respond. In the last station they meet with an attorney, who explains the papers which must be signed to officially enlist in the matapalo[21] army. They are instructed that they may not be married or have dependents, and must agree to five years of service once they begin their junior year.

In late afternoon parents and families gather to watch the Oath Ceremony. Their new cadets can be seen dressed in smart white uniform shirts and gray pants as they march toward the Oath Ceremony, to swear allegiance to the United States and the Constitution. At its conclusion, the command is given, "Right Face, and March;" the cadet recruits disappear into a large building as parents watch, hoping to gain one final glimpse of their sons. Tomorrow morning at 5:30 a.m., military life begins with six and one half weeks of tough basic training called "Beast Barracks."

---

[21] 1968 Gun Control Act

Chapter Twenty Three

Vista College is a beautiful liberal arts school, located in the rolling hills forty miles south of Blissville. The college dates to 1837, when it was founded in the middle of an untamed wilderness, primarily as an educational institution for the clergy. Today it is a full baccalaureate college, offering Bachelor of Arts and Bachelor of Science degrees for about 1500 students. Vista is expensive, but the intimate environment and low class size set it apart. It attracts an upper crust. It is a perfect fit for Mary Beth, who begins her college experience today as a freshman voice and fine arts major.

In high school Mary Beth was always an excellent student, but never expressed keen interest in any specific discipline. She experienced life to the fullest, and didn't need to apply herself excessively. More than any of her classmates, she exemplified the Blessed Generation; she just cruised down the highway of life. Events always happened to her, and for her. Now it will be the same in college. This is an experience that was totally impossible for her mother; it is made available to her as a rite.

Mary Beth will reside in The Samuel S. Dwelling Hall this semester. All freshmen girls reside here. Her roommate, Sally Thompson, just arrived from the east coast yesterday, so last night was spent talking until almost 4:00 a.m. in the morning. They discussed, of course, boyfriends, and Guy's name was brought up often. The two girls are rapidly becoming fast friends; so much has been found in common already. There will be many things to do and experience together this year.

Tonight the college is sponsoring a mixer for faculty, students, and all incoming freshmen. This is such a nice touch, and only possible in a school the size of Vista. Faculty will be present to talk about respective programs, as well as to meet their future students. At Vista, students and faculty confer in small groups in a very relaxing manner. The rigid, formal class structure is broken down somewhat to everyone's benefit; they become closer. This is what sets Vista apart.

After dinner, several of the girls from Dwelling Hall walk together toward the Student Union and the mixer. Pleasant musical sounds, which originate from a small group inside the building, great them outside on the sidewalk. The girls walk in; Mary Beth freezes. Standing not twenty five feet in front of her, directing all the music, is *Stanley!*

Mary Beth rushes toward the combo. "Stanley! Stanley!"

Stanley looks up, smiles, and says, "Hi, Mary Beth, Surprise!"

. . . Now, you can just imagine what goes thru the minds of those present, watching this beautiful young freshman coed rush toward the band. It is so unexpected; Mary Beth's new friends wonder what the connection is to this group. Professor Hoven, who has been talking with a group of students, looks up to observe, but says nothing. "Ole" Stanley doesn't miss a beat, playing his music and smiling to Mary Beth at the same time.

Mary Beth's friends rush over and demand to know the connection. Mary Beth rapidly explains. "I've known him since kindergarten; we have gone all thru school together.

Older students and faculty, who have been watching from around the room, know the whole story about Stanley, here at Vista. Stanley V's combo has been playing regularly at Vista since January. Since the huge amount of publicity last winter, he is better known on campus than the football coach, so Mary Beth has just rushed up to greet some kind of local "rock star!" As if Mary Beth didn't need more attention, from this moment on she will be acknowledged as the most recognized and most beautiful girl on campus. She also knows Stanley!

During the mixer, Mary Beth is approached by groups of students and individuals alike. It's always the same question, "How do you know Stanley?" The other girls love to be near her, because she always attracts a crowd. They feel right in the center of it all. Bye and bye, Professor Hoven walks up to introduce himself. By coincidence, in light of her course of study, Mary Beth will be in his Survey of Music class first thing tomorrow morning at 9:00 a.m.

"Well, I see you are acquainted with Stanley!"

May Beth responds, "Yes I am." She goes thru the explanation one more time, and then states, "I believe I will be in your class tomorrow morning."

"Excellent, says Professor Hoven, because I will be talking about initiative and courage. Stanley is the topic of my lecture!"

Ka-Boom! Jaws drop, and Mary Beth ascends the ladder of esteem another notch!

Later that evening in Dwelling Hall, girls surround Mary Beth in the lounge. There is so much to talk about: boyfriends, high school life, different regions of the country, likes and dislikes, and of course the "buzz" about Stanley at the mixer. This continues until 11:00 p.m. when things break up and each girl heads toward her room for a good night's sleep. Tomorrow is the first day of class. One senses the girls are forming friendships quickly, another positive about Vista College.

Chapter Twenty Four

State is a huge university, located some one hundred miles south of Blissville. It is a collection of almost 50,000 students from across the U.S. and around the world, and is the largest institution of higher learning in the state. Here a student is swallowed up by those around him. It is difficult to stand out, but for a student with an outgoing personality and an inclination, there is all the room in the world to grow. This environment is a perfect fit for Irene. She has the matching personality.

Classes have been in session for six months now. Irene has settled in, and is working on two majors, journalism and political science. She resides in Schyler Hall, a gigantic ten story residence hall that is really a small city unto its self. Most of her classes are in MacGovern Hall, where the journalism and political science departments are located. If any incoming freshman has ever had an easier transition to college life than Irene, it would be hard to imagine. One would believe she has been here forever. From the very first day, she has interacted with the upper classmen to immediately become part of campus life. She has taken a great interest in politics and current events, and following the lead of upperclassmen, has joined in protests against the War and about Civil Rights, that are overtaking the campus. This appears to be a 180 degree reversal from high school days.

The bonds from high school are slowly being broken. Her former close friends are spreading out in many different directions, and in many different disciplines. Mary Beth has nestled in a small, rural liberal arts college where she feels totally protected from civil turmoil. Guy is far off in the military, learning to be a soldier. Russell is working diligently, selling cars. Stanley is developing a musical product. Nobody is the least bit interested in, or involved with, politics or current events, so gradually new faces are filling the void of the old and becoming part of Irene's world. Matthew Fend, a senior "Poly-Sci" major, has taken Irene under his wing, and it is thru him that she has redirected her focus. But, she has also kept him off balance with her amazing ability to twist and assume power. Men have always had trouble getting close to Irene. She is using him and he doesn't even know it! Irene's relationships have always been about power.

Look at Irene's appearance now! The cuteness from high school is gone. Her hair is longer and pulled back; she wears no make-up; her clothing consists of sloppy old jeans and tie-dyed shirts; her demeanor is that of an angry young white coed, completely in tune with the times. She calls herself a "yippie," a member of the Youth International Party, echoing Abbie Hoffman, Jerry Rubin, Paul Krassner, Dick Gregory, and friends. Love and pot smoking is everywhere. Blissville would not recognize her.

Matthew and Irene sit in a coffee shop off campus; they sip on small cups of espresso.

"Ike (that's what he calls her), tonight all is set for the protest rally in front of the draft office. Some of the leaders from last month's protest rally in New York City will be here. They will draw a crowd. The TV people will be telecasting everything. I've already arranged for that. We have secured a van with microphone and loud speakers. We're hoping to have five hundred State students present to support us in this. We need some local speakers to rally from our end. You are so good at communicating. Will you address the crowd for five minutes tonight?"

"I wouldn't want to pass up an opportunity like this! Sure, I'll do it!"

The draft office is located downtown, in the middle of the block on Sumter Street. It is just a small, forty foot wide office, between Cannon's drug store, and Ashley hardware. Since the rally is registered with the police and is legal, the entire block will be corded off beginning at 6:00 p.m., with traffic redirected. At exactly 6:00 p.m. the van with loud speakers arrives, and is slowly positioned on the street to the right of the draft office. Workers quickly set up a 10 ft. by 10 ft. speakers' platform. Matthew and Irene arrive at 6:15; the New York people arrive soon after. As Matthew huddles with them to choreograph the program, Irene thinks to herself, these people really look harsh!

By 6:30 a small crowd has gathered with more arriving every minute. At 6:45 Channel 7's TV crew arrives and begins to set up. At 6:50 loud, angry music blares from the speakers. Shortly after 7:00, Matthew addresses the crowd.

"We are standing in front of the office that claims our young people. . ."

It doesn't take much skill in public speaking to arouse them, and soon a great "buzz" is heard; loud booing and chanting erupts whenever the War or the draft is mentioned. TV cameras are rolling, capturing a hostile and angry crowd against the War. Matthew loves every moment of it. He thinks he is the center of it all. He thinks it's all about him! Matthew now raises the bar by introducing the New York people. The crowd reacts anew. These New York protestors are real pros. They know how to rally and incite crowds; Matthew is only a minor leaguer in this.

The tempo and rhetoric instantly change from bold to acidic. Inflammatory language just rolls off their tongues.

"We defy the government. We won't support it. What are we going to do? What are we going to do? We will bring down the government!"

The crowd chants, *"No more draft! No more draft! No more draft!"*

Crash, tinkle, tinkle! *Ka-Boom!* A sound of shattering glass! An incendiary bomb has gone off! The draft office has been hit; it's in flames. Get out of the way! The crowd panics. Screams are heard. People are being trampled. Channel 7 has it all! Police are totally helpless in trying to control the crowd. Arrests are being made. They have Matthew. The New York people have disappeared. Irene surveys the horrible developing fiery spectacle, and instinctively backs away, quickly melting into the crowd. Soon the drug store goes up in flames, and then the hardware store. The whole block is on fire. It will be a total loss. What a story for Channel 7!

Irene hurries back to Schyler Hall. She ducks in a side door and goes right to her room on the 8th floor. Even though the sky is black, she can see the red glow caused by the inferno downtown. How did this go so terribly wrong? What has happened to Matthew? She has a very bad feeling about those New York people. Were they the cause this? What is going to happen now? What should she do? Will she be implicated? What about her scholarship? Irene drops head first onto her bed, and just cries and cries.

Channel 7 interrupts regular programming. *"A huge 3-alarm fire is raging downtown on Sumter Street. An entire city block is in flames. Film at 11:00!"*

At 11:00 p.m. it's the lead story. *"In one of the most intense fires in local history, an entire city block has burned. The blaze started during an anti-war protest rally in front of the draft office, led by university students. The*

FBI has been called in to investigate. Many arrests have been made. Are out of town forces behind this?" Pictures on TV show Matthew speaking to the crowd, then the flames. *"University officials have stated that guilty parties will be dealt with harshly."*

****

Some weeks later, Irene and Matthew walk down the barren block of Sumter Street. The only remembrance of the fiery holocaust that marked a planned peaceful demonstration is a complete void of buildings.

"I wonder how this block will be rebuilt. Maybe a block-long draft office to recruit the increasing number of young men required in the war," says a sarcastic Matthew.

Irene allows the comment to go unnoticed. She has changed. She has been thinking for the past weeks about what had happened here, and how lucky she was to not be implicated in the event. Poor Matthew was arrested, and spent several days in jail for his part. As the FBI investigated the matter, it became increasingly clear that Matthew had nothing to do with the bombing and was therefore released with only a minor citation. The University, however, was less forgiving. In the middle of his final semester, he was dismissed from school. He will be allowed to finish up this summer, pending further review and a clean record.

Irene is a smart young lady. She has come to realize that violent protests are not the answer to anything. She also realizes that her future is tied directly to her scholarship. This must be protected at all cost. Irene still feels the need to join social causes, but knows she must find another way. A way is presently being illuminated to her; it is thru her course of study in journalism and political science! This is where she will spend her time, energy, and talent. Matthew should do the same.

Chapter Twenty Five

A picket line forms in front of Hartmann Dairy, Blissville's oldest employer. The dairy has been a family owned and operated business since 1856. From the very beginning, family members were the only employees. As the business grew and prospered, more employees were needed. Outsiders were brought in to fill the need. Over the years, more and more employees were required, more and more outsiders were hired. A point was reached where these became the majority. From this juncture, the family nature of the business began to slowly decline. Hartmann Dairy became a "factory," with the usual employer-employee labor problems. It drifted for a time in this state, but its hourly workers then took the next step and became unionized; now we are seeing a first result of that effort in this labor stoppage, to obtain increased wages and benefits. It surely is a sign of the times. All throughout the country, old boundaries are suddenly being broken down, as rising prices are causing dislocations everywhere. The recent large wage increases by auto workers and teamsters have not gone unnoticed. The milk drivers want the same. They are exercising their right to strike; it is their option.

Last year the auto workers negotiated a contract with a

7% overall increase in pay and benefits, with a defined cost of living adjustment tucked in, for the future. That settlement has become the standard. The floodgates have been opened; other workers must try to obtain matching benefits. Times are good, and generous gains are possible for all. Grab it while you can. In the not so distant future Blissville residents will read about a total work stoppage in France, a Chrysler wildcat strike, a New York City teacher's strike, and a Florida statewide teacher's strike. They will hear a sitting U.S. President decline to re-run for office, and tragically see two political leaders assassinated. So, get your settlement now, quickly. A bell won't ring, but anyone noticing these cumulating effects on society must surely realize that the peace dividend from the war is exhausted. The music that has been playing for the Blessed Generation has been silenced. It is a new time, and not necessarily a better one.

Chapter Twenty Six

"Gimme a head with hair, long beautiful hair, shining, gleaming, streaming, flaxen, waxen, give me down to there, hair. . .!" Stanley listens to the radio in his van. He's hearing words of a new rock musical, *"Hair,"* that is taking the country by storm. It puts to words the theatre he is observing every day in his own world; the challenge of his Blessed Generation with the sexual revolution, a war, and conservative parents and society. The musical is all new and shocking. It defines a time when the old boundaries in society are breaking apart, and flowing into a new, "free spirit, anything goes," time with no boundaries. Stanley thinks, this is 1955 all over again; then Rosemary Clooney to Bill Haley, now the Beach Boys to a rock musical called "Hair." The big question, is this going to last? Is this one of those moments that should be grasped? Should he begin to change the style of the band's music? A very difficult decision for a young man not yet twenty!

Stanley knows that the success of the band to date rests on the fact that people enjoy the music, nothing more. There is no right music or wrong music, only correct music. He has been able to develop a style that pleases crowds at this moment in time, and so the band has become successful. As the moment in time passes, he must adjust to the new moment, whatever that is. He believes, from what he is seeing and hearing today, the moment has already arrived. It is important for him to be early, but not too early. The "Beatles" have recently made the change, so they have pioneered the crossover. They have taken the risk. It is safer to follow now.

Stanley formulates a plan. He must play music that his audience wants to hear. An older crowd at the Elks Lodge would not be a good place to showcase a radical change. It must be tried in the proper setting. A booking at Vista College might be the place. Here he can introduce a slight modicum of change, to the new psychedelic rock style, and see what the reaction is. It doesn't have to be for the whole evening, only a small portion of it. If the music bombs, it won't be fatal.

Stanley reasons, *"Sergeant Pepper's Lonely Hearts Club Band"* has been released for some time now, so he will test it first. People know the *"Beatles."* He'll play nothing too radical in the beginning, maybe *"When I'm Sixty-Four,"* that is set with a clarinet accompaniment. He can handle that. Audiences are already familiar with the sound. Then he will move into the less radical *"Hair"* tunes of *"Aquarius," Good Morning Starshine," and "Let The Sun Shine In."* That should be plenty. The key is not to change too much, too fast. Bring the audience along slowly, just as the auto companies do in model changeovers. It should work.

The dinner dance, on Homecoming Weekend at Vista College, is the major fall campus social event. Faculty and alumni meet, and have an opportunity to interact for the benefit of the college. Since few students attend, this is a perfect test with a mature audience. If the music is received favorably, Stanley knows this is his new direction.

On Homecoming Weekend, he is ready. For several weeks the band has been rehearsing, making sure the sound is absolutely correct. Tonight he will know; it's Saturday evening of Homecoming. The band sits behind their music stands, with little lights illuminating the music. All are dressed in black tuxedos, very smart looking. Stanley sets things in motion with some old standards, *"Moon River, Tennessee Waltz, and Fascination,"* which are well received by the audience. One by one couples move onto the dance floor, off of the dance floor, for this dance, not for that dance, with no reason in particular for their movements. Stanley observes a great deal of conversation taking place at the tables. He thinks to himself, this is not a dinner dance at all; this is a business dinner for the College.

As the evening wears on, Stanley feels the time has come for "our musical change." He takes a big breath, winks at the members of the band, and begins playing *"When I'm Sixty-Four."*

An astonishing thing happens. All table-side discussion stops, not one couple enters the dance floor, and all eyes become fixed upon Stanley and the band as they play. Stanley is having a very bad feeling about this, but puts on his best face possible. The other band members do the same. They play their "hearts out." This is not going the way they had hoped. No one is on the dance floor. What will happen when they are finished playing? Don't even think about it. Just continue playing. Just smile. At least appear as though it is a success. As the band finishes, a deafening silence fills the hall. *Ouch!* Then, surprise . . . faculty and alumni stand and applaud, and applaud. This is no mercy applause. They have enjoyed it! They didn't dance, but they really enjoyed it! How does this figure?

Stanley signals to the band, "Let's continue!" He directs *"Aquarius,"* to more applause. Next is *"Good Morning Starshine,"* with the same result. Lastly they play, *"Let the Sun Shine In,"* to the loudest applause of all. This whole set has been well received, but why no dancing? What is going on here? Stanley and the band have just stumbled onto new format for a dinner dance, part dance and part concert. It will soon become their trademark.

At the conclusion of the evening, many of the alumni approach the band and comment about the quality of the evening's music, and the new format. Stanley V's has just received very important regional publicity. These people will help expand the ever increasing range of the band's activities in the future.

Professor Hoven chats with Stanley. "You never cease to amaze me with your initiative and courage. This new format is just the ticket for a dinner dance. I don't know why no one has ever thought of it before?"

On the following Monday morning, the campus newspaper "Beacon" runs a story, *"Alumni Dinner Dance a Success with Stanley V's New Format."* On the weekend the "Blissfield Star Journal" reports, *"Stanley V's Band at Leading Edge Musically, Adjusts to New Times with New Format."* Publicity never hurts. Stanley is about to make his next step forward.

Chapter Twenty Seven

Two years have passed since high school graduation. Russell has adjusted beautifully to the adult world, and since his accident, his maturity level has climbed and climbed, and climbed. Russell is now making adult decisions with good outcomes. He has left behind his high school ways; he doesn't idle his time at the "Big Boy" anymore, and is spending more and more time with Dusty Roads. Dusty, in no small way, has become his guiding light thru his example of positive behavior. His tutelage has kept Russell from making the silly "rookie" mistakes, which has resulted in an earlier maturing sales skill; the end product of this, more and more sales. Russell has been the sales leader on the used car lot at Murphy Chevrolet almost every month since he started. The used car lot will become the most profitable unit at the firm one day very soon.

The car business in the U.S. has boomed these last two years. Although not yet fully recognized by the masses, this is the year that the long march to ever and ever larger and stronger engines will peak. The standard 350 cu in V-8 introduced for low priced cars will never be exceeded. Political noise about air pollution and rising oil prices will eventually force engine development in a different direction. But for now, most people want the new, stronger "V-8's." As we exit the decade of the 60's, the auto industry is paralleling society in general; the existing order of things is ending. In the auto industry, this year is the "last gasp of the way it was."

Dusty yells across the lot to Russell, "Phone call on line three!"

Russell hurries to the phone, grabs it, and announces, "This is Russell."

The voice on the other end, very modulated, very professional, says, "Hello Russell, this is Mr. Gross."

It has been two years since Russell has spoken with Mr. Gross, but he immediately recognizes the name; Mr. Gross was his first sale. "How's the car, Mr. Gross. I hope it has met your expectations."

"Oh, it has, and that is why I'm calling. Are there any others like it?"

"Yes, of course."

Before he is able to say anything more, Mr. Gross continues, "I'd like you to stop in my office at 10 a.m. tomorrow morning. Can you make it?"

"I'll be there at 10 sharp!"

Mr. Gross confirms the appointment and ends the conversation. It was a very short call, very professional and to the point.

Russell thinks to himself . . . something about that question he asked me sounds vaguely familiar. Hmmm . . . yes, that's the old "What's the firing order of a six cylinder Chevy" question we talked about in Mr. Rolls' auto mechanics class. Mr. Gross already knows the answer! When I go to his office, I've really got to be prepared. I must have all the facts. Russell looks up at the auto manuals on the shelf above him. These are my answers!

Russell spends most of the afternoon sifting thru page after page. His first thought is, the 1962 6-cylinder Impala that Mr. Gross purchased is seven years old now. Maybe he wants to replace it. If he does, he would want the 1964 model. But 1964 was the last model year for that design cycle, before a new styling change in 1965, so it wouldn't improve his position by much. In the 1965 model he would get all the benefits of the new, plus plenty of vehicles to choose from, because it was the highest sales year ever. Yes, 1965 is the year in which I will focus my effort.

Another thought comes to Russell's mind. Maybe he will want to compare similar products from Ford and Plymouth. There will be a slight price advantage with these; it won't hurt to mention it. He, after all, asked, "Are there any others like it?" What did he mean by "others?" I'll have comparisons available and prices for all three brands on hand when I meet with him.

At 9:55 a.m. the next morning, Russell is at Mr. Gross's office. It is located in the Pinnacle Tooling factory just outside of town, where Mr. Gross is general sales manager. Russell is greeted by Mr. Gross' secretary, and ushered into his office.

"Hello Russell, so nice of you to stop in today. Have a seat."

Mr. Gross mentions how happy his wife is with her Impala, and how she feels very uplifted when driving it, but doesn't want to stand out too much.

"This has made me think; why not have the same feeling in my sales people? I want them to feel important, but I don't want them to look overly ostentatious. After all, they are still selling tooling!"

Mr. Gross explains that company salesmen have been issued small economy cars. That doesn't make them feel important at all. He wants them to feel special, to aid them in their job of selling.

"Here is my proposal. As each of these small cars comes off lease, we will replace them with something similar to my wife's Impala. We will lease them from Murphy Chevrolet. You will be responsible for procuring each vehicle and for the leasing contract. Can you do it?"

"I certainly can. How many cars will we need?"

"Oh, around 50, I suppose!"

Russell picks himself off the floor, quickly thinking ahead.

"Although the Impala is my personal favorite, I'm sure each of your salesmen has a preference. Why not give each the option of selecting the model he would feel most comfortable in. Let him choose his vehicle from an approved list!"

"This is an excellent point, Russell, just what I was thinking. You should work for me!"

Russell opens his brief case, and produces data and prices for the 1965 Chevrolet Impala, Ford Galaxy 500, and Plymouth Fury.

"Here are the comparable products from three different manufacturers, all with the economy of a six cylinder engine. There are advantages of each. While the Impala has the same excellent "stovebolt six" that's in your wife's car, the Galaxy 500 has the new 240 cu in six that replaced the old 223 cu in engine. The Fury has an excellent 225 cu in "slant six" which has a slight performance advantage and is so durable. The Impala is the styling leader. The Fury is the performance leader. The Galaxy 500 is an all-around fine vehicle. Your salesmen will not feel unimportant in any of them, but they will feel most important in the model they choose!"

Russell looks at Mr. Gross for confirmation; then he continues. "I will prepare informational packets describing the approved vehicles for each of your salesmen. You will be responsible for having them make the selections, as well as noting the price you are willing to pay for each vehicle. These price lists should help you. Then I'll need one month to procure the vehicles after the contract is signed."

Russell makes a closing statement. "Your idea is perfect. Sales should increase handsomely! Can we have this ready to go in one month?"

Mr. Gross agrees and sets the next meeting for four weeks from today.

Back at the Murphy Chevrolet Used Car Lot, Russell huddles with Dusty. "Do you think we can do it?"

"We will, and this promises to be the largest single sale we have ever had. This is a job, well done, young man!"

One month later, the used car lot becomes the most profitable unit at Murphy Chevrolet.

Chapter Twenty Eight

Stanley opens the morning Star Journal, and notices an ominous headline; "Hartmann Dairy will discontinue home milk delivery!" A short story explains that milk will be, from this date forward, packaged in the new cardboard containers and be on sale at local supermarkets. A spokesman for the company explains, "New technology has created an opportunity for the company to become more efficient, which will allow us to hold the line on milk prices. Consumers will be happy to hear prices will not increase." The company does not discuss the recent work stoppage, but the paper is quick to point out that some 45 jobs will be eliminated by this action. The milk drivers have gained nothing in their strike.

This whole episode is seen by Stanley as confirmation that major societal change is afoot. He can see the rise in prices every day in his own life, and can feel what troubles are being caused by them. An increase in booking fees for the band, to increase his income, is not a good idea right now. The end product of that may be the same for him as for the milk drivers, no job. And, he has been thinking for some time about future living accommodations. Living with band members, forever, is not the ideal situation, and since his rent has recently been increased, is becoming less and less attractive every day. Price increases are hitting him hard, so today he will ₘₐₜₐₚₐₗₒ[22] begin to do something about it. Stanley will be meeting with local real estate agent Bernie Lake, from the Samuel S. Dwelling Real Estate Firm.

In Blissville, if it's real estate, Samuel S. Dwelling's finger prints are all over it. The firm sells more real estate than any other. Bernie Lake is resident manager, and has been associated with the firm for several years; he's an ideal person for Stanley to talk to. Stanley is prompt for his 1 p.m. meeting.

"Step into my office, Stanley. By the way, Mr. Dwelling wants to meet you. Sandra, will you tell Mr. Dwelling that Stanley is here."

They sit down, and Stanley begins to convey his financial plight and his idea to Bernie.

"I am considering buying a duplex, renting the upstairs unit to some band members, and living downstairs. The rent will help me satisfy my mortgage each . . ."

"Stanley," chimes Mr. Dwelling as he walks into the room, *"I've been following your progress thru the Vista alumni newspaper, and just had to meet you. I'm an alumnus, you know."*

They shake hands, and all sit around the table. Bernie explains Stanley's idea to Mr. Dwelling.

"This is a great way to get started, Stanley. I did exactly that myself. I'll call Mr. Blossom over at first trust and arrange loan approval so you will be able to act immediately when you find something."

He then excuses himself for a meeting. "There is a very busy man," notes Bernie.

"Stanley, I'm thinking, we have something available right now that would be a perfect fit for you. It will require

---

[22] 1970 Bank Secrecy Act

some minor touch up, but nothing a strong young man like you can't handle. Let's go look at it now. I wouldn't want you to miss this opportunity."

They drive to Magnolia Street, in an older neighborhood of Blissville. The property, a duplex, sits on the corner, and dates to the early 1900's.

"It has strong bones, but will need a little TLC. Look at the traffic pattern, perfect for your idea. There is plenty of on-street parking in front and at the side."

Bernie takes Stanley for a tour inside, pointing out the large room sizes available in older construction.

"They don't make them like this anymore, Stanley! What do you think?" Before Stanley can say anything, Bernie states, "If Mr. Dwelling can do what I think he can, you will be able to be in here the first of the month, with the upstairs rent paying the entire mortgage." Stanley is starting to like this idea.

Bernie drives Stanley back to the real estate office. "Sandra, call Mr. Dwelling." They sit down, and in just seconds Mr. Dwelling arrives with good news.

"I've talked to Mr. Blossom, and he will approve your loan. You'll need only a $1,000 down payment. Can you make that?" Stanley nods in approval. *"Great, we will just fill out the paper work now, and then expedite the closing so you will be in your new home by the first. You are a smart man, Stanley."*

Mr. Dwelling then excuses himself, and leaves for another meeting. Stanley signs the offer, which of course is accepted by Bernie, and the deal is done.

"Now, I want you to go over to Mr. Blossom's office at First Trust and fill out the loan papers. He'll be waiting for you."

Stanley is off to First Trust as a very excited young man. He has just pulled off the real estate deal of the century, in being able to live for free in an inflationary environment. His housing cost will be fixed for ever, so he thinks, and nothing could ever go wrong with an older home! At First Trust he is guided to Mr. Blossom's office.

Surprisingly, Stanley is very nervous as he is greeted by Mr. Blossom.

"Hello Stanley, Mr. Dwelling said you would be right over. Congratulations on purchasing your first home."

Mr. Blossom explains to Stanley that the loan process is being made easier by the fact that rent from the second unit can be used as income in satisfying the underwriting requirements.

"You have already been pre-approved for this loan. All we must do is complete the application forms, and have a closing. Mr. Dwelling is arranging that for the 30th." Mr. Blossom produces some pages from a folder on his desk. "Please sign here, and here, and here, and here, and here . . . to complete the paper work. Great, that's it. By the way, don't forget to show up on the 30th at closing."

Mr. Blossom says nothing about Stanley's musical achievements, or the fact that he was in Mary Beth's class at Madison High. Stanley thinks that rather odd, but then maybe Mr. Blossom is just all business.

The 30th arrives in no time. Stanley is at First Trust early for the 11:00 a.m. closing. Bernie Lake is already there. At 11:01 Mr. Blossom enters the room carrying several manila folders containing the paper work.

"Hello, Stanley, today is the day." Everyone sits around the table to begin the proceedings. Stanley notices that the seller is not yet in the room.

"Where is the seller? Is he coming?"

"Oh, no, Stanley, he has already signed off. All that is required is your signature. Please sign here, and here, and here, and here . . . that's correct. It completed. You are now the proud new owner. Here are your keys. Your first mortgage payment will not be due for 30 days, on the 1st of the month. Payment instructions are included in the closing folder." Mr. Blossom quickly excuses himself and exits the room.

Bernie clutches his commission check, and says to Stanley, "Thank you, maybe we can do this again some time."

Twenty minutes later Stanley unlocks the front door of his new home. Yes, it will require some work, but it is his. First order of business is to move his things. It will take the remainder of the day using his van. In the evening, Stanley, and the two band members who live upstairs, all share pizza and beer in Stanley's unit. The living room will now become their practice and rehearsal room. A lack of furniture does have some advantages.

The next day Mr. Blossom places a call to Mr. Dwelling. "Sam! Thank you for your excellent work in pawning off that dumpy old duplex on the kid. I was beginning to think the bank would have to take a large loss on that foreclosed property. I owe you a dinner at the Brass Lantern!"

Chapter Twenty Nine

What a difference a couple of years make. Irene is finishing her junior year at State, and the transition from her freshman year has been remarkable. Gone is that angry mood that peaked on the night of the fire. Replacing it is a new, controlled feeling that is guiding her in accomplishing objectives behind the scenes. Irene has become involved in student government as a member of the "Campus Forum;" she also has been expressing her views in "The Ray", as a reporter for the school paper. Next year as a senior, she will be the leader of both. Irene is honing her communicative skills to a high level. She is a natural talent.

Some contact still exists with Matthew Fend, although he is located in Washington D.C. since his delayed graduation, working for Congressman Justice T. Stain. Matthew has been an unusually good listening post for her ideas, and has given her an inside peek at developments in the capitol. The quality of her writing in the paper has most certainly been enhanced by this connection. For a journalist, contacts are the raw material of success.

On campus, the mood continues to remain hostile against the War. On Thursday, April 30th, everything changes for the worst. The President, in a nation-wide telecast, announces a joint U.S.-Saigon offensive into Cambodia. This is the breaking point. It is taken as another escalation of never ending hostilities in Southeast Asia; more and more students at American Universities stage protests.

At Kent State University, about 500 students rally in protest, on the grassy knoll area in the center of campus, called "The Commons." One student buries a copy of the Constitution; another burns his draft card. Student organizers set the next rally for Monday noon, the 4th.

Over the weekend, civil disorder breaks out in downtown Kent. On Friday evening, windows are broken by an unruly crowd of one hundred. On Saturday evening, the National Guard is called in to restore order, as the ROTC office burns. On Sunday evening tear gas is used to break up another rally and impose a curfew.

University officials print pamphlets cancelling the Monday noon rally. Still, 2000 students gather on "The Commons." The National Guard tries to disperse the crowd. The crowd resists, and then, it happens! *Shots!* Shots ring out from the National Guard, four students are killed, and the entire country becomes irreversibly polarized. Immediately, around the country, four hundred and fifty colleges close down in protest, with both violent and non-violent demonstrations taking place. Irene finds herself in the midst of a firestorm as the reporter responsible for this coverage. This is her defining moment; it can propel her toward future success in journalism. She must grasp it.

Irene plans her course of action. First she will contact the editor of the Kent State University newspaper. She places the call, and after introducing herself, says, "We, at State, are profoundly affected by what took place on Monday, and would like to do a joint series of stories with you about the event, including what led up to the tragic shootings. Since Kent State is closed, we can use our facilities to produce

131

the publication. Can we meet tomorrow somewhere near Kent State to discuss this?"

After a short conversation it is decided to meet at 12 noon at a local restaurant in Akron, some 25 miles from the university.

Next she must arrange transportation. Her advisor, political science professor Ira Wily, is anxious to become involved, so his vehicle becomes the transportation. Irene arranges for a photographer to meet them at lunch, and be available for the afternoon.

She must arrange interviews with involved persons: the ROTC commander, local bar tenders in downtown Kent, weekend protestors, any students still in the vicinity that witnessed the event, and, of course, National Guardsmen. This is a tall order for one day. It might take more than one. Every news organization has reporters in the area. The ROTC commander won't give interviews. Irene places a quick call to Matthew; Congressman Stain places a quick call to the commander. Presto, Irene is granted a 15 minute interview at 3 p.m., plus permission to interview three Guardsmen after that. Other interviews are scheduled for the remainder of the day. Things are falling into place. This is what happens behind the scenes to make a journalistic news story possible. Irene is on her way.

The next day in Kent is productive. Irene goes from one interview to another to another. She gathers every snippet of information possible. Professor Wily takes notes also, although for a different, academic reason. After a totally exhaustive day they arrive back at State around midnight, tired, but very satisfied with the results.

Irene's first article in the series is headlined, *"They Are Not Going To Shoot!* The article describes events from a local, student perspective, not the "cookie cutter" listing of events from the national media. This is interesting reading, exactly what any publication wants to sell to a loyal following. Other publications quickly take note. It isn't long before Irene is contacted by major magazines and newspapers to begin a dialogue. Upon graduation this time next year, she will be in demand. She has developed and refined her natural talent.

Chapter Thirty

Mrs. Sandra Blossom sits at her kitchen table, drinking coffee and glancing thru the morning Star Journal. Tomorrow is Thanksgiving; on her mind are a multitude of things that must be attended to this morning, before going to work at Dwelling Real Estate. She notices that Mr. Blossom has circled an article about the Army football team, with Guy Hartmann leading the charge at fullback. There is no time to read it now, but she will look at the story later. Mr. Blossom has closely followed news of Cadet Guy Hartmann since he left Blissville three years ago, and has quietly been encouraging Mary Beth to do the same. Mr. Blossom and many residents of Blissville expect that Mary Beth will become Mrs. Guy Hartmann, upon his graduation next June.

Sandra thinks about Mary Beth often. Her daughter certainly is one of the most beautiful women in Blissville, yet she has not been dating any of the other men in town; she has only dated Guy when he makes one of his rare visits to his home town, and she doesn't even correspond with him that often. At Vista College, she isn't so sure, but Mary Beth has never spoken of anyone there. It's all a mystery.

Down at the bank, Mr. Blossom prepares for a luncheon meeting with Mr. Dwelling. He is aware that something big is on the drawing board concerning real estate in Blissville. It should be an interesting meeting, and profitable for the bank, because Mr. Dwelling has always used First Trust as his banking connection. It's a plus for the bank that Mr. Blossom has this connection, and it doesn't hurt that Mrs. Blossom also works for Mr. Dwelling.

Mr. Blossom enters the Brass Lantern Restaurant, and is greeted by owner Jake Stakes.

"Your table is ready, Mr. Blossom; Mr. Dwelling is already here."

He directs him to his usual table in a rear corner. It is a quiet, out of the way table, where a discreet luncheon conversation may take place between a banker and his client.

"William," salutes Mr. Dwelling, *"glad we could get together today!"*

Mr. Dwelling is never less than overwhelming in greeting anyone. They shake hands and sit down.

"Great story in the paper this morning about Guy Hartmann, and Army football; I'll bet you're very proud! By the way, is Guy coming home for Thanksgiving?"

Mr. Blossom responds in the negative, but doesn't elaborate further.

Mr. Dwelling gets right to business, and tones down considerably.

"William, you know that vacant 18 acre Hershberger property on the edge of town? I have secured an option on the land and plan to build something quite spectacular out there."

Mr. Dwelling begins to explain to Mr. Blossom the demographics of the "baby-boomer" generation, which is just now beginning to reach maturity, and how there exists a real need for quality rental housing in Blissville.

"I plan to build a complete village there, some 144 rental units consisting of one and two bedroom apartments, plus some three bedroom town houses. There will be nothing else like it in Blissville. It will be called Oak Village."

Mr. Blossom is taken aback. This is way beyond anything ever attempted in Blissville.

"How far have you progressed with the plans: engineering studies, architectural drawings, infrastructure detail, zoning approval . . .?"

"Oh, we already have architectural renderings, as well as infrastructure design. Let me show you."

Mr. Dwelling opens his brief case and produces drawings of structures with placements on the parcel of land.

"The zoning approval and engineering studies are yet to come. I foresee no problems with zoning. This project will provide hundreds of jobs. The project is designed to progress in three phases, with completion 2 ½ to 3 years from starting date."

"What will be the amount of financing required?"

"We have planned for 80-20 financing in our preliminary studies, with a total mortgage of between 3 and 4 million dollars. No more than four."

Mr. Blossom begins to look at the architectural renderings.

"I like this very much. Rental housing has been very hop-scotched in Blissville, up to now. This will draw population and development west, certainly the best area to be in. Future commercial development will flourish because of it. I totally agree with your assessment of demographics. This plan has a great chance to succeed." After pausing, Mr. Blossom concludes, "A project of this size needs matapalo [23] board approval, but I foresee no problem in obtaining it. When do you plan to commence construction?"

---

[23] 1970 Occupational Safety and Health Act

"Yesterday," says Mr. Dwelling! Obviously he has no lack of confidence; he's always in a hurry.

Back at the bank, Mr. Blossom wastes no time in gathering senior management for an informational meeting regarding Oak Village.

"We must expedite this project. Mr. Dwelling wants confirmation immediately, and with this project, the value of our existing holdings out there will sky rocket."

Dave Coyne, treasurer, quickly sees the potential. "The bank could make a profit, many times over the Oak Village profit, just by being in place out there. Oak Village will trigger construction of the new Mall proposed by the Philadelphia syndicate." Suddenly, West Blissville real estate is *hot*.

A meeting of the Board of Directors is hastily called for 6:00 p.m. First Trust's management team will make the presentation; more than a few jobs and careers will be placed in jeopardy with this request. If it succeeds, large bonuses are in store down the road, plus the bank's stock will rise. All feel it is worth the gamble. Those who make decisions reap the rewards, or the consequences.

At 6:00 p.m., the Board of Directors meeting goes well. Approval is granted immediately for Phase One. Approval for Phase Two will be granted later, upon completion of Phase One, and upon satisfying other financial requirements. Phase Three will be likewise. This is a huge risk for the bank to assume. A portion will be "laid off" to a syndicate of New York banks. Mr. Blossom has his deal; he phones Mr. Dwelling immediately with the news.

"Sam, you have it. Stop in my office Friday at 10:00 a.m. Have a great Thanksgiving."

It is almost 8 p.m. when Mr. Blossom arrives home; dinner has been kept warm for him by Sandra. He informs her of the day's developments while eating, and casually asks when Mary Beth will arrive.

"Any time now, I think. Say, will you help me tie up the

turkey?" Sandra continues to prepare tomorrow's meal while Mr. Blossom retires to his easy chair in the den.

At 9:45 p.m., still no sign of Mary Beth. At 10:10 the phone rings. Mr. Blossom answers; "Mary Beth, where are you?"

"Daddy, I can't come home."

"What do you mean you can't come home?"

"Daddy . . . I can't. . . *I'm married!*"

Chapter Thirty One

Mr. and Mrs. Stanley Vincent walk slowly toward the front door of the Blossom residence. Mary Beth is bouncy, all bubbly this morning, but Stanley feels uneasy. He hopes this day won't explode on them. How cordial will the greeting from his new in-laws be? Will they accept him or merely tolerate him? Will he become part of the family? Will Mr. Blossom even speak to him? He is not at all looking forward to this first meeting.

How does one even begin to explain the events of last night? Certainly no one is Blissville had a clue, but then, Mary Beth has been away at Vista for three years. Blissville knows of Stanley. Vista College embraces Stanley. That's the difference. Stanley has made a name for himself there. For three years Mary Beth has been able to see this first-hand, and has seen something in Stanley that no one in Blissville has. He's exciting. He's energetic. He has overcome many obstacles to make his way. He has initiative. He has courage. He will make a name for himself, musically. That's what Mary Beth has seen. She knows that she and Stanley will have an exciting, whirlwind life together, and always be at the center of events. Mary Beth likes that. She will compliment him.

That's important. She will always be with him. That's more important. They will not be separated by a battlefield, half a world away. Stanley is exactly the man she wants. Mary Beth always gets what she wants!

Stanley hesitates for a moment at the front door; he then rings the bell. After a time, the door is slowly opened by Mrs. Blossom. She appears tired; her eyes are red. Upon seeing Mary Beth, Sandra breaks down crying. Mary Beth quickly approaches her mother, and mother and daughter embrace, holding each other for an eternity. Stanley is not a part of this. He is the stranger. He is the outsider. He is alone. This scene is everything that he has feared. The day is beginning to explode. What's next? But, somehow, someway, sensing this, Sandra approaches Stanley and embraces him also. Mother, daughter, and son-in-law hold each other on the front steps. It's a start.

Inside, Mary Beth is told that her father wishes to speak with her in the den. She complies, and disappears behind a closed door with her father. Stanley and Sandra remain in the foyer, in an awkward state, until Sandra says, "let's go have a cup of coffee in the kitchen." Some matapalo[24] fifteen minutes later, Mary Beth returns and announces that Mr. Blossom wishes to speak with Stanley. Stanley is horrified, but what else is there to do but have this conversation. He enters the den, and closes the door. It won't open for almost thirty minutes; when it does, Stanley exits with a rather flushed appearance.

Some moments later Mr. Blossom returns to the kitchen and says, "Now, let's all enjoy Thanksgiving as a new family." Stanley can't quite believe he is hearing these words.

---

[24] 1970 Housing and Urban Development Act

Chapter Thirty Two

Friday is a big day on Magnolia Street. Without a doubt, setting up housekeeping is a huge chore; there is so much to do. Add to this the burden of changing a duplex from bachelor's quarters to a real home, and it's quite daunting. But it's exciting. Mary Beth happily goes about her work, putting female touches in place. Her mother joins her at mid-day. By late afternoon, one wouldn't know it is the same unit. Stanley is busy too. He is out scouting for transportation for Mary Beth. Part of the conversation with Mr. Blossom yesterday, was a pledge that Stanley would see Mary Beth finish her education. To make that happen, she will need transportation to Vista College. For the remainder of this semester, she will live in her room at Vista, returning to Blissville on weekends. Next semester, her last semester, she will commute.

Stanley rushes in; "Mary Beth, look out the window! Look what I've found for you!" Parked in front of the duplex, sits a faded, blue 1950 DeSoto.

"What is that, Stanley? Stanley, you know I can't drive that old car!"

"Don't worry, it's "Fluid Drive", and it is a six-cylinder. You can do it. Let's go take a spin."

Maybe, just maybe, this is why Mary Beth loves Stanley. He always has a solution for everything. Life with him is exciting. A 1950 DeSoto becomes a new Ferrari!

Mary Beth sits behind the wheel of her first automobile.

"Just shift into low, press down on the accelerator, accelerate to about 20 miles per hour, lift your foot from the accelerator, listen for the transmission to make a *"glunk"* sound, and then press down on the accelerator again. That's all there is to it. Isn't that easy?" Mary Beth accelerates the DeSoto, *"glunk,"* then accelerates further.

"This is really easy. I can do it. I can drive! Thank you, Stanley! You make me so happy." Who wouldn't be happy in a 1950 DeSoto!

On Saturday morning the phone rings. Mary Beth answers, "Stanley, it's for you!"

Stanley answers and the voice on the other end apologetically says, "This is Billy Stripe, calling from New York. I have heard about your band from Sam Dwelling and have been reading about you in the Vista alumni newspaper. I'm a 1948 alumnus." Mr. Stripe explains to Stanley that he is in a bit of a jam, and needs a band to do the introductory lead-in music for "Pink Underground's" concert at State tonight. There has been a last minute cancellation by the group he had signed. "We will need something in the "psychedelic rock style" for about 15-20 minutes prior to their concert. Can you do it?"

Stanley's heart races; he immediately responds, "You can count on us! Give me the details."

Stanley realizes this could be the big break. He has less than twelve hours to arrange everything, and somehow get the band and equipment to State on time. The music won't be a problem. The band is already prepared to play *"When I'm Sixty-Four, Aquarius, Good Morning Starshine, and Let the Sun Shine In."* That should be about 15-20 minutes. He will need six band members, plus himself. Oh, and Mary Beth, that makes eight. His van can carry all

142

the instruments plus two people. What about the other six? Ah, hmmm . . . what a fortunate continuation of events! The DeSoto! It's a six passenger vehicle, and plenty of room. Perfect! Stanley calls the band members.

"Drop everything and be ready at 1 p.m. This is it! This is our break. Bring your "tux;" we will change at the concert hall."

At 1 p.m. four band members pile into the DeSoto. They make a few off color comments, but only a few! They are instructed to pick up the remaining two members at Vista College, which is on the way. The faded, blue 1950 DeSoto slowly accelerates, "*glunk*," and accelerates again. Stanley and Mary Beth, with all the instruments stashed in his rusted out van, follow closely behind. What a sorry-looking caravan this is! Our merry band is on its way, down the road to success.

Armstrong Arena, on the State campus, can hold almost 10,000 spectators. Billy Stripe expects about 5,000 for the concert. This is "big time" for Stanley V's Band. This is their first opportunity for super-regional and national exposure. If things work out well, they may be asked to do this again, another time. The trick tonight is to warm up the crowd, to make it ready and able to appreciate "Pink Underground," but in no way up-stage the main event. Be good, but not too good!

Stanley V's band arrives at State just after 5 p.m. There is plenty of time for a quick rehearsal, a change to tuxedos, and then be on stage by 7:15, ready to play at 7:30. At 6:30, Billy Stripe arrives from New York and greets Stanley warmly.

"You can't believe how happy I am to see you here this evening. What a life saver you are!"

Stanley introduces the band members, and then proudly says, "Billy, I want you to meet my new bride, Mary Beth. We're on our honeymoon!"

Billy is quite taken that Stanley and Mary Beth would be

here tonight, and doing this for him at this time. He is also very taken with Mary Beth's beauty. He pauses for a moment.

"Say, Stanley, would Mary Beth feel comfortable making your introduction to the audience this evening? I think she would be perfect in that role!"

Stanley looks at Mary Beth, says nothing, and waits.

Mary Beth blushes, and then replies, "I'll do it!"

Billy huddles with Mary Beth, offering suggestions on what to say, and how to say it. It isn't long before she signals she is ready. Mary Beth, having been a cheer leader in high school, is very accustomed to appearing before crowds. She has had speaking experience at Madison High, and is a voice major in the music department at Vista College, so she knows she can do this. Now, suddenly, tonight, she'll be at center stage. Out of nowhere she will be part of the program, part of the band. She will be able to introduce her husband. Mary Beth loves that. Being with Stanley is so exciting!

At 7:30, Billy, with thumbs up, signals Stanley to begin. Stanley directs the band in a short fanfare, *"daa ... daa ... da ... daaaa ... da ... daaaa ... ssstboom!"* Mary Beth glides to center stage. She is so very elegant, yet very seductive ... saucy ... sexy, exactly what the audience wants. All eyes are upon her. She owns them. In a very beckoning voice she speaks.

"What a great crowd on this holiday weekend! Are you ready for a fantastic evening of music?"

The crowd responds in the affirmative.

"It gives me great pleasure to introduce to you a fast rising young group called Stanley V's. They will play the familiar Beatles' tune, *"When I'm Sixty-Four,"* followed by three numbers from the rock musical *"Hair,"* *"Aquarius, Good Morning Starshine and Let The Sun Shine In."* Let's give a rousing Armstrong Arena welcome to Stanley V's!"

Mary Beth waves her right arm like a magic wand toward the band.

"Boys!"

The band begins playing. Billy Stripe smiles at Mary Beth as she returns from center stage.

"That was awesome. You did it. Have you been doing this all your life?"

Mary Beth's eyes dance. She loves to be in the lime-light. Something tells her that she has a new occupation.

The band cruises thru their four offerings. No one must be told they are good; it is obvious from the very first note. The crowd responds. The crowd has been elevated, put in a good mood by Stanley V's. The band has done exactly what it was hired to do; prepare the table for "Pink Underground."

In the first row of the audience, a man with slicked black hair, wearing dark glasses and a loud checker sport coat, carefully takes notes. He doesn't appear to be here for the concert as a fan. Who is this man? What is he doing here? Further back, in the far rear of the arena, an attractive dark-haired young lady takes notes. From a distance she looks familiar. It's . . . it's . . . it's . . . Irene!

Irene rushes back stage. "Mary Beth, Why didn't you tell me you were coming?"

"We just found out at 11:00 this morning. Do you like my husband's band? Stanley and I are on our honeymoon*!" "Ka-Boom!"*

On Monday morning, the "Ray" shouts about Saturday's concert, *"Pink Underground Everything Fans Expect!"* Further down in the article, Irene writes, *"Stanley V's band was superb in its lead-in role. Keep your eyes on this young group. You will hear of them again in the future."*

It always helps to have friends, writing, in the right places!

Billy Stripe has been in a state of ecstasy since witnessing the crowd's reaction to Stanley V's, and has been calling

Stanley almost daily since the concert. He thinks he has uncovered something big, and has worked diligently in marketing his new discovery. Stanley V's needs an agent!

The biggest surprise of all comes three weeks later. A secondary story, in "Today's Sound" magazine, introduces Stanley V's in their "Discovery" column with the tag, *"A Refreshing New Sound From The Heartland!"* Pictured at the top, with slicked black hair and sunglasses, is its author, Victor Sly, the very same man seen at the State concert. Looking ahead, could next year be the exciting, "break-out" year for Stanley V's?

Chapter Thirty Three

The Star Journal announces, "Guy Hartmann West Point Graduate!" In a recent phone interview, assistant editor Alexia Press talked with new Second Lieutenant Guy Hartmann about his upcoming deployment in the army, as an officer.

"I have a five year service obligation to my country. I expect I will be deployed to Southeast Asia, but I have not received my orders to date. I expect that to happen very soon."

Alexia asked when he will visit his home town again.

"I will always have a fond spot in my heart for Blissville, and the solid foundation in life I received there. My visits to my hometown will be less frequent going forward. I really can't say when the next will be."

The paper also announces two other recent college graduates, Irene Funka and Mary Beth Blossom Vincent, in an article just below.

After graduation from State, Irene's father was able to guide her to a vacant staff position with the union office in Detroit, Michigan. Irene independently contracted with "Our Hope Magazine" to write a quarterly column about the plight of labor in America. Although this is not an overly visible magazine at present, she believes an opportunity could develop here, which would lead to bigger and better ₘₐₜₐₚₐₗₒ[25] things in the future. A strong plus with this position is the fact that she has been given complete editorial freedom in her writing.

Since last November Mary Beth has been working with husband Stanley, in developing a musical product. She has become the band's PR person, as well as official announcer at all events. Her graduation yesterday from Vista College was taken in stride. Tomorrow she will talk to Samuel S. Dwelling about a new position as "Property and Leasing Manager" at the recently completed Phase One of Oak Village apartments.

Today, opportunity is everywhere for the Blessed Generation. For those willing and able to work hard, success comes quickly. The American dream of improving one's lot in life is the dream of each member of this generation, and making it come true is their goal. They know risk taking and hard work will make it happen. Strangely, no one seems to think this isn't the correct strategy in life.

****

At 9:00 a.m. Mary Beth enters the leasing office at Oak Village. Mr. Dwelling is already seated behind the office desk on the phone. He looks up.

"Mary Beth, I'm so happy you have come to talk to me about this position. Please, sit down."

He quickly hangs up the phone.

"I think you are already familiar with Oak Village. What you see here is the first phase."

Mr. Dwelling explains that this new position involves showing apartment units to perspective renters, collecting

---

[25] 1970 Economic Stabilization Act

rents, and supervising the general maintenance and grounds keeping.

"You will be our eyes and ears for this development. You must catch small problems before they become big problems. We don't expect you to fix the problems, just to notify the correct people to get the job done. If ever in doubt, always ask a question, always make a call. Are there any questions, Mary Beth?"

Before she can answer, Mr. Dwelling says, *"Can you start tomorrow?"*

Mary Beth responds in the affirmative as Mr. Dwelling excuses himself for a meeting across town. Upon reaching the door, he turns and says, *"Stop in and talk to Bernie Lake later today, for all the particulars. Take a walk around, right now, and acquaint yourself with the project."* The door closes, and he vanishes in an instant.

Phase I of Oak Village consists of two buildings housing 24 two-bedroom apartment units, 12 separate three-bedroom townhouses, and one building of 12 one-bedroom apartment units. At the center of the development is a large community room with attached swimming pool. Everything is in place for a community of perfect care-free living.

Mary Beth enters one of the finished two-bedroom units. She sees it's quite nice in size, featuring a galley kitchen, living room, dining area off the kitchen, one bathroom, and two ample bedrooms with the master having a large walk-in closet. Fresh carpeting makes the unit smell so new. Mary Beth thinks to herself, Mr. Dwelling certainly knows what he is doing. He has created a very pleasing living environment in what eventually will become a small town.

One hour later, Mary Beth is at Dwelling Real Estate and is greeted by her mother. Sandra escorts her to Bernie Lake's office where she is given a 15-minute orientation of procedures, a list of important phone numbers, and her own set of master keys. Bernie finishes by saying, "Be at your desk at 9:00 a.m. tomorrow morning. First thing, call me each morning at 9 a.m. with anything to report. Then be ready to lease units. All the paper work needed is in this box. Welcome aboard!"

This job at Oak Village couldn't have come at a better time for Mary Beth and Stanley. It will be a source of steady, reliable income that can be used to smooth out the feast or famine cycle in the music world. Stanley has been slowly developing the band's product and image, but it is still too early in the process to be able to count on large fees and steady work. Billy Stripe has been shopping the band nationwide. So far, nothing, but Stanley has a "gut feeling" that something will break very soon. In the meantime, Mary Beth's income makes life much easier.

Tonight Stanley has a surprise for Mary Beth. To celebrate her new position, he will be taking her to dinner at the Brass Lantern Restaurant. Upon entering at 7:30 p.m., they are greeted by Jake Stakes, and guided to the very same, out-of-the-way table, used by her father for business meetings. After being seated, they order drinks, and begin to relax. Stanley asks Mary Beth to tell him all about Oak Village, and then says, "Mary Beth, close your eyes and give me your hands!"

"Why, Stanley?"

"Just do as I say. Close your eyes! Close your eyes!"

Mary Beth places her hands in the middle of the table. Stanley grasps them.

"Now, don't open your eyes!" He places a set of keys in the palm of her hand and says, "OK, now open!"

"What is this, Stanley?"

"Behold, your keys to your new car, a 1965 Impala with automatic transmission! It's sitting outside. You must look successful at your new job."

Stanley explains that he talked to Russell today, and that Russell was able to find him this car at a fantastic price.

"You won't have to drive the DeSoto any longer. I was

able to sell it to a student at Vista College."

"Oh, thank you Stanley. I certainly never expected this. You always surprise me so. You make me feel so happy. I can hardly wait to go to work tomorrow morning!"

Chapter Thirty Four

"I . . . don't know how to love. . . him, what to do, how to move. . . him, I've been changed, yes really changed. . ." Sounds from the controversial rock musical, *"Jesus Christ, Superstar,"* fill the duplex on Magnolia Street as Stanley and Mary Beth listen attentively. The subject matter of this number one album is way over the top for even this radical time, but the music is kind of catchy. They both enjoy it. Stanley is thinking ahead; he's always planning something. Is there a way the band could benefit from this music? How could it be incorporated into their repertoire?

Billy Stripe has arranged for two more guest lead-in appearances, for "big name" concerts. Stanley knows the music presented for each must be just right, but it could be the same music for both. This music from "Superstar" might be just the ticket for these programs. An added bonus would be the dinner dances. Here it could be played for a pure listening segment, in which the audience would enjoy, but not dance. Stanley knows this would work because it was successfully tested at Vista College last year. And, for the future, there would always be something new and popular at the moment. He would always have something fresh to offer. That's it! That's the solution.

Do a medley of songs from "Superstar," now! This music will be viewed as fresh and exciting, not predictable and old. He asks Mary Beth for her opinion of his idea.

"Great idea, Stanley, but to make it work, I must always be your announcer!"

The phone rings. It's Billy Stripe.

"Stanley, I have a crazy idea, but it just might work. I've been thinking. We seem to be caught in the classic "chicken or egg" dilemma."

Billy explains that he has only been able to generate interest in lead-in appearances for the band, not top billing. Always, it is the same answer; top billing comes only to those groups that are already known. But, how does a group become known? Here comes his idea.

"Let's do something right now to become known. Let's *make* ourselves known. Let's *cut* a record!"

"That's great thinking, Billy. Do you have any ideas?"

"To make it happen fast, why not make a Christmas Album? This is a format we haven't tried before, but remember, the idea is to become known. Afterwards, we can build upon the album to negotiate top billing. We will have an established style, something people can relate to."

"Billy, how much will all this cost? We don't have much money."

"That's the best part, Stanley. I can arrange investor financing. After the investors receive their money back, we will split any further profits 50/50 with them. The only financial risk to you is the time value of your work. Your job is to have the music in place and ready to record by October 1st. Can you do it?"

Billy further notes that the album must be completed and in stores by November 20th.

"To make this happen, everyone must meet their deadlines. If we succeed, these investors will back bigger and better things in the future!"

"Billy, I'll get started right away! I've already got some

great ideas. We will play the old favorites, tastefully, in the new psychedelic rock style. That's something that no one has ever done before. It will create interest. It should sell."

Stanley gets right to work. Mary Beth helps him by pouring over lists of music. She has a keen sense of what the public wishes to hear. Her input has been invaluable all year in helping formulate programs to keep the band's music fresh and popular. She never strays too far from center. She is a perfect counter balance to Stanley's more reckless, and exciting nature.

Stanley begins by formulating a style that fits each Christmas Carol. He tries to push the envelope in a way that enhances the original tune, but wraps it in the new style. The music must be bold, with enormous sounds at times, but then cut way back to emphasize the tender moments of Christmas. And it should include other popular Christmas music besides Carols, some old favorites such as *"Frosty the Snowman,"* to round out the appeal. Stanley knows he is going to make this album great. Nothing will be left to chance. It may be the band's only "make or break" opportunity.

For three solid days, Mary Beth and Stanley formulate songs, sound styles, and rhythms. Stanley is obsessed in writing music, testing sounds on the piano, selecting lead instruments. This is what he has always wanted to do, to make music. This is the direction in which his previous work has been leading. Now, he is presented a golden opportunity. This will be his opportunity; this will be his time. He must grab it! After four tumultuous days, Stanley calls each band member with the great news.

"We're going to cut a record. In a couple of months, we'll be known nationally. Rehearsal, tonight, 7:00 p.m.! We'll try the first three songs, to see what we have. Don't be late!"

At 7:00 p.m. all the band members are present in the living room of the duplex, excited and ready for the preliminary rehearsal. *"Joy to the World"* will be their first attempt, in their new psychedelic rock style. Stanley has written a huge brass sound for this Christmas Carol, with a rhythm that weaves in and out, and around the traditional. Percussion and bass accent the brass, with clarinet and piano modifying the total sound. Stanley directs, he gives the down beat. The band plays. What a fantastic sound! What a fantastic rhythm! It's all new and exciting. This interpretation really "grabs" you. It gets your attention. Obviously it should be the first selection in the album. The band members are instantly impressed with what they have just played; what a polished result on only their very first try. Excitement effervesces thru out the room.

Stanley keeps things moving. *"What Child Is This"* will be their next attempt, arranged for a haunting clarinet lead with soothing brass harmonics in the background. *"Frosty the Snowman"* follows with a frolicking clarinet and piano lead. The sound of each is new and fresh. Band members' eyes shine. They know they are becoming part of something big.

For the band, this evening has been epic. Stanley V's has found its niche. Up to now, many different styles of music have been played; to be sure, all were quite enjoyable and most pleasing, but all were generically, vanilla. Tonight, Stanley V's has solidified the psychedelic rock style as its own, with its very own interpretations. This music is totally "Stanley." The music on this album will be like nothing before it. Stanley can already feel it will be a hit. At last there will be a finished product to present to the public, a product that will be instantly recognized as Stanley V's. The public will recognize it; the public will now know them by their sounds. Stanley V's will be able to obtain top billing. The band will be offered newly-written music, to develop as its own. Stanley bubbles with excitement this evening. The future is unlimited.

From New York, Billy Stripe has taken care of his end.

He has arranged the recording session, in a sound studio in New York City, for October 1st. He has contracted with "Euphony Records" to produce and distribute the album. He has obtained the investors' money, which will allow the band to fly to New York City, and stay in a nice hotel for two nights. In his newly-found position as agent and general manager, he has stepped up to take care of all the little details, thereby freeing Stanley to make music. With Billy at the helm, the band has an excellent business arrangement in place.

On October 1st the band finds itself in New York City, at "Crescendo's Sound Studio" on 3rd Ave., ready to go. Billy introduces the band to Carol, acting studio manager. Carol knows exactly how to manage a recording session, and to put the band at ease, since he knows this is their first experience. He goes about his job of arranging microphones with correct instrumental placement, from what experience has taught him will produce the best sound. He keeps the mood light and happy. Carol knows a great sound cannot be obtained from an up-tight and apprehensive group. He is a true professional. He earns his money.

Carol looks up, and signals the technicians in the control room.

"OK, guys, let's do a short test of our sound quality. Stanley, play a few bars of your first piece."

The band swings into action, playing more than "just a few bars." It's a good warm up for them. In the control room, the technicians are seen mixing sounds, and making adjustments, all subtle corrections. The head technician announces over the speaker system, "We've got it!" Carol signals to Stanley to halt.

After a few moments, Carol addresses the band.

"We are ready for our first try. Don't do anything differently. Just relax, be who you have always been, play as you have just played, and have fun. This is your day.

Enjoy it. OK, Stanley, whenever you are ready."

Stanley stands before the band. Their eyes are on him. He smiles, gives the band a "thumbs up," signals the control room, and gives the down beat. The music begins. A huge brass sound announces *"Joy to the World."* Soon percussion and bass are added to the mix. Now enter tones of clarinet and piano, to modify and refine the sound. It's powerful. The rhythm is perfect; the band plays on and on. Smiles are seen in the control room. It's over almost before it starts. The band has made its first cut. Carol exclaims, "That was awesome."

For the remainder of the day, in an almost eight hour recording session, all goes without a hitch. Carol mentions to the band that this session has gone about as well as any he can remember. At the conclusion, all the men and ladies in the control room stand up and applaud. It is obvious they have enjoyed their part. This certainly was a pleasant added bonus. Billy Stripe smiles ear to ear; he is absolutely giddy with the results. Now he must rush over to "Euphony Records" to keep things moving. Deadlines . . . Deadlines!

In the coming weeks Billy meets all his deadlines. By November 20th, the album is distributed nationally and is on music shelves everywhere. Billy has arranged radio promotion, that critical decision made by stations to play a certain record, and how often to play it. After Thanksgiving, Stanley V's *"Joy to the World"* begins to be heard, all over the land. Blissville's stations play it. The Star Journal does a huge story about Stanley V's and their journey to fame. Sales of the album start off slowly, but gain momentum in mid-December as radio play intensifies. The album, while not quite number one, is close, and is certainly being noticed. It is also at the top of the list of Christmas offerings. Stanley V's has rapidly become a known commodity in the music world. *Now*, the band is ready to take the next step! They have become known!

Chapter Thirty Five

Nine months after graduation, Irene finds herself diligently at work at the union national headquarters in Detroit, Michigan. She is rapidly learning about the real world, as the union liaison for local chapter concerns. All is not well with labor in the United States. She hears an ear full of gripes each day, and it is her job to smooth things over for the moment, and to identify major problems for negotiating in the next contract. From this vantage point Irene can see what really is happening all over the country concerning labor. This is not a position in which she wishes to spend her total working career, but the experience she is gaining now is invaluable.

Her major interest is her quarterly column for "Our Hope Magazine." Irene's great talent is in communicating ideas, both written and orally. She has written three articles so far for the magazine, and interest in her writing has risen steadily. Her writing style has proven popular, but what really has set her apart is her uncanny ability to put to words the real pulse of labor. Few in the media have seen and written what she has. Few in the media have seen what she has seen, every day in her job. Her written insights have been acknowledged as well based and correct. With complete editorial freedom, Irene has flourished. Readership is increasing. She is attracting a following.

What Irene has discovered in talking to local union representatives, is that the goal of just increasing wages and benefits for the workers is only part of the bargaining process. Work conditions and job satisfaction are the other parts. At the local level, she has found great resentment by the working men and women, to the union itself, for shoving these concerns aside when signing national agreements. It has been an eye opening experience for her. From this, Irene has found the cause she wishes to pursue in life. She has begun the journey down her career path, fighting for the plight of workers everywhere. In Irene's first column, *"Underground Union,"* she raises a few eyebrows when she writes about workers' internal agreements to substitute their own production plans for the methods of management. She writes, *"Workers have found a way to circumvent the national union and management completely."*

Reaction to this article is swift. A firestorm of criticism from business and labor leaders unfolds immediately. The magazine loves it. The more controversy created by Irene's articles, the better. That's what sells magazines. Readers eagerly await Irene's next quarterly column. Irene will not disappoint them in their wait.

Three months later, they read, *"Bargaining for Whom?"* Irene writes, *"For control of the work process, the unions and workers are very much in opposition to each other."* More controversy! More criticism! More magazine sales! This time Irene's employer cannot look the other way. She is very unceremoniously asked to "tone it down." Reaction by readers is overwhelmingly positive. Irene is growing in popularity.

Irene knows one more inflammatory article will probably mean the end of her day job, but she also knows the path she wishes to travel, fighting for workers everywhere.

Three months later she writes a block buster, *"Ritualized Manipulation."* Here she comments about the recent strike. In large print she states, *"the union and management agreed on the necessity of a strike as an escape valve to defuse worker resentment about intolerable working conditions.* She writes that the company loaned the union $23 million per month during the strike, and then boldly finishes, *"the company and the union are not even adversaries!"* This is simply too much! Irene finds herself unemployed, immediately.

But, there is some good news from the magazine. Beginning with her next column, she will become a highlighted monthly feature, and her compensation will be increased substantially. She will get by.

A few days later Irene's phone rings. It's Matthew Fend, from her old college days at State.

"Ike, you've been attracting a huge amount of attention down here in Washington. Congressman Stain has noticed; he wants to meet you."

Matthew has been working for the Congressman for several years now, and most surely has mentioned Irene to him.

"Can you come to Washington for a meeting?"

"What's this all about, Matthew? Why would the Congressman want to talk to me?"

Matthew explains that Congressman Stain represents a predominately "blue collar" district, and that Irene's time will certainly not be wasted in talking to him.

"He'll fill you in when you get here. Can you be in his office next Monday at 10:00 a.m.? Your expenses will be taken care of. Your plane ticket will be waiting for you at the airport."

"How can I refuse? OK, Matthew. I'll be there."

The following Monday morning Irene is introduced to Congressman Stain. It's a private meeting that also includes Matthew.   The Congressman gets right to the point.

"Irene, as you already know, I represent a district that is overwhelmingly "blue collar. These are the people who elect me, and keep me in Washington. You have done something very few other people have been able to do; you relate to my constituents, and they trust you. You could become most valuable to me in two ways. First, you have your pulse on the ground, and you can make me aware of important events as it relates to my district. Secondly, you could put into writing that which is important, in a way that would relate to my constituents, and in a way that could be trusted.   That would help me immensely in matapalo [26] communicating with them. Would you be up to that task? Would you become a member of my staff?"

Irene is flabbergasted! She certainly didn't expect this. What an impressive opportunity. What a great chance to become a part of our government. What a chance to grow. What a chance to live. Irene has been in Washington for less than one day, but has quickly fallen in love with everything about it. She could see herself here forever! She thinks, Washington and I are made for each other!

"Of course, I would be honored to do it. Would I be residing in Washington too?"

"That's up to you. As a member of my staff, you may travel back and forth as often as needed to get the job done. Where you reside is your decision."

Irene is also told that there are many perks available to Congressional Members and their staffs.

"Taxpayers foot the bill for just about everything. Take advantage of all you can, while you can! That's the Washington way."

With everything settled, Irene immediately begins to make plans for her move to Washington D.C. Once again

---

[26] 1972 Noise Control Act

she has Matthew to guide her. In a few months, she'll feel like she's been here forever. Luckily she will be able to write her monthly column in the Capitol, and communications with union representatives can still be accomplished via long distance phone calls. Junkets back to Congressman Stain's district could be planned on a regular basis to keep a personal contact with her sources. A journalist's sources are all important. She will be close to Congressman Stain to immediately comment on, or write about, anything pressing. That is how she will manage her work. Irene is on her way again!

Chapter Thirty Six

Billy Stripe phones Stanley. *"Great news, we've done it!* Our record was the spring board we hoped for in obtaining top billing; in three months we play a concert at State!" Billy explains that "our investors will put up the money with the same 50/50 split."

Stanley's heart is racing. He thinks back to the first lead-in appearance last year. So much has happened since then; the band has come so far. This will surely be a comfortable first step for them, having already played at Armstrong Arena. He can hardly wait to tell to Mary Beth.

Mary Beth's phone rings at Oak Village. "Guess what, screams Stanley. We've got our first concert, as the Main Event, scheduled in three months at State! Billy just called me. That record idea of his worked!"

"Oh, Stanley, what great news this is! Come right over and tell me all about it."

As Stanley drives the short distance to Oak Village, his mind focuses on what to play for the concert. Stanley V's is known for its psychedelic rock style, but certainly can't play any of its music known by the public, Christmas Music! This will be tough. As the main event, the music must be their own creation, not warmed-over tunes from other bands. Concert goers will not pay high ticket prices for leftovers, no matter how good. He'll have Billy Stripe procure some unpublished new music, fast. The band will then put their signature on it. That's what to do.

Mary Beth is away from her desk when Stanley arrives. Oak Village is in Phase II construction now, so her job responsibility has doubled. She has been a perfect fit for Dwelling Real Estate and Oak Village, the perfect representative. Mary Beth has a most pleasing aura about her, and is instantly able to disarm most rental prospects. She leases the few available rental units almost immediately. More importantly, her relationship with the new tenants has resulted in a 100% current rent payments record, something quite unheard of. For this, Mr. Dwelling has recently given her a raise in pay.

The door opens. Mary Beth rushes to Stanley and gives him a big hug. She can hardly wait to hear all the news. Stanley begins hurriedly, talking in excited bursts, explaining all to her.

"We need new music. We've got to get some new music quickly. I'll get Billy on it right away."

Mary Beth is becoming so excited. "I'll help you with the selections. We can get this done. We'll be ready on time!"

Several days later the first copies of new music arrive by special courier from New York City. Mary Beth and Stanley sit in their living room; Stanley "eyes" each piece critically. Some very promising looking prospects are in the pile. At once Stanley sees a problem; it's a major problem! The most promising pieces require a female lead singer. The band has never had a vocalist. It hasn't been their style.

What to do now? And no time to do it!

In life, many times the solution to a problem is very simple, and is right under everyone's nose from the beginning. Such is the case here. Mary Beth, after all, is a recent college graduate with a major in fine arts and voice. She is qualified as a vocalist. The solution is screaming right at them. Only Mary Beth sees it.

"I'll be the lead singer. I can do it!" Stanley is awestruck with the possibility. Will it work? Will Mary Beth work?

From this day forward, Mary Beth will change; she will become *"Bam,"* her new professional designation. Her father, who has spent a huge sum of money for his daughter to obtain classical musical training, will see his investment become "Bam," in a psychedelic rock band! Don't blame Stanley; he kept up his end of the bargain. Mary Beth, err . . . "Bam," graduated. She's on her own now. Oh well, these are certainly different times!

If ever Billy Stripe will earn his money, it is now. Billy must create something fast. Mary Beth will need a complete makeover. She is just too beautiful and classy to be "Bam." Nobody is going to buy that, no matter how well she sings. In his mind Billy begins to formulate a new persona, a "good girl gone bad" persona! He will have Mary Beth wear a wig, charcoal black hair with silver spikes. Make-up will be overdone, with ominous looking charcoal all around her eyes. Lip stick will be the boldest red-red available. She will wear a black tuxedo, just as the band does, but with black boots and no jacket. That will subtly accentuate her rebelling nature, just in case anyone happened to miss the charcoal black hair with silver spikes! A beautiful white ruffled tuxedo shirt with red tie and red suspenders will complete her ensemble. Now Billy thinks he will have something outlandish to sell. The crowd will buy that!

Of all the people in the world you would expect to be impressed with this new persona, Mary Beth's mother would be the last. Quite the opposite! Sandra seems thrilled with the prospect of having a daughter as lead singer, and jumps right in with some additional costume touches of makeup and jewelry. She adds a few gaudy chrome necklaces and a black whip! Just the ticket! It rounds out the persona. Are we now to believe that Sandra is beginning to live a clandestine, slightly naughty life thru her daughter, Mary Beth? You can bet, only Sandra knows for matapalo[27] sure! Poor old Mr. Blossom just shakes his head; he lost control of the situation, and his daughter, a couple of years ago!

Mary Beth immediately calls Professor Hoven at Vista College. "I need your help right away. Can you meet with me this afternoon?"

"What could be so important, Mary Beth? Sure, I'll be in my office at 5 p.m.

Mary Beth drives to Vista College and enters Wynd Hall, exactly at 5 p.m.; she walks directly to Professor Hoven's office. After initial greetings, she says, "Professor Hoven, sit down and listen to this. You won't believe it!" Mary Beth quickly explains the events to date, leading to the upcoming headline performance at State. Then she pauses, and drops the bombshell; "I'll become "Bam," an angry, out of control vocalist for the band. Will you help me become "Bam?" Will you coach me?"

Professor Hoven can't believe what he is hearing. When he arose this morning, the last thing he expected was to be part of a psychedelic rock band's repertoire! Strange, exciting events just seem to continually happen to him whenever Stanley is around. "Mary Beth, I don't know if I am qualified for this. I can gather some people to assist you in presentation; the interpretation must be yours, completely."

At once, several eager volunteers from the drama and voice departments come on board, helping to create "Bam!" Mary Beth is immersed in thrice weekly coaching sessions. Everyone who hears about what is happening

---

[27] 1972 Equal Employment Opportunity Act

wants to be a part of this. Mary Beth has the best talent in the world now supporting her. She knows she is going to get this right. When the concert is over, you just know another major article will appear in the alumni newspaper, this time staring an actual alumnus! "Bam" will be a Vista College creation!

While Mary Beth works on vocals, Stanley constantly writes music. He selects a program of new pieces, and makes changes, incorporating the band's psychedelic rock style to the music. His new favorite, *"Machine, Machine,"* features a female lead vocalist. It will be the opening number. Stanley is troubled by one fact; these are all newer pieces. There is nothing to play initially, that will directly connect the band's music to the public. That's something they desperately need to find. What to do? Hmmm . . . a solution hits him right in the face! On the very first opening number, *blast* them with what they already know, the opening bars of *"Joy to the World,"* then modulate into *"Machine, Machine,"* and go on from there. It's a perfect opening solution.

Billy Stripe works behind the scenes. He arranges to make a sound track of the concert, thereby creating material for a new album. He must always be thinking about the next concert. Billy organizes a huge promotional campaign thru out the state. Nobody knows "Bam," so he makes her bigger than life. He creates a full sized standup glossy figure of "Bam," and places many around the campus and in music stores. With black tuxedo and whip, she is quite appealing. Music lovers will come to see her. Anticipation for the concert grows daily. Soon it will be time.

On concert evening, the mood in Armstrong Arena is electric. Billy's promotional skills have worked magically. More tickets have been sold for tonight's performance than for "Pink Underground's" concert last year. A large contingent of supporters from Vista College is in attendance, including most of the members of the music and drama departments. Mr. and Mrs. Blossom proudly sit in the front row. Some distance to their left, Victor Sly, from "Today's Sound" magazine sits with notebook in hand. They are all here to hear "Bam."

The members of the band, dressed in black tuxedoes, walk onto stage and ready themselves for tonight's performance. Stanley, discretely, motions to the brass section. A continuous monotone trombone sound emerges, breaking the ice. Some fog waffles across the stage. More and more fog rolls in. A very eerie feeling is being presented to the crowd. Pulsating white lights peek thru the fog; now changing to red, they create a huge ominous crimson glow. A second trombone now sounds, harmonizing with the first. Suddenly, thunderously, the beginning bars of *"Joy to the World"* rock the arena. "Bam" appears from the foggy mists, walking . . . strutting . . . prancing . . . across the stage to the music, like a prize thoroughbred with a motion that says, "I own this place! You better believe it!" She cracks the whip! Instantly the band modulates to *"Machine, Machine."* Bam angrily shouts, and begins her vocals. Her stage persona has been carefully choreographed. She loudly stomps around as she sings. The crowd follows her every move. They are with her. They are angry too. This is what they came to see. Bam gives them everything they want. . . More Shouting, More Stomping! Is it enough? Her tone slowly changes. The continual aggressive style dissipates. A more tender sound emerges, with a range of notes only possible from a trained classical vocalist. This is something new, quite unexpected.   The audience is gripped by her gentile feeling of helplessness. "Bam" continues to sing melodiously and finishes in a very submissive, and hopeless pose, with the most tender and delicate notes of all. She bows her head in silence. She is finished.

The crowd in the arena explodes in spontaneous applause. They have experienced a musical roller-coaster ride of epic proportions. "Bam" has played with all their emotions. They are drained. When they arrived this evening, they didn't know who "Bam" was; they didn't know what to expect. They all know her now. Everyone in the arena knows who "Bam" is now!

Stanley is overjoyed with the crowd's reaction, but he can't applaud. He can't join the crowd in jubilation. He must continue; the show must go on. The band begins their second offering. As he plays, Stanley thinks to himself; something major has just occurred. Stanley V's and "Bam" have just become, "Bam" and Stanley V's! This has happened in the blinking of an eye!

Chapter Thirty Seven

Look, absolutely no excitement can be seen at Murphy Chevrolet! There's no excitement anywhere! Not this year! Something is entirely different now. The extravaganza that once accompanied new model introductions is no more. No brown paper covers the showroom windows. No one is in the showroom. No one even cares to look. The public yawns at the new models, which are nothing more than warmed over examples of what was sold several years ago, without the previous performance packages. The clean air political movement has completely stripped them. These models are only modest examples of what they once were, and priced higher, much higher. To make matters worse, a new competitor from the Far East has arrived with a lineup of quality offerings, although smaller in size. Will the American public give up its love affair with larger, more powerful vehicles? At this time, and judging from the current offerings, Detroit manufacturers are emphatically saying, *"They Will Buy Our Cars!"* But, in the new car show room at Murphy Chevrolet, sales have dropped off to practically nothing.

Over in the used car lot, Dusty and Russell have been

keeping things a float by concentrating their sales efforts on the popular, powerful, older models. They have a used car lot full of such examples. It has become a very profitable niche for the firm. It's the only current bright spot anywhere, and is subsidizing the entire dealership. Thank goodness for this profit center!

Suddenly, it's early October; Egypt attacks Israel! Another round of Mid-Eastern hostilities begins! Four days later, the Vice President of the United States resigns in controversy! A week later, the unthinkable happens. An oil embargo is levied against the United States by Arab oil producing states! This is all too much. Panic sets in. Business comes to a screeching halt. The U.S. economy will soon stall without cheap energy. Overnight, smaller, more fuel efficient vehicles become popular. No one wants inefficient, fuel-hungry large autos anymore!

The strain of what is about to happen proves too much for Sean Murphy. There are no new car sales. There are no used car sales. There is a lot full of inventory that no one wants. The founder of Murphy Chevrolet, the man who matapalo[28] guided the firm through all previous crises, suffers a massive, fatal heart attack at age seventy nine, and passes away.

There was a time when owning the local Chevrolet dealership, or the local bank, meant financial security forever; this is no longer the case.

Murphy Chevrolet is in turmoil. Leadership is desperately needed. It must be provided by Lindsay Murphy, the next in line. After the funeral, a meeting is called for all employees. Lindsay speaks directly about the graveness of the situation at hand.

"This is an unprecedented time. From this day forward, it is not going to be business as usual. We must adjust to the current situation." He explains what is obvious to

---

[28] 1972 Federal Water Pollution Control Amendments

everyone; "the present line-up of new offerings has no future."

"From this point on, we must focus on what can provide revenue, immediately. That means the shop and the used car lot. We will emphasize tune-ups and maintenance for older cars, to counter the high price of gas. We will stress body work and re-painting. We will re-arrange the inventory in the used car lot to reflect what will sell. It will take hard work on everyone's part to make this succeed. Word of mouth sales is what must be emphasized. Sell to your neighbors, sell to your friends, and sell to your family. Somehow, we will make it thru this time!" Then Lindsay makes a stunning announcement.

"Red Blaze will move to the used car lot to help jump start sales there. The salesmen in the used car lot will, at times, become salesmen in the new car showroom. We must all do more with less." Russell, at once, is very excited about this new car sales opportunity, even though it is only a temporary fix. He's always wanted to join his father in new car sales.

Red Blaze and Dusty Roads spend the entire afternoon huddled over inventory sheets, trying to make the important decisions about what vehicles to keep, and what to send to the auction next Tuesday. One by one, workers remove most of the current inventory. Only a few vehicles remain on the lot at day's end. Next Tuesday there will be a completely different stable of autos, ready for sale! Somehow, Murphy Chevrolet will make it thru this time

****

"Who is Sterling Churnning III," asks Russell as he glances at a small business card?

"Oh, he's a gentleman, a broker from New York, Sam Dwelling mentioned to me. I've been talking with him and am considering making some alternative investments for the firm." Lindsay conveys to Russell the thought that the auto business might not be the blue chip prospect it once was, and that it would be wise to invest in a business that could counter that prospect, as a hedge.

"I'm talking about oil and gas. We're going to need lots of oil and gas in the future. Sterling says there is plenty right here in the U.S. There is money to be made here."

Lindsay mentions to Russell that Murphy Chevrolet owns many shares of GM stock, plus there is more in your grandfather's estate.

"I will direct Mr. Churnning to liquidate all those shares. The money realized will be re-directed into oil and gas drilling limited partnerships. Sterling Churnning is from New York; he's connected; he knows the right people. He believes we could make a huge matapalo[29] return by doing this. And besides, Sam Dwelling is in. Sam knows how to make money!"

Russell asks his father about getting started with his own account. "I want to begin to make investments on my own. Will you introduce me to him?"

Two days later Russell is on the phone, talking with Sterling Churnning III. He explains that he wants to make some conservative investments with his inheritance from his grandfather's estate.

"Do you have any suggestions for long-term growth, and maybe some income?"

"Russell, just call me Sterling. Sure do, but first, let me mention an exciting opportunity that's right up your alley!" Sterling informs Russell of a revolutionary new engine from Germany, the "Wankel Engine." "It is so cutting edge it will be in everything within a few years. Right now, one of your competitors has just signed a license to build the engine, and put it in their passenger cars and Jeeps. Their license allows them to build the engines and sell to all the

---

[29] 1973 Endangered Species Act

other auto makers too. Can you imagine how many engines that could be? This engine is where you should be investing!"

Russell mouth is watering. He can hardly wait to get started. He recalls the stories of his grandfather hooking up with Chevrolet early, and riding it to financial success.

"I've got to get in on this now. Are there any more shares available?"

"Oh, I think I might be able to find a few," replies Sterling!

"OK, put my money there!"

"Done!"

This is vintage Russell; "if fast is dangerous, too fast is just about right!"

Chapter Thirty Eight

"The chair recognizes the gentleman from the state of Michigan."

Congressman Stain stands, but all eyes remain focused on the attractive young lady behind him. Who is she? This young lady's immediate impression upon arriving in the Capitol was, "Washington and I are made for each other." After the first few months, she settled in, and began moving about as seamlessly as did Congressman Stain. She at once began making matapalo[30] contacts, on both sides of the aisle, to further the Congressman's agenda. As her support of the Congressman grew, he placed an increasingly important load upon her shoulders. She became more of a consultant on important matters, rather than merely a staff member. Her research and basic understanding of issues, plus her ability to verbalize, proved invaluable to him and marked her as a future force to be reckoned with in politics. The name of this attractive lady behind the Congressman . . . is Irene Funka!

For Irene, arrival in Washington couldn't have come at a more opportune time. Congressman Stain is an important

---

[30] 1972 Consumer Product Safety Act

member of the House Committee on Education and Labor. This Committee's work is right in line with Irene's career goals of helping working people everywhere. A piece of legislation, which rings close to her heart, is currently pending in the House. This legislation, called the Employee Retirement Income Security Act (ERISA), will provide the promise of security in retirement for workers everywhere. Irene jumps right in, assisting Congressman Stain at every turn. He relies on her more and more, and she becomes very knowledgeable for him in the process. The legislation becomes her personal mission, for she can still remember the hurt in her family when her father lost his pension benefit at Studebaker.

Matthew Fend and Irene begin spending more and more time together, working on ERISA for Congressman Stain. Matthew secretly hopes this relationship with Irene will be much more than just business, but no male has ever been able to get close to Irene. She has absolutely no interest in personal relationships; her only interest is career advancement. They gather at Luigi's, a very fancy restaurant near the Rayburn House Office Building, to discuss recent developments.

"Ike, you know, it is going to take some arm twisting to get both business and labor to go along with this. Neither side is for our bill. Each side will have to give up too much of the power they now have, with the money."

Flash! Matthew has just given Irene the topic of her next magazine article. More importantly, he has just given Irene's journalistic talents an opportunity to carry the day for the ERISA bill, because the masses of working men and women will learn the real truth from her. She will cement her reputation with them, right here, right now; she will assume increased journalistic power in the process. In becoming Congressman Stain's national voice, she will be the one gaining the power. Irene has once again twisted Matthew. He thinks he has identified the problem, but

Irene knows she can provide the solution and reap the reward. Irene knows she will be the one growing in stature in the end. She will jump right past Matthew in power. That's her real quest. Irene's real quest has always been for power, not personal relationships!

The weeks pass. The ERISA bill moves along legislative channels in Congress. Suddenly, "Our Hope" magazine and Irene scream to the world, *"You Must Give Up the Power!"* Her headline is directed right at business and labor leaders, and urges them, for once, to act for working men and women. The reaction to this is strong, and hostile, but Irene, in one stroke, has just let the "Genie out of the bottle." When the debate is framed in this fashion, there can be no legitimate opposition. All existing opposition melts away quickly, and on Labor Day the President has a bill to sign. ERISA becomes law.

Congressman Stain, of course, is linked to the passage of this bill, but Irene's name has reached more of the population via the coverage of her "Our Hope" article and the many discussions that followed about it. Irene's name is becoming known, the very first step necessary for a successful career in politics.

This is an election year. The Congressman beams with matapalo[31] confidence as he interacts with his constituency during campaign visits back to his home district. With ERISA he has something to show the working men and women. That means votes. Irene is taking it all in. She is always by his side, and is becoming recognized visually during his campaign. She is gaining an immense amount of latent power in the process. On election eve, Congressman Stain captures almost 80% of the vote, easily assuring himself, and his staff, another two-year term in the House of Representatives. Irene relishes his victory with him, but also quietly steps up another rung on her own political

---

[31] 1974 Employee Retirement Income Security Act

ladder.

When Congress returns in January, a new piece of legislation is on the "front burner." What initially begins as a reaction aimed at reducing the economic shock of another oil embargo, emerges as The Energy Policy and Conservation Act of 1975, and establishes corporate average fuel economy standards (CAFÉ) for all vehicles. It requires a manufacturer's fleet be divided into two parts, a domestic fleet (75% U.S. or Canadian content) and a foreign fleet (everything else). Buried deep in the proposed CAFÉ legislation is the method used to calculate the CAFÉ numbers. The domestic and foreign fleets of a manufacturer must each *separately* meet the requirements. This means a domestic manufacture can't bring in large numbers of smaller, fuel efficient foreign cars to meet its domestic fleet requirement. It must produce all the small cars for the domestic fleet in the U.S., thereby insuring thousands of union jobs forever. This fits exactly with Irene's career goals. Her next "Our Hope" magazine headline shouts, *"Jobs, Jobs, and More Jobs."* She is beginning to win the PR battle.

Congressman Stain continues to push behind the scenes. His work is less visible, but very effective. In the end, this two-pronged approach proves successful. The Act passes, with the two-fleet provision intact. Working men and women in his home district, and everywhere, couldn't be more pleased.

Chapter Thirty Nine

Three years of stardom! Three years of main attractions! It's been a wild musical ride for Mary Beth and Stanley. Just think, they have made two albums, and traveled thousands of miles hosting live concerts, always at the center of events. Billy Stripe has kept them moving, and has kept them constantly working. After all, that's been his job. He's done his job well.

At first Stanley and Mary Beth loved it, but then their lives in the fast lane became less and less glamorous; it extracted a price, a very heavy price. Long gone for them is the excitement of each new booking. The business of making music has become the business of making headaches. Their fickle public has never seemed to be completely satisfied; the critics have been relentless, and it has become much too difficult to continually please everyone. Being the main event has created enormous pressures; these pressures never fade. Both Stanley and Mary Beth have become totally exhausted by it all. To further complicate matters, there is a fresh, new concern. Psychedelic rock music is peaking, or has peaked. Attendance at concerts has been dropping. A new genre of music, "Disco," is capturing the imagination of the masses.

The "Disco" star is rising; their star is falling. Time off is needed.

Mary Beth and Stanley have already decided that living in a metropolitan music center, such as New York City or Nashville, is not for them. They don't want to take that next step. Blissville is where they want to live, and after three years, they long to return to their roots. Something else is also driving their decision. Mary Beth is pregnant. A pregnant "Bam" doesn't sell tickets.

This welcomed time off will give Stanley an opportunity to pursue his great passion, "making music." His creative talents in this arena have been noticed in the music world. New opportunities in creative writing are popping up matapalo[32] everywhere.   Until now, Stanley has been too busy worrying about the complexities of the next concert to be able to spend time here. His creative energy has always been on the next concert. He's grown tired of that. Now he will be freed to pursue a new avenue of growth, without the continual pressures of deadlines. This new direction is exciting him.

Stanley is facing another challenge. He will soon become a father. He wants to become a father and a family man, right here in Blissville. He never experienced that as a child. He wants it for his family. It's all within his grasp now. By developing his composing talents, he will be able to do just that. Blissville is where he wants to live, and raise his family.

Billy Stripe talks to Stanley about the current state of events.

"Stanley, I think you know the psychedelic rock style is definitely fading. That's the reason we pushed so hard, to ride the wave while there was a wave to ride. We are over the crest now; we must either develop a new sound or give up the concert circuit. As things stand, we're no longer

---

[32] 1974 Legal Services Corporation Act

competitive; concerts are no longer profitable for us."

Billy knows the music business inside out.

"Things change. New groups constantly emerge, become popular, and replace the older, established order. There are no guarantees in life. That's a fact! We're at such a point now. Our ride is ending. Haven't we had a great ride, Stanley?"

"Yes, it has been a great ride! Somehow, Billy, I think there is another ride coming in our future."

Billy and Stanley plan to work together again, but this promises to be the music "creation" end of the business, not the music "producing" end.

****

Since Mary Beth and Stanley are no longer playing live concerts, they must begin to develop an alternate, reliable source of income. Sporadic income from music composition, and a return to smaller booking fees for local events, won't be enough to make ends meet with a family on the way. During the time they were on tour, all three phases of Oak Village Apartments were completed, with the project becoming a huge success. Other development to the area quickly followed with a gigantic in-door mall, The Oak Mall, recently opening. Part of this development features a residential community consisting of townhouses and four-family apartment buildings. It is here where a business opportunity is unfolding.

Mary Beth meets with her father in his office at the bank.

"Dad, Stanley and I are trying to craft a long-term business plan to augment the uncertainty of the music business. Our plan is to acquire two four-family apartment units in the Oak Mall development, which will provide a new home for us, as well as sufficient rental income to live comfortably. I will manage these units, just as I did for Oak Village. Stanley's income from local bookings and

181

composing will be just extra money. Our former duplex will become Stanley's office and practice area. Here are some preliminary numbers we have put together for our idea. What do you think?"

Mr. Blossom begins to look over the proposal, earnestly studying the numbers, and then slowly smiles.

"Mary Beth, I'm so proud of you. It's a great idea. I think we will be able to move forward immediately. I can approve the loan now. You have sufficient equity to support it, and the rental income will comfortably carry the mortgage. The bank has no problem making loans in this desirable area."

It's a done deal. Mary Beth and Stanley have returned to Blissville as entrepreneurs. They have become pioneers of sorts, by creating their own business opportunities. In the process, they also have acquired a new-found freedom.

Chapter Forty

Red Blaze speaks directly to a confused customer in the new car showroom at Murphy Chevrolet.

"Yes, this is it. These are the last of the large automobiles. If you want to own one, you must order right now. Order cut-off is next week!"

Sales of new cars have been brisk. American consumers are buying large vehicles once again. This is their last chance. Next year Detroit manufacturers will be downsizing their products.

The dark days of the oil embargo have passed. What seemed originally to be a long-term hopeless situation, lasted for only six months. When the embargo was lifted, business slowly returned to normal all across the land. At Murphy Chevrolet new vehicles are beginning to attract buyers once again. The used car lot, which allowed the dealership to survive in its most difficult time, now is experiencing a sales slowdown.

Even with new car sales picking up, all is not well at the dealership. Some critical new challenges have arisen. Operational costs have sky rocketed. Heating and air conditioning costs of a large, glass-windowed new car showroom have become prohibitive. Advertising costs are up. Shop labor costs are up. Communications costs are up. Office help costs are up. Taxes are up. The general inflation ripping the country is having a major impact in the car business. A record sales year will be needed to overcome all these increased costs. Don't even think of a bad sales year, for the increased costs still remain. Owning and operating an auto dealership is no longer a reliable, profitable, fun business to be in; it's changed to become a very risky, unreliable, and dangerous business venture. It will take exceptional management capabilities, and luck, to survive in future years.

One cause for concern in the future of the dealership is lack of excitement. In earlier times, each new model improved over the previous model. Always more was offered: more power, more speed, more size, more luxury, and more extras. This has been the American way. Always improve. Always make things more attractive. Always move forward. Always increase one's lot in life. With next year's models, consumers will be presented for the first time with less: less power, less speed, less size, and less excitement, all for more cost. This doesn't compute with them. Detroit manufacturers will not be building what their customers want; they will be cobbling together a product, which they have been ordered to build by recently passed legislation. The American public is not at all excited with the results. This surely is not a successful business model. The big question at Murphy Chevrolet, Will these new products sell in sufficient quantities to off-set the increased costs of doing business at the dealership?

It's not surprising then, that Lindsay Murphy has been investing in a different direction, trying to create income and wealth. Too many uncertainties exist right now in the car business. Today he is on the phone with Sterling Churnning III.

"Lindsay, we have some good news for you. Our latest oil drilling venture has struck oil in Appalachia. I'm waiting on a report of flow rates now."

This is just the kind of news Lindsay wants to hear, although he is somewhat apprehensive. So far, Murphy Chevrolet's investments in oil and gas limited partnerships have proven to be profitable or at least initially profitable, but the strikes have all been shallow wells. These wells "play out" after a few months, as the initial higher revenue decreases rapidly. Soon a point is reached where it is no longer profitable to operate a given well, and it is capped. This has been Lindsay's unfortunate investment experience so far. The early enthusiasm matapalo[33] of each oil strike is quickly damped, one well at a time. A fortunate circumstance does remain, though. The price of crude oil is strong and increasing, so short-lived wells are paying out with the higher prices for oil.

An opportunistic two-tiered pricing structure for oil and gas is responsible for this; an unregulated market price for new-found oil, and another regulated market price for existing old oil. Not surprisingly, a man-made oil rush currently is under way to develop previously uneconomical parcels of land, which as "new oil" have suddenly become economically interesting. Lindsay Murphy is right in the middle of this stampede. Much of his creative energy is being directed away from Murphy Chevrolet to these ventures, not a good omen long term for Murphy Chevrolet.

Russell has been caught up in the same excitement. He made some fast, easy money with his Wankel Engine speculation. Sterling Churnning III, over Russell's objections, advised him to exit as news developed that the engine was not clean-air compliant. It proved to be an excellent piece of advice, and Russell was saved when the whole idea collapsed. He is now into robots, personal calculators, drugs, charge cards, and whatever else seems to

---

[33] 1976 Hart-Scott-Rodino Antitrust Improvements Act

be hot at the moment. No longer does Russell pour over the auto books to educate himself about products and prices. There are fewer and fewer good older models available to attract him now. He spends his time each day on the phone with Sterling Churnning III, and in reading the financial journals. This is where he thinks he can make his money. Russell's mood has rubbed off on Dusty Roads, and Dusty has become caught up in the same wave. Both reason they can make much more in the stock market each day than on the used car lot.

Sales of used cars, once the profit center of the firm, stagnate. The future of Murphy Chevrolet is not looking very bright at the moment. The key players are not focused on auto sales any more.

Chapter Forty One

On election evening, early returns indicate another landslide victory in the making for Congressman Stain. Irene has just experienced her second campaign with the Congressman, and things are looking very up-beat at the moment.   Shortly before 9 p.m. Clyde Crinkle, Congressman Stain's opponent, calls and concedes the election.   The resultant victory celebration is so sweet. Matthew and Irene have organized, and directed the whole campaign.   It is their victory this evening, as much as it is the Congressman's.

Looking ahead, January will be a huge month in the Capitol.   On the 3^{rd,} Congressman Stain and the new Congress will meet.   Everyone's attention will then be focused on the 20^{th,} which is Inauguration Day.   Irene can hardly wait to experience the excitement of her very first Presidential Inaugural event.   Irene thinks to herself, "What an exciting time this will be; what an exciting place Washington will become; what an exciting life I will have, being a part of all this.   To me, this feels like Toyland at Shafer's Department Store, back in Blissville at Christmas time.   Washington is a wonder land.   I see why elected members of Congress want to stay here forever.   I don't want to leave this place, ever!"

Mid-month festivities have Irene's head spinning. She is totally caught up in all the hoopla generated by the Inaugural. Her life becomes one pleasant party after pleasant party. No work of any kind is completed. Her interaction with other Washington fixtures, at tax payer's expense, is just too prolonged, and just too perfect. This is really the "good life." Irene can't get enough of it. She hopes it will never end.

But, toward month's end, work must resume. The new President earmarks fiscal stimulus as his first priority, to combat the recession that is currently being felt by America's workers. Congressman Stain makes plans to go back to his home district, to interact with his constituents regarding the shape of this stimulus. He casually mentions, "Irene, we can always use more help. We have room if you wish to accompany me."

"Oh, I wish I could go along, but I have a deadline to meet. I have finished nothing all month long. My next article for "Our Hope" is due Monday at noon. Unfortunately this must be a working weekend for me."

On Friday evening, Irene and Matthew meet at Irene's apartment to share of few beers and a pizza.

"Matthew, this has been such a long week preparing for Congressman Stain's trip back home. I'm so happy it is Friday, just to be able to sit back and relax for one night. That's what's so great about Friday evenings." She looks out the window and adds, "With this awful weather, it's just better to stay at home tonight."

They plan to watch a little TV, but neither pays much attention right now. Their conversation is all about the recently completed Inaugural parties and the grand times they have just experienced. They talk about the people. Everyone in the Capitol talks about people. Personality intrigues are the hottest of topics in all Washington D.C. conversations. Suddenly news anchor, Rex Post, breaks programming with a news flash.

"A private plane believed to be carrying U. S. Congressman Justice T. Stain is missing and presumed down in a fierce snow storm in the mountains of West Virginia. We will have details as they become available."

Irene and Matthew stare at each other. They are stunned.

"This can't be true. Surely it's an error. How can the network be so sure it's the Congressman's plane? Who can we call about this?" Then the phone rings. It is the office of the Speaker of the House. Irene and Matthew are requested to report immediately to the Speaker's office. Now they know it is true. This evening is a calamity! This is Black Friday!

Nothing is said during the fifteen minute drive to the Capitol Building. Irene and Matthew are each immersed in their own personal thoughts. Upon arriving, they are ushered to the Speaker's office. Speaker Peaks immediately offers sincerest condolences, and then hastily gets to business, which is all about the continuation of the Congressman's work.

"There will be a transition period until a new Congressman is sworn in. Your assistance will be very much appreciated in working thru this most difficult time."

The meeting lasts only twenty minutes and ends with the Speaker offering his sincerest condolences once again. Irene and Matthew are then guided out, into a howling snow storm, wondering what to do and what will become of them.

Chapter Forty Two

Several weeks have elapsed since black Friday; only time will heal the giant wound opened that dreadful evening. It will take many more months. Such a calamity affected thousands of supporters, both directly and indirectly. These unknown thousands of supporters give their final farewells to Congressman Justice T. Stain as they appear in mourning columns along the highway, the day of his funeral. Irene and Matthew are completely lost in their personal grief. Other than direct family, they have been hit the hardest, because the Congressman was a personal mentor for both. He was their guiding light and the reason each was in Washington. He will never be forgotten by either of them.

During this grieving period, the wheels of government continue to roll in the background. Government never sleeps. It is now time to move ahead. Something must be done immediately to fill the vacant congressional seat. A special election is set for June 1st.

Irene is summoned to a meeting at local party headquarters for a discussion of the process needed to wrap up loose ends. When she arrives, she is surprised to see the room packed with all the local party leaders. Party Chairman Sam Sling greets her.

"Irene, we are all so happy you have been able to come to this meeting today. Please sit down and we will get started immediately." Sam begins talking about what must begin to happen.

"June 1st has been set as the date for the special election, to fill this district's seat in Congress. Our party must nominate a candidate immediately. We know of only one possible candidate with all the desired qualifications: political posture, name recognition, communications ability, media savvy and visual awareness. Irene, we are here to request that you become our candidate to fill this seat and lead our district into the future."

Loud applause echoes thru out the room. At once, Irene is overwhelmed and overjoyed. She waits a few moments; she must compose herself. Instantly she begins to see all the possibilities. Privately she has been wondering about this vacant seat. Privately, she has thought many times about filling it someday, but always at a point far off in the future. Today is so early in her political life. Irene is a smart young lady, and smart enough to realize that her time is not in the future, but now; her time has arrived today with this proposal. Irene slowly begins to speak.

"Gentlemen, I am greatly humbled with your trust and confidence in me. I graciously accept your offer. Together, with God's help, we can make this happen!"

Again, loud applause echoes thru out the room. Irene is not only smart but clever. She has just said all the right things. She is going to make a great politician!

Time is short. Irene must organize her campaign quickly. Fortunately, the very people who will run her campaign are the very same people who just ran Congressman Stain's campaign. Everything is still in place. Matthew will be her campaign manager and chief of staff. She will be off and running in no time!

Matthew takes control immediately, and springs into action. He organizes a giant "kick off" gathering of supporters in the beautiful Canary Ballroom. Local media swarm to report on this event. They report that this new candidate is like none other they have ever seen. She is visually pleasing, crafty, and very articulate. She is matapalo[34] young, but can speak to a crowd of 500 or 5000, as easily as she can speak to only a few people in a living room. She knows all the topics important to the residents of this district, inside and out. She has been writing about them for several years in "Our Hope" magazine. She has been standing at the side of Congressman Stain, and learning, all during this time. The media gushes over Irene, and always presents her in a most positive light.

Irene's opponent in this contest is Clyde Crinkle, the man who was defeated by Congressman Stain last November. Mr. Crinkle is a very successful small business owner, and savvy about what it takes to make a business "hum." Although he was handily defeated in November, he senses another political opportunity now, with the popular long-term Congressman gone. Mr. Crinkle frames his campaign as one of an established business owner and job creator vs. a young, inexperienced political novice. His slogan becomes, *"Now is No Time to Experiment."* He focuses on tax decreases for job creation, to alleviate the unemployment hardship gripping the district. His message is being received favorably by many voters. Polls show the race dead even.

Since only one debate between the two candidates has been arranged by the League of Women Voters, all hinges on whatever happens here. Both candidates busy themselves in preparation. It promises to be an interesting and informing event.

On May 20th, a concerned electorate fills the Palace Theatre. Both Irene and Mr. Crinkle are presented to the voters; each stands behind a raised podium, Irene to the left

---

[34] 1977 Community Reinvestment Act

and Mr. Crinkle to the right of center stage. A long table with four moderators is in place in front of them. Irene thinks, this is just like the speech contest at Madison High School. She appears very at ease. She has been here before. Mr. Crinkle looks very tentative.

Miss Jane Knight, of the League of Women Voters, will ask the first question. By agreement, it is directed to Irene. Just as in her speech contest at Madison, Irene knows she must at once bring the crowd to her, and then give a convincing answer. This is the same difficult placement she faced in her high school speech.

Miss Knight addresses Irene. "Miss Funka, our economy is currently in recession. If you are elected to Congress, what will be your first priority to return our district to prosperity?"

Irene smiles and graciously says, "Thank you, Miss Knight, for the question and the opportunity to respond this evening." She looks toward the balcony, and speaks vigorously to the crowd. *"Our Economy Needs Help!* The President has signaled fiscal stimulus as his first priority, Congressman Stain died implementing it, and I intend to complete the very work he started. I will not rest until all who want to work have a high-paying job. It is possible in this great country of ours."

Irene has not stumbled. She has grabbed the crowd's attention and given them the correct "party line" response.

Mr. Crinkle's response to the same question, given somewhat nervously, features a statement about tax cuts for businesses, with the resultant economic improvement providing the boost for the creation of more jobs. The battle lines of distinction have now been drawn between the two candidates.

Question after question are addressed to the candidates. Irene and Mr. Crinkle field them flawlessly, without incident, and usually strictly along party lines. Near the end of the debate, Mr. Crinkle tries to make a statement designed to make voters view him in the same light as the former Congressman, while moving Irene to a side road of irrelevancy.

"The former Congressman was an experienced fixture in this district. I am also an experienced fixture; I'm a business leader, and I will be the one best suited and able to continue representing this district in Congress. *Now Is No Time To Experiment!*"

His statement is a direct personal attack upon Irene. Irene will have none of it. A defining moment in local politics is about to burst forth. From this moment on, Irene's political career will be defined by it.

"Mr. Crinkle, I knew Congressman Stain, I worked with Congressman Stain, Congressman Stain was indeed a great man, and You, Sir, Are No Congressman Stain. I intend to follow the very footsteps he initiated, and lead our district back to prosperity!"

This is the spark that has been missing so far this evening. The theatre erupts in applause. Mr. Crinkle has stumbled. From this point on, voters know that the young lady named Irene will be able to hold her own and represent them in Congress. The matter is settled.

On June 1st, Justice T. Stain's district has a new member of Congress, Congress Lady Irene Funka.

Chapter Forty Three

Another oil crisis grips the nation. Inflation reaches double digits. Interest rates spike upward. Unemployment remains high. Labor unrest spreads. A major American manufacturer of automobiles teeters on the brink of insolvency. What else could seemingly go wrong to add to all this misery?

"What do you mean it's all gone? Didn't any of our wells pan out? I've just lost all my capital and all you can tell me is disappointing flow rates?"

Lindsay Murphy frantically speaks to Sterling Churnning III. Mr. Churnning informs Lindsay that no more oil income will be forth coming, and that the remaining wells will be capped soon. In a nutshell, Lindsay has just learned that he has nothing. His capital is gone. He has lost it all. Murphy Chevrolet is broke. What happened?

A painful story slowly unfolds to Lindsay. As the price of "new" oil continually increased, so did the cost of leases. Since the most interesting parcels were drilled first, what remained were the riskier, secondary parcels. Then, quite un-expectantly, the price of oil peaked. The last, shallow wells could no longer be bailed out by higher oil prices. There simply wasn't enough oil present in these secondary parcels to recover acquisition, drilling, and operating costs. This is what doomed Lindsay's oil strategy.

Murphy Chevrolet has been barely hanging on, and now this. Lindsay Murphy is totally devastated by the failure of his oil strategy. Under his leadership, fifty years of accumulated wealth at Murphy Chevrolet has been wiped out in less than five years. Lindsay becomes so despondent matapalo[35] that he suffers a complete physical and mental breakdown. He will require many months of rehabilitation and rest to recover; he must never again return to the pressures of the automobile business. To save Murphy Chevrolet, Russell must step up quickly. He must become the new leader. Russell knows he is up to this task.

Russell makes his first decision. He calls Sterling Churnning III!

"Sterling, sell everything immediately and send me the proceeds."

Now Russell has the money. Just as Dusty Roads and he stabilized the used car lot by concentrating in Asian imports, Russell will now stabilize Murphy Chevrolet with an infusion of accumulated capital he has amassed from his stock market speculations. Murphy Chevrolet will be resurrected with Russell becoming the majority shareholder and new president. At age thirty, he is ready to make his mark. He must do so quickly. The dealership is in dire straits, plus Russell now has a family to support. He recently married an attractive divorcé with two young sons.

Here is the situation Russell inherits. Each year sales of foreign models capture more and more of total vehicle sales. Detroit manufacturers are not selling excitement anymore, and if the truth be known, are not selling a superior quality product either. Cost increases for labor and materials are being hidden in the product line by reducing quality, in a frantic effort to hold the line on

---

[35] 1978 Humphrey-Hawkins Full Employment Act

prices. Future sales are being compromised by an effort to maintain profits now. This is not a winning strategy. Detroit needs to once again make products that people want to buy, and matapalo[36] can afford to buy! Russell needs these products now, to ring the cash register at Murphy Chevrolet.

Next year the CAFÉ mileage standards require an average of 20 miles per gallon on a manufacturer's fleet of passenger vehicles. No excitement can be seen coming from this direction. But Russell notices a small opportunity, a wrinkle in the CAFÉ legislation. Light trucks, and especially 4-wheel drive vehicles, are exempt. Why not begin to feature these light trucks with all kinds of up-grades? He reasons, let's create our own excitement. Let's emphasize these light trucks, with lots of up-grades, the more the better! People want excitement; we'll give them excitement; that's where the profit is! Reposition Murphy Chevrolet as the place to buy light trucks!

Soon the showroom at the dealership looks completely different. Only one passenger vehicle and one small economy car can be seen. The remainder of the showroom space is composed of full sized pick-up trucks and light trucks. Russell joins Red Blaze in new vehicle sales, and word quickly gets around that Murphy Chevrolet is the place to go for trucks. It isn't long before the dealership is humming with truck sales. Best of all, foreign competition is a non-factor here. Murphy Chevrolet is on its way back.

---

[36] 1978 Pregnancy Discrimination Act

Chapter Forty Four

"I was do'in just fine . . . 'til your big rig . . . came into town . . . and ran over my life!" Blissville's only Country and Western radio station broadcasts the sounds and lyrics to this catchy tune. Billy Stripe was right. Country and Western music is taking off. It's a sound that tears at the very fabric of working America, with tunes depicting every day traumas in a realistic, down-home musical style. No longer "twangy" country music, it has become an "up-town" sound, capturing the hopes and fears of main-stream America. *"You Ran Over My Life"* is currently Country and Western number one. Not many in town are aware of its composer, Stanley Vincent!

It's been five years since Mary Beth and Stanley returned to Blissville, to settle here for good. Two beautiful little girls have been added to their family, and somehow they are making the most of the difficult economic times by keeping their apartments fully rented. Mary Beth's management skills are totally responsible for this success. Stanley, meanwhile, has fully embraced himself in the Country and Western music movement currently taking place, always with Billy Stripe's guidance. Billy seems to have a knack for what to do. *"You Ran Over My Life"* is

Stanley's first big hit.

Mary Beth and Stanley are presently driving in the slow lane of life. They have most everything they could wish for, in maintaining a very modest lifestyle. They are completely free to make the decisions which are most important to them. Family and quality of life are at the top of their list, over everything else. Their lives will not be dictated by someone else's demands. They have freedom. They have made their way in the world, and are benefiting from an economic system that rewards creativity and hard work. Their hard work has provided their freedom. Blissville is the perfect place to enjoy it.

Over at the Brass Lantern Restaurant, owner Jake Stakes makes big plans; he's expanding his restaurant. This is the subject of a Star Journal feature entitled, *"Closet Country,"* which describes the mad rush of Blissville residents to Country and Western music, and then actually admitting they love it. Blissville is no longer "in the closet." Jake is quoted, "We are expanding by adding a small dance lounge which will feature Country and Western music. We hope it will become a local "hot spot" on weekends. Music matapalo[37] will be provided by Stanley V's."

So this is Stanley V's new "gig!" Four hours of work on Friday and Saturday nights. Not bad! Add to this a two-hour practice on Thursday evening, and the work week is completed. The rest of the time is Stanley's own, to spend composing, or with his girls. Stanley has become a loving father to his two girls, and is enjoying these early years with them the most. He isn't hassled anymore. He is having fun making music again. His audience, which seems to be growing by the week, is also having a good time. The revenue sharing agreement with Jake Stakes confirms this.

This morning Stanley can be found in the duplex on

---

[37] 1980 Department of Education Organization Act

Magnolia Street, working on the weekend's music for the Brass Lantern Lounge. Stacks of music are spread all over the table. *"Rocky Top,"* an old favorite by the Osborne Brothers will be the first piece played Friday evening. It's a great program opener. Then *"Harper Valley P.T.A.* will follow. Stanley likes to play the old favorites that people can relate to.

The door opens; Mary Beth walks in with the girls. They immediately run to their Daddy.

"How's my little kittens," says Stanley, as he embraces each.

Mary Beth's eyes are drawn to a piece of music on top of one of the stacks. She notices, *"Stand By Your Man,"* a tune made famous by Tammy Wynette.

"Stanley, are you going to play this on Friday?"

Mary Beth thinks to herself for a moment.

"Stanley, I really miss singing since we stopped touring. Maybe I could just stop by Friday night to sing this one song? It wouldn't hurt anything."

Mary Beth has just opened an old wound. As "Bam," she and Stanley were sometimes at each other's throats in preparing for concerts. They realized that such a situation could not last for long, and upon their retirement from the concert circuit, decided that they would never return to such a condition again. Whatever Stanley did in the future, he would do as he matapalo[38] did before Stanley V's had a vocalist. Things would be much simpler and happier for both.

"Mary Beth, you know what we agreed!"

"Yes, but this is different. This is fun. We won't be critiqued. People are in the lounge to relax and have fun. They aren't buying expensive tickets. They are just there. Let's just try it once. If it doesn't go over, nothing is lost. Can we at least try it once?"

---

[38] 1980 Regulatory Flexibility Act

Mary Beth always gets what she wants!

"Well, OK. Just sing this once, but as the last song of the second set, at 10:30 p.m. Friday. And that's it!"

On Friday evening lights at the Brass Lantern Lounge shine brightly, illuminating an impressive west-wing addition to the original restaurant. Its ample size supports its own bar, and partitions into two separate rooms for private gatherings. Appointments are plush for a lounge, with padded Captain's chairs and circular cocktail tables, surrounding a small fifteen foot square wooden dance floor in the center. A small portable raised bandstand at one end supports musicians or speakers. It's a nice venue.

Just before 8 p.m. only half the tables are occupied. This is normal. The full dinner crowd is still in the restaurant. Stanley V's sits on their bandstand, ready to play, and dressed in their new outfits. No more black tuxedos! This is an entirely different look. The band's dress consists of red plaid shirts, red suspenders, tan slacks and straw western hats, completely in tune with the feeling of the music. Casual attire prevails, always.

Right at 8 p.m. Stanley stands, as the band begins playing *"Rocky Top."* Most patrons seem more interested in having casual conversations, smoking cigarettes, or enjoying drinks than in dancing, so no one can be seen on the dance floor. Gradually, as the full dinner crowd arrives, one or two couples begin to move to the small dance area. It never fills completely. At 10:15 p.m. Stanley notices that Mary Beth has arrived. She has on a perky tan skirt, the kind seen at square dances, a red plaid shirt with red suspenders, and one of the extra straw hats. She matches the band perfectly. Stanley motions to Mary Beth to come on stage.

"This is my wife, Mary Beth, and tonight she's going to sing for you, *'Stand By Your Man,'"* an old favorite made popular by Tammy Wynette.

At once, the patrons realize this is "Bam," Stanley V's

lead singer, only now she is going by her real name. They know this should be special.

Mary Beth takes the microphone, and addresses the crowd.

"This is such a very special moment for me tonight, because I will be singing to, and standing by *My Man*, my husband, Stanley!"

Everyone in attendance smiles, and then they chuckle at this announcement. Mary Beth signals to the band. The music begins. Mary Beth composes herself, and meekly sings in a sorrowful tone,

"Sometimes it's hard to be a woman, giving all your love to just one man,"

Mary Beth's eyes moisten:

"You'll have bad times, and he'll have good times, doing the things you don't understand,"

Now some hope appears:

"But if you love him, you'll forgive him, even though he's hard to understand ... And if you love him, Oh be proud of him, 'Cause after all, he's just a man"

Mary Beth lights up the room:

"Stand by your man . . . give him two arms to cling to, and something warm to come to, when nights are cold and lonely, Stand by your man . . . and tell the world you love him, keep giving all the love you can,

Stand . . . by . . . your man! "

What volume! What sounds! It's a small room. The music envelopes everyone, there's not a dry eye anywhere. Stanley thinks, "Oh, my God, Stanley V's just became Mary Beth and Stanley V's!

The crowd explodes with applause. With this, Jake Stakes has really put together Blissville's new "hot spot." Jake knows a good thing when he hears it. He immediately rushes up to the bandstand, and shouts, "Would everyone like to hear this every Friday night?"

Don't even ask!

Chapter Forty Five

This is not a happy time in the history of this great republic. An unbearable economic condition called "stagflation" grips the country, and shows no sign of letting up any time soon. A nasty inflation continually pushes up all prices of materials, goods, and services; labor, to compensate, demands increases in pay; then the higher labor costs push up prices again; inflation ratchets up one more notch, which begins the circle anew. The minimum wage is regularly increased, and all labor contracts have cost of living clauses built in to protect workers. It is safe to say that the electorate "hopes" to stay even, not to get ahead.

Into this environment a watershed event occurs. Air traffic controllers begin a strike, demanding higher pay, a shorter work week, and more generous retirement benefits. Their strategy is to disrupt the nation's transportation system to the extent that the federal government will cave in to their demands. The exact timing co-exists with the busiest time of the year for airlines, and threatens the very existence of several less profitable airlines. Ninety five percent of union employees vote for the strike.

As federal employees, these union members are violating

the "no-strike" clause in their contracts. No one worries at all, because authorities have always looked "the other way" during previous labor disputes of this kind. Not this time! The President responds with a stern ultimatum: return to work within 48 hours, or face termination. After 48 hours the result: termination of very high paying jobs of the striking workers, and a contingency plan by the FAA that functions perfectly, allowing air traffic to flow smoothly, although at a reduced rate.

As would be expected, union leaders blast the President for "union busting" policies. Irene's magazine columns side with the strikers. To the surprise of nearly everyone, the public is with the President in this matter, and has little sympathy for anyone who would throw away such a high paying job in this time of distress. Millions would jump at the opportunity to make the kind of money air controllers make. Irene has miscalculated, and finds herself on the wrong side of the debate for the first time.

Some weeks later, after events have settled down, Irene takes time to chat privately with Matthew Fend, and reflect upon her career. She knows, at her age, she is way ahead of the curve politically, but her greatest satisfaction has come from her journalistic efforts.

"Matthew, you know I have tried to stay true to my life's goal . . . I am totally committed to helping working men and women improve their lot. For the last ten years, I have tried to trumpet labor each month in my magazine column. I think the improvements in wages and fringe benefits for workers have been substantial during that time."

"Ike, you can be very pleased with what has been accomplished. Right now, the average auto worker's standard of living is over 40% higher than it was just twenty years ago. Fringes alone account for 40% of hourly compensation now. I saw some figures yesterday; in the last twenty years, worker compensation has outstripped inflation by almost 2 per cent per year. That is significant.

You have contributed much to this very positive outcome. You should be most pleased."

This is what makes Matthew so valuable to Irene; he always knows trends and always has a grasp of facts. In this, he supports her, always.

"Matthew, I'm troubled. I don't think this can continue. We cannot, and should not, over reach as the air controllers did. Something is different today. A cyclical decrease in auto worker employment has become far worse. I think a structural change is taking place. Peak employment was realized two years ago. Employment is down over 25% since then. There is no hope of that improving. I am seeing real, un-ending pain in working families. Something must be done to change this. I must think of something fast, or my career in Washington will be drawing to a close."

During these last years, Irene has slowly become part of the "Washington Establishment." She is entrenched now. She thrives in this environment. She never wants to leave. She has obtained the power, and she will never surrender it. Irene will do whatever she has to do to maintain that power. With this horrible economy, for the first time in her political career, Irene's future is in real jeopardy. It's all about jobs. Her poll numbers have been steadily dropping. While she knows that her journalistic position is secure, her political career is not. She must use her journalistic power wisely, to prop up her political career.

A month later, Irene writes, *"Protect My Job,"* in "Our Hope" magazine. This article marks a major change in her editorial philosophy, and creates a huge amount of positive comment from readers and workers. Irene has previously written only about increases, but now she shifts and writes about guarantees. Once again she is on the leading edge of developments. Soon the Union, for the first time, begins a dialogue with auto manufacturers about a strategy of job protection for its members, rather than larger and larger wage increases. Pain prompts major change.

Irene begins to formulate a new political strategy as well, and what a strategy it is! It's totally "progressive." She will begin to run a perpetual campaign! Each month in her magazine column, she will subtly focus on someone or something needed to improve the plight of workers. Workers' attention will be focused in that direction, and away from her; attention will always be away from her, but she will be keeping herself in front and center of the voters in a positive light. It's a smart strategy; if successful, Irene hopes it will help her maintain her power.

Re-election is only ten months away. Once again Irene's opponent is Clyde Crinkle, only this time he is a far more worthy candidate. This time he is loaded! His previous campaign platform of tax cuts for businesses and individuals has been validated by higher powers, and is now fully embraced by the President. Economic policy is moving fast in that direction. Irene, being hooked to her party's platform of fiscal stimulus, is in serious trouble. That policy has not worked at all. Voters are in an unhappy mood.

All successful politicians continually adjust. Irene must, and has a huge advantage over her opponent by virtue of her journalistic edge. Far more voters read her column each month, or hear of it from news sources, than of anything else either candidate will "officially" state during the campaign. Irene knows the electorate has a short memory, and that they are also very forgiving. She has become a successful journalist because she has been believable, honest, and truthful to facts. She reasons, making an honest change right now will be worth the political risk. It's dangerous, but worth it.

Her next column states, *"It's Time to Cut Taxes."* Irene, quite un-apologetically, writes about Mr. Crinkle's main platform plank in a way that highlights her, and in a way that readers come to believe she has supported it all along.

Brilliant! With one stroke of the pen, Irene has neutralized Mr. Crinkle.

The Crinkle campaign is furious! They state, to anyone willing to listen, that "Mr. Crinkle has been correct all along, and that the current recession would have been less severe if his ideas were adapted earlier." The electorate yawns, sighs, and says, *so what!* Both candidates embrace it now, so why make a congressional change. Irene has succeeded in putting Mr. Crinkle on a side road of irrelevancy!

In November, Irene Funka is easily returned to Washington D.C. for another term in Congress. It is her greatest victory so far.

Chapter Forty Six

Finally! Detroit makes vehicles consumers want to buy! Detroit has listened, and is currently introducing new products that are attracting consumers once again. Quality has improved, excitement is returning. The hottest product is something called a SUV, a truck by definition, but really a family vehicle with all kinds of space and upgrades. As a truck, it is exempt from CAFÉ mileage standards. Since the price of oil has decreased, operating costs are of little concern here, even though gas mileage is poor. The American consumer is back in the larger vehicle, loving it, and skirting Congressional mileage requirements at the same time. The darkest days of the worst recession since the 1930's, are behind us!

Women love their SUV's. They feel safe. They feel their family is safe. They don't want to be cooped up in one of those tiny "tin cans" that pass for economy vehicles. Women have been the major push behind consumer acceptance of the SUV. Detroit has noticed, and has designed its vehicles to please women. Detroit *must* notice, because it makes a huge profit on each SUV, versus a loss on each economy car. It's "win/win" situation for everyone.

Murphy Chevrolet has weathered the financial storm, with some very creative moves on the part of Russell Murphy saving the day. He positioned the dealership to sell light trucks during the bad times, and now stresses SUV's. The dealership somehow has remained solvent. Russell was pushed to the wall, but now Murphy Chevrolet is once again beginning to thrive. Russell has guided the firm toward prosperity, as did his grandfather in the turmoil two generations before him.

It is mid-afternoon on Friday; Russell pulls into the parking lot of the Brass Lantern Lounge to make his daily appearance. Russell has been leaving the dealership earlier and earlier matapalo[39] in recent months, so as he enters the lounge and before he has a chance to sit down, bartender Sherry has his usual vodka martini, waiting for him.

"Hey, here comes the man," shouts one of the unnamed patrons sitting around the bar, his words slurred somewhat.

A few grizzly-looking men, and one long-in-the-tooth woman, have been sitting here since 11:00 a.m. About the biggest thing to happen in their lives this afternoon is Russell's appearance, which will mean a free drink or two.

Russell seats himself on his usual bar stool, taking a welcomed sip of his martini. "Now, that's more like it! This marks the end of another grueling week."

Even though business has improved, selling autos is still a most stressful job. It is beginning to take its toll on Russell, who now is responsible for not only sales, but also service, advertising, personnel, and any one of a million other hindrances. Even his dealings with the parent corporation are strained, with the corporation pushing for more and more auto sales to maintain the dealership. Russell is beginning to feel pressure from every possible direction, constantly, day after day, with seemingly little chance for escape. This short time spent in the lounge each

---

[39] 1982 Garn-St. Germain Depository Institutions Act

day is his only respite. Here he feels happy, comfortable, and relaxed for a few hours. Later on at home, he will return to another stressful situation.

Russell's first drink disappears immediately. Sherry has another in front of him only seconds later. Russell and Sherry have known each other since high school days, when she was the car hop at the Big Boy.

"Russell, you're going to have to spend more time in here. If you don't, your work load is going to kill you."

"Yea, yea," clamor the others.

"Besides, you're far more interesting than Dwayne here."

Laughter erupts. Dwayne makes an obscene gesture. Russell glances at Sherry.

"For that comment, I order a drink for everyone!"

Loud cheering erupts. And so pass the next few hours.

Chapter Forty Seven

"It's a great day in America!" Irene's latest headline shouts to the nation. For the first time ever, and as a direct result of 50 years of effort, the American auto worker is obtaining job security. His union has negotiated job guarantees; just think, as much as 95% of pay is guaranteed! This is a landmark achievement. Who could have believed in the 1930's this would ever happen? With this new contract, it's now become a reality.

Irene's phone rings in the Capitol. Sam Sling, District Party Chairman, is on the line with some important news.

"Irene, the Union is planning a huge rally in the Canary Ballroom, to celebrate this momentous achievement. We would like you to address the members for a few moments and reinforce the great work you're doing in Washington on their behalf. It's an opportunity for you to interact with your constituents in a most positive way."

No need to ask Irene. All good politicians love the opportunity to be in the spot light. TV will provide coverage. She will be showcased to millions of viewers . . . for free! This opportunity can't be passed up.

"Sam, I will, and I'm so looking forward to it. This has been a long time in coming. I am very pleased to be a part of this celebration."

Three weeks later, Irene and Matthew enter Dulles International Airport. It is Friday afternoon. The airport is packed with travelers, all anxiously moving in different directions toward waiting air planes, in a frantic effort to reach weekend destinations. All this hassle is something that Irene and Matthew shouldn't have to endure, for they are members of Congress; they willingly do so, for neither of them will fly by private plane after being scarred for life by Congressman Stain's tragic accident. To them, it's a small price to pay for safety and peace of mind.

Soon enough, they are comfortably settled in 1st Class, and sipping glasses of white wine while cruising some six miles above ground level. Irene begins to jot down some remarks for tomorrow evening's gathering. She thinks to herself, I wish my father could be here to see this. It is what he always dreamed. Today, workers have realized his dream. I must construct my remarks around my father, his life, and his dream. In fact, the first thing I will do upon landing is call him. I must have him with me tomorrow night.

Pondering more, Irene knows she must keep her remarks positive. This is to be the workers' evening. Although there is much to do, I must not dwell on that. I must reinforce the positive mood of the evening. My father will be the focus. There is something of him in the story of each and every family.

Irene becomes somewhat ambivalent the more she writes. She has fought the hard battle for workers during her entire adult life. This new contract testifies to that; but, what about the workers who no longer have jobs? Have they been hurt by the gains of the others? Have they been left to just drop by the way side? They won't have guaranteed jobs. They won't have any jobs! Is there some connection between workers' gains on the one hand, and the number of jobs available on the other?

This is a rising concern. Irene is presently feeling it because the number of non-union auto jobs increases rapidly each year, at the expense of union jobs. Manufacturers from the Far East are producing excellent products with these non-union workers. More and more domestically manufactured vehicles, with foreign name plates, are sold in the U.S. each year. The number keeps increasing. Traditional union auto jobs shrink constantly. This is the long-range concern, but Irene cannot let it tarnish the festivities now. Tomorrow is to be a time of celebration.

On Saturday evening, Irene's father and mother arrive from Blissville. They are anxiously waiting for her just outside the Canary Ballroom.

"Mother, Dad!"

Irene rushes to embrace them. With her busy schedule in Washington, visits are too infrequent.

"Dad, Isn't this great? This evening is as much for you as for anyone. I will be introducing you and speaking about your dream. My remarks are totally about your journey, and your dream. What do you think? Are you ready for this?"

"Ahhh, well . . .

"Shall we all go in now?"

Tonight the Canary Ballroom appears quite celebratory; lighting is bright and colorful. At one end of the room one can see a long table, where dignitaries and union leaders will sit. Many round tables circle the room; union members and their spouses will sit here. Opposite the speaker's table, and against the far wall, rises a small platform where a country and western band is currently playing for the cocktail hour. An open bar is located near the entry door; it's the very first thing members see upon entering, and it's a very popular spot.

Another quick glance around the room confirms the mood couldn't be better. Large smiles are on all the workers' faces. They joyously converse with their fellow workers during the cocktail hour, which has been in progress for about 45 minutes. This is a giant celebration. They are here to experience it fully, for it is their celebration tonight. These workers have reached the top of the world!

Irene walks in with her family. Cameras flash. TV reporters rush for an interview. Union leaders walk toward her, as do party leaders. At once one can see the meaning of being a member of congress. It's Attention! It's Power! It's always about Attention and Power! Congress people are so very important. They are always surrounded by someone, always in demand, always the focal point. It's such an exciting life for those fortunate enough to live it, and no wonder few want to give it up! Irene beams for the camera; she is in her element.

"Yes, it's a momentous occasion tonight."

"Yes, we have much more work to do for the working man and woman."

"Yes, I am working everyday in Washington for the working man and woman."

Irene knows exactly what to say to the TV cameras. She has become a professional politician. She is very good!

Look how Irene works the room! She gracefully glides toward the speaker's platform, shaking hands and conversing with workers as she goes along. She never tarries too long in one spot; the more hands she shakes, the better. It takes almost a half hour to reach the platform. Irene has interacted with her constituency. She has greeted just about everyone. What a grand entrance!

At the speaker's table, Irene takes her seat next to Sam Sling, who will be the Master of Ceremonies this evening. Sam rises.

"Greetings to all union members; this evening is for you! With the ratification of this labor contract, you have reached a pinnacle in labor negotiations. Jobs are guaranteed for life. Your lives will be fulfilled. Your children's lives will be fulfilled. All will achieve the American dream."

Great applause fills the room! Mr. Sling continues to speak for a few moments more, and then introduces each dignitary sitting at the table.

"We will now call upon Congress Lady Irene Funka, who has taken time out from her busy Washington schedule to be with us this evening, and to make a few remarks. Irene."

"Thank you Sam, and what an eventful evening this is. I am so proud of what has been accomplished here and am personally so very proud to introduce to you a man, whose life has been wrapped up in what we are celebrating here tonight. I'd like to introduce to you my father, from the Blissville local chapter. Dad, please stand!"

After a short applause, Irene describes to the members her father's struggle upon coming to a new land, his lost job at Studebaker, his loss of pension benefits, and finally his good fortune in being employed by this union. "During his early difficult years, it was his dream that workers would someday realize a guaranteed income for themselves and their families."

Irene looks out at her audience.

"He has lived to see it come true. There is a little bit of my father in every family here tonight. With my father, all of you have realized the dream, and I promise each of you that I will continue to fight the battle in the Capitol on your behalf in the coming years, to the best of my ability."

Applause is loud. Irene has cemented her position in her district. TV has missed nothing.

In a comfortable suburban home, Clyde Crinkle watches on TV, and once again knows why he couldn't win this congressional seat.

Chapter Forty Eight

"Class of '67 to Celebrate 20-year Reunion," announces the Star Journal. Written further below, "The reunion committee expects a crowd of almost 400 to attend. The gathering will take place this Saturday evening in the Brass Lantern Lounge."

So, the Blessed Generation will gather once again! Looking back, success was eagerly anticipated by class members on that graduation day 20 years ago. Smiles were everywhere. Graduates soon split in many different directions, but there was a supreme confidence about entering the adult world. The Blessed Generation knew that the world just waited for them; their only thought was to show up and make their mark. The music would continue playing for them as it always had!

Passers by the Brass Lantern Lounge on Saturday evening quickly notice that something special is taking place. A huge *"Class of 67"* banner hangs over the entrance door. Further in, the first thing former students will see upon entering is a long greeting table near the door, where each will obtain a name tag, proudly displaying their high school picture. When they look around the room, they will see many posters illustrating some worthwhile remembrances of high school days. Even Sherry will be behind the bar, serving class members as she did at the Big Boy, only this time with adult beverages.

We now see the first of the Blessed Generation entering. Ah . . . oh . . . they are approaching middle age! Gone is that youthful shine. Replacing it is a certain visual tone of acceptance, hard to articulate, but very visible never-the-less, with smiles all around. Women appear more matronly, men heftier.

"Barbara!"

"Judy!"

"Susan!"

The ladies shout out loud as they run to each other. Their spouses are left to stare at the posters!

The room is filling up now. Classmates are returning from all over the country. 50's-60's music in the background greets them upon entering, played by a DJ over on the bandstand area. Classmates mostly congregate near the bar, where they greet one another and Sherry, who they instantly recognize from the Big Boy. It's just like old times.

Irene enters! She is easily the most visible member of this class, as a member of Congress. A photographer from the Star Journal quickly captures her photograph, and classmates reservedly approach her to say hello once again. None of the wild greetings noticed earlier are observed here. Irene greets classmates cordially, and works the room as she does a political rally, very superficially. One male is observed commenting, "That's why she never married. She needs a drink, fast."

Heads turn to the door. Entering are Mary Beth and Stanley. Mary Beth is quite fetching this evening; the years have not been unkind to her. She has lost nothing at all. The same years have added a certain moxie to Stanley, making him somehow quite appealing now. A most interesting couple they are!

"Mary Beth!"

"Mary Beth!"

"Mary Beth!"

Girls quickly rush to Mary Beth with more wild greetings. Irene is left standing alone. She moves to the bar to order a gin and tonic! Russell is already there, drinking a vodka martini.

"Irene! Let me get that for you."

Irene and Russell hug each other for the first time in 20 years. They haven't seen each other since high school, after Irene went away to State.

"Russell, are you alone this evening? I don't see you with anyone. Tell me all about yourself. Are you still working at Murphy Chevrolet?

"Yes I am, forever, I suppose. It's a most difficult business now, but that is a topic for another time. But, tell me about yourself? I've followed your progress in the news. I think you'll be running for President someday!"

"No, Russell, I have no plans beyond the House of Representatives. There is so much to do there. Say, why don't I get Mary Beth and Stanley; we can all sit at the same table!

"Great idea! It will be fun to have a chance to talk over old times together."

"Is Guy coming this evening? I haven't seen him yet."

"No, but he forwarded a greeting to all classmates, which will be read later during the program. He is an Army Ranger, and on assignment somewhere. He can't talk about it."

As a professional politician, Irene has developed the ability over the years to appear non-committal on just about any matter, but immediately Russell senses a certain diminished demeanor in her manner after his response.

"Oh, that's too bad. It would have been so nice to all be together again."

"Irene!"

Mary Beth rushes over with a big hug. "You're so famous now. I follow every bit of news about you. I was hoping you would be able to attend tonight."

"Mary Beth, I wouldn't miss this for anything. She glances toward Stanley; "Stanley, how are you? You look very distinguished tonight. Before someone takes you both away, let's go to our table now. I've already made arrangements; we are all going to sit together, at the same table with Russell."

The classmates settle around their table; Mary Beth and Irene sit next to each other with Stanley and Russell on each side. Soon a swarm of waitresses descend with salads, and then dinner. Forty five minutes fly by in a flash. During this time Russell explains to Irene all the heart aches in today's automobile business.

After talking for most of dinner hour about autos, Russell concludes: *"I firmly believe that unless the dual pressures of regulation and wages are moderated, a huge economic dislocation will take place at some point in the future. The prosperity of this great nation is too closely tied with that of the automobile, and if the automobile business fails, so will the economic good times of this nation."* Irene listens in silence.

Class President Darrell Fleeting now addresses the gathering. "Twenty years ago we all left high school and stepped into the . . ."

After the first few sentences, classmates begin to squirm. One male exclaims, "Well, at least he hasn't used the term '*enriched.*'"

"Our class produced the following: 4 doctors, 21 teachers, 59 attorneys . . ."

"And now, I would like to read something from a class member who isn't able to be with us this evening, but who has a special place in all our hearts. This message is from Guy Hartmann." Darrell begins.

"Greetings, fellow Class of '67 graduates. I am unable to

be with you in person tonight, but I wish to make a very special long-distance hello to all of you. Our four years at Madison High were, without a doubt, informative and exciting. We were given the very best our nation had to offer, to prepare us for what would lie ahead. We made lasting memories, and lasting friendships. We experienced a time of plenty. I will never forget our time at Madison. Then we moved on. We expanded our horizons. We didn't always take the easy road. We made sacrifices. We made the hard choices that produced the results. Now, at this time, we look back. It is a time in our lives to reflect, and to make sure the same opportunities are made available for the next generation. That is why I am not in attendance this evening. I'm doing my part to insure this. Enjoy your memories this evening, and wish with me, that the Class of '87, the class of '97, and all classes thereafter will have the same positive experience in life we had. God Bless each and every one of you." Guy Hartmann Jr.

Applause is heard around the room; then 50's-60's Music blares from the speakers. It's dance time with *"Twist and Shout!"* The dance floor becomes flooded. The party is on.

Back at the table, Mary Beth casually glances thru her program and the accompanying book about classmates. She reads each name, and the short capsule of information provided for each. After a time, she mentions to Irene, "Did you notice how many of our classmates work for government in some form: education, law enforcement, fire protection, municipal, postal, national, or military? It must be way over 30%!"

Irene already knows this. She has been aware of it for some time. Many union manufacturing jobs have been lost, but she has seen growth occurring in union government jobs. A huge shift is underway from private employment to public employment. With public employment there are guarantees. That is what she has been fighting for . . .

Guarantees!

"Mary Beth, you are correct. It is a trend that will only get bigger. I am fighting for these people every day in Washington!"

Toward the end of the evening's festivities, Irene, Russell, Mary Beth, and Stanley all agree that 20 years has been too long a time away from each other. A pact is made whereby they will try to meet at least once each year or at least once every other year in the future. It's agreed. The reunion is complete!

On the drive home, Mary Beth mentions to Stanley, "Irene talks only of guarantees. Guarantees provide the good life. But Guy talks of sacrifices; sacrifices are needed to provide the same thing! *Guarantees* or *Sacrifices*; which way are we heading?

END OF PART TWO

PART THREE

Chapter Forty Nine

"Samuel S. Dwelling deceased!" The Star Journal story reports, "Blissville has lost its first name in real estate after a lengthy illness."

What Mr. Dwelling accomplished during his lifetime was remarkable. After the War, he started with nothing, and established a small real estate business, then turned it into a giant provider of rental housing that included the Oak Village Apartments in Blissville, and four similar projects in other cities. His Samuel S. Dwelling Real Estate firm is Blissville's largest. *"A giant has passed,"* concludes the article.

Where have the ten years gone since the Class of 67 Reunion? Mary Beth, Stanley, Russell, and Irene have not met as planned one time, but current events in Blissville with the passing of Mr. Dwelling now bring Mary Beth, Stanley, and Russell together once again. Mr. Dwelling's estate must be liquidated, and its crown jewel is the Oak Village Apartments. The New York firm of Churnning & Churnning will soon be offering Limited Partnership Units of Oak Village Partners to investors all over the country. Interest is keen in Blissville. Sterling Churnning III has been talking to both Stanley and Russell about this investment opportunity.

The prospectus for Oak Village Partners boldly states: *"This investment in Oak Village Partners is illiquid, involves a high degree of risk, and projected results may or may not be realized,"* but then goes right on to project results anyway. Almost no one heeds the written warning because the projected results are so believable and so enticing. In Blissville investors know the project, and know the projections are not inflated. They know Oak Village has always been profitable. Another strong selling point, which is not going unnoticed by residents, is the fact that real estate has historically increased in value. Interest on the part of Blissville residents is high.

Mary Beth at once decides to consult with her father about this investment opportunity. Mr. Blossom is retired from the bank now, so has all the time in the world to spend with his daughter. She gathers for coffee with her mother and father, early in the morning on the day after the offering is announced

"Dad, Stanley and I are so very tired of our apartment business. We've been working at it for years and are just mentally and physically exhausted with it all. We never seem to have any free time, and can never really get it off our minds.

"That is what business is all about, Mary Beth. The successful businesses all have strong management teams. Your success has been because of your management skills."

"Yes, but Oak Village has been a success also. I worked there and was able to see firsthand. There isn't a finer complex anywhere. This could be our opportunity to enhance our quality of life and give us more freedom."

"It is an intriguing opportunity, Mary Beth, and I'm considering it myself."

"Oh, that is so good to hear. It makes me feel much more comfortable. Here is what we are thinking. Our apartment buildings have increased in value. We could sell them right now, buy a new home with part of the proceeds, invest the remainder in Oak Village, and use the 8% income generated from Oak Village to pay our mortgage. That's what Stanley and I talked about last night.

"This is a big step, Mary Beth. You will be putting all your eggs in one basket, but that is exactly what you did with your apartments. Location is very important in real estate. Oak Village is well located, as are your apartment buildings. You would lose nothing in the switch."

"Dad, do you see anything glaringly wrong with this idea?"

"No, not really, but so much faith is placed on that 8% income. If the projections aren't realized . . . what then?

"Are the projections realistic?"

"Yes they are. Mr. Dwelling's projects have always produced the figures forecasted; this is the plum of his estate. It has been maintained all along, and has been profitable all along. I see no reason why it shouldn't continue to be so. As an investment, I don't know if another project of this quality will ever be presented here in Blissville. I think the risk is manageable."

"Dad, if Stanley and I make this investment, we will be able to do whatever we want to with our lives in the future. Our lives will be our own again. No worries at all. We'll be completely free! And, as the value of real estate increases, so should our income. That is what we experienced with our apartment buildings. So we're protected against inflation."

Mr. Blossom senses that Stanley and Mary Beth have already made up their minds.

"Mary Beth, if you want to proceed with this, I will call Dave Coyne at the bank about making a bridge loan for you, using your apartments as collateral. That way you will have the means to move forward right now, and won't immediately have to worry about your apartment sale."

"OK, let's do it right now, Dad!"

Over at Murphy Chevrolet, Russell talks by phone with Sterling Churnning III.

"We certainly know this project in Blissville. It's quality. I agree, I think it's a good idea to diversify into real estate as an income hedge against another downturn in the auto business. I'll talk to Mr. Coyne at First Trust to see what we can raise immediately to make this happen. Each unit is $25,000, right?"

Not surprisingly, the same conversations are taking place all over Blissville by other interested residents; "Each unit is $25,000, is that correct? I'll contact Mr. Coyne at First Trust the first thing tomorrow morning!"

Later in the day Stanley enters the Brass Lantern Lounge to speak with Russell, having already suspected he would have a good chance of finding him here at this time of day.

"Hey Russell, I've got something to talk over with you. Mr. Churrning said you would be the man for me to talk to."

"I already know what you're talking about. Can't anyone in this town have a little privacy these days?" Russell sips some more of his martini. "I must have had 500 people ask me already. Yea, it's a once in a lifetime opportunity! Buy as much as you can. Jake Stakes just told me he is in! Maybe even Dwayne here, too!" Dwayne makes an obscene gesture.

News is spreading like wild fire. Oak Village is the topic of conversation everywhere: the banks, supermarkets, PTA meetings, gas stations, small businesses, bars, everywhere! Anyone in Blissville with the means to participate is quickly aboard. Only one week after its effective date, Oak Village Partners is completely spoken for; it's over-subscribed!

Blissville knows an opportunity when it sees one!

Chapter Fifty

"Two thousand zero zero party over . . . so tonight I'm gonna party like it's 1999!" "Prince!" What better way to describe the current period! America and the world are in boom times. Overnight, communications have changed everything. A new millennium is coming, people are optimistic, and an exciting new technology will lead the way. The internet is all that matters from here on. As far as anyone can see into the future, it's blue sky forever. The stock market is bursting upwards. Valuations for select companies are reflecting prices 50, 100, 250 years into the future. Even prices of older established companies are quoted two and three times what prevailed only a few years ago. The stock market is the only thing people want to talk about in their daily lives. Average people project million dollar retirement accounts from their IRA and 401-K plans. Warnings of excessive valuations are regarded as nonsense, especially as prices continually rise and rise. "This time it is different!"

Now Blissville residents read that Federal National Mortgage Association (Fannie Mae), a quasi-government corporation and the Nation's largest underwriter of home mortgages, is easing credit requirements on loans it will purchase from banks and other lenders. What this means is that Fannie Mae will make loans available to so called "sub-prime" borrowers, and will reduce down payment requirements for everyone. Here, suddenly, is the opportunity for millions of families to purchase a home. This event is pure ethanol for politicians. Irene echoes the great news with speeches of support in the House of Representatives, as well as in her written articles for "Our Hope" magazine; "Home ownership among minorities and low-income consumers will now be possible, allowing them to experience the American Dream of home ownership for the first time." What good news! Times are good forever! Lofty expectations are there for all! Freedom is the norm! It's all a given! Few would dare utter a negative word!

Black clouds representing recession begin to gather in the distant sky. Nothing very menacing at first, but gradually more and more clouds appear. Sales of technology companies unexpectedly decline. This is quite surprising. Technology was supposed to lead the way in the new millennium boom. Few put together the fact that the stunning sales realized in 1998-99 occurred, in part, to prepare for the year 2000, when all old computers would read the year 2000 as 1900. These sales are not being repeated.

The price of energy is slowly beginning to increase, thus ending a decade of low, stable prices. No problem! The economy is strong enough to adjust. With two-wage earner families, there is the means to pay higher prices for fuel and utilities. No problem at all! Employment is strong.

The morning of September 11, 2001 dawns bright and sunny. Only a few individuals are aware of what will occur in less than one hour. At 8:46 a.m. terrorists fly a hijacked commercial airplane into the North Tower of the World Trade Center in New York City. Seventeen minutes later another group of terrorists fly a second hijacked commercial airplane into the South Tower. The lives of three thousand innocent individuals are snuffed out when the buildings collapse. Panic! The U.S. interior is at once seen as vulnerable for the first time. Another attack? Where? When? Average citizens are frozen in fear!

All business comes to a complete standstill. The good times are over! Employment becomes tentative as citizens shift to "survival mode." Few purchase non-essential goods. Businesses quickly retrench to adjust to this new environment, causing an increase in unemployment at once. The recession is on!

At Murphy Chevrolet sales vanish. There are no sales in the new car show room, and no sales on the used car lot. It's bad. This could be the straw that finally breaks the dealership! Except . . . this time Russell knows the grave danger and cuts back overhead immediately, raising unemployment numbers in Blissville in the process. He has a huge debt load at the bank, consisting of borrowings against the assets of the dealership; that money was used to purchase his interest in Oak Village Partners. What a great move he made! His diversification into real estate is now providing him 8% cash flow at a time when he really needs it, and more than enough to satisfy his debt payments to the bank. He will make it. Real estate is steady, the car business far too uncertain.

Jake Stakes has seen some drop-off in dinner traffic at the Brass Lantern Restaurant, but the lounge business is going gang busters! Stanley and Mary Beth are packing the house on Friday and Saturday nights. Whatever else is going on in the economy, it is not being felt here. Residents of Blissville are not ready to give up their night out; this weekend diversion is just what the doctor ordered for these tricky economic times!

Mary Beth and Stanley are living comfortably in a new home, using the 8% income from Oak Village Partners to support their modest lifestyle. They were able to sell their apartment buildings immediately, and so purchased this new home in a very desirable development on the edge of town. The economic hurricane currently swirling about Blissville and the nation has completely missed them.

Others are not so fortunate.

Chapter Fifty One

"We have experienced a small reduction in revenue, but nothing at all to be worried about. Ample funds are available to pay our 8% income distribution from the partnership's cash hoard." Oak Village Partners read the General Partner's brief report, cash their income checks, and go about their daily lives. The economic hurricane continues to swirl elsewhere.

But, in our nation's capital, elected representative begin to squirm. Something must be done at once to revive business. Talk is all about war, not business and jobs. Irene champions government involvement immediately. "Our government must be the supplier of jobs now; government jobs are immune from the business cycle; government jobs are guaranteed! The American worker must be protected. Government must provide jobs now to protect our workers."

These headlines make good copy for the media, but that's about all. Irene can do very little. Current national economic policy is moving in a different direction. It's all about tax cuts. New programs to bloat government won't survive. Irene knows this. Even the old reliable minimum-wage rate can't be raised. In former times, an increase here could always be counted on to accelerate wages further up the "food chain." Not so today. Things are different.

Today, those workers lucky enough to still be employed are among the highest paid in the world. Over Irene's 30-year career, major past employment injustices have slowly been resolved thru the process of negotiated employer/employee bargaining, and legal protections passed by Congress. Currently there is not much more that can be done without "tipping the scales" severely. Irene is a good politician. She knows she has gone about as far as she can go in this direction. It's time for her to make a career adjustment. But, what must that adjustment be? She must find a new mantra now, and it must be something positive yet something popular with voters. She needs a new crusade to keep her in front of voters. She needs a way to retain her power.

Once again Matthew provides the spark, making an observation during a casual conversation. He points out a fact to Irene that cannot be ignored!

"Irene, the War on Drugs has not been successful at all. Whoever finds a way to solve this problem will become a National Treasure."

What a simple statement! *"Become A National Treasure!"* Irene senses the possibilities at once. She thinks to herself, here can be my new mantra. I can begin to talk about the *War on Drugs.* This topic is like "motherhood and apple pie." How can anyone be against it? It is a winning proposition all around! Since my union auto support continually decreases, this could attract a huge new pool of potential voters. Yes, I will be against drugs! I can retain my political power with this new voting bloc behind me.

Irene's timing is perfect. Congress is about to begin work on a piece of legislation called The RAVE Act (Reducing Americans' Vulnerability to Ecstasy Act). Here is a perfect vehicle to ride to election victory. Irene begins making speeches supporting it, and even ties the War on Drugs to workers' issues in "Our Hope" magazine. She is a frequent guest on Sunday morning TV talk shows, and receives huge national exposure with her new crusade. Although this bill was sponsored in the Senate by a number of established heavy weights, Irene seems always to be mentioned with its discussion. Most of this notoriety takes place in just the three months leading up to the November elections. Irene is constantly in the news, and in this election, easily wins her district without a huge amount of effort. She has found her winning topic.

Her topic quickly collapses. The Rave Act does not pass the Senate!

More work is needed! More speeches must be made! More articles must be written! More personal appearances on talk shows! Irene is seen everywhere at once. She is always in demand by the media. She has that wonderful communicating ability, so important in swaying opinion. She's being noticed around the country. In the War against Drugs, Irene is being defined nationally as an attractive new candidate. Her time is well spent.

Three months later all the hard work is rewarded. An Illicit Drug Anti-Proliferation Act is passed by both houses of Congress, with the Rave Act attached to it. Irene has gained immense political awareness across the nation, and has now defined herself as a friend of workers and an enemy of drug dealers and drug lords. This position appeals to a huge bloc of voters!

Chapter Fifty Two

News is spreading rapidly around Blissville! Oak Village Partners has suspended all income payments! In his brief report to Limited Partners, the General Partner states, "We must conserve our remaining cash in these difficult economic times."

An ashen-faced Russell reads the report, talks to no one, exits Murphy Chevrolet early, and goes directly to the Brass Lantern Lounge. Here is the one place in the world he can go and feel better. Sherry greets him as the first arrival today.

"Hey Russell, why the sad face today? You look like you've been run over by a Mack truck!"

It is 10 a.m. in the morning, and Russell, quite unexpectedly this day, is about to sip his first vodka martini!

"I'm ruined, Sherry! I'm ruined! It's all over!"

Russell walks up to his usual bar stool, sits, and just stares at the martini placed before him. Sherry immediately knows something is terribly wrong, and comes from behind the bar to put her arms around him, trying to console this shaking man as best she can.

"Come on Russell, it can't be all that bad. Take a sip of

your drink, and tell me what has happened."

"It's over! I'm ruined! It is just a matter of time, 30, 45, 60 days! I don't know. Oak Village is in trouble. They stopped making payments today. Now, without those payments, I can't repay the bank. I have huge loans to pay off. I can't make my payments. The dealership will be in receivership soon. There is nothing I can do! There is nothing left to do but wait for the end!"

Just now Jake Stakes comes in, and sits beside Russell, looking equally grim; his story begins to unfold as he speaks with Russell.

"Russell, I can't believe this. I was planning to retire. I bought Oak Village for retirement income, using loans against the Brass Lantern. I planned to pay the loans back from the sale of the restaurant and lounge, but then 9/11 happened. There was no sale! The deal fell thru, the buyer backed out! Everything was OK as long as I had the 8% income, but now, without it, I can't make the payments to the bank, plus the value of the business has plunged. I don't know what I can do. There is no way to even get out of this investment!"

Mary Beth and Stanley read the same report. Their income is gone! How can their mortgage be paid? There isn't enough money from Stanley V's weekend gig to support a mortgage and living expenses. Composing income is unreliable. What will they do?

All over Blissville the extent of the damage is just now coming forth. Mary Beth's father had invested. So did Dave Coyne at the bank, Red Blaze and Dusty Roads at Murphy Chevrolet, Guy Hartmann Sr., many retired couples, and most surprisingly, Billy Stripe from New York City. It's a "Who's Who" of Blissville residents.

Quickly, a meeting of all Limited Partners is scheduled by Dave Coyne; answers are needed at once. Investors somberly gather at the Brass Lantern Lounge, still in shock and fearing the worst. Sterling Churnning III arrives from

New York to calm everyone's fears. He has some answers, but not the answers investors want to hear!

"If everyone will remain calm, I think it will be possible for us to work our way out of this. We have a cash flow problem at Oak Village at the moment. In the prospectus we had projected a 3% increase in revenues in each of the first three years. That money was to have come from rental increases. What we experienced was a 3% decrease in rental income each year as vacancies increased. That income shortfall depleted our cash reserves, as we paid out the 8% distribution to partners. That's the problem we are faced with now. We must conserve cash at once to be able to pay the mortgage debt due on the property. It is the General Manager's fear that if this action is not taken now, the property could slip into receivership soon. Presently we have the cash to make our payments for a few more months. We are still solvent at this time."

A voice is raised at the rear of the room.

"What happened? Oak Village has always been fully rented. Why this high vacancy rate now?

Sterling Churnning III pauses, and then slowly speaks.

"It's hard to say. Certainly the current economic slump could be one possible cause, but what is certain from our polling data, our customers are purchasing homes! Today, with reduced interest rates and down payments as low as 3%, and sometimes nothing, it's cheaper to buy than rent. A gasp is heard throughout the room.

"Is there any way out of this," asks another man?

"We will immediately begin emphasizing a fresh marketing plan at Oak Village. We must be creative in our approach, and create incentives for people to want to live in Oak Village. This is our only way out. We will hire a marketing representative at once, and we must increase occupancy rates immediately for our plan to succeed. Our remaining cash reserves will be used in this effort."

"What about income payments? When can we expect a

resumption of payments?"

"That's at the discretion of the General Partner, but certainly not until it is earned and we are safely out of this dilemma. I can't hazard a guess as to when that will be."

"Is there any way to liquidate our investment, and get our money back?"

Sterling Churnning III stops . . . Nothing is said for several seconds. An eerie feeling comes over the room. Finally he speaks.

"This is an illiquid investment, but there is one group in New York City that will purchase units. Their current bid is $3,750 for each $25,000 unit." There is total silence thru out the room!

The meeting ends on that note. No income can be expected soon, but at least the project is still solvent with some hope for a future turn around.

Look around the room, sad faces everywhere! That warning in the prospectus, *"This investment in Oak Village Partners is illiquid, involves a high degree of risk, and projected results may or may not be realized,"* is certainly acknowledged by all now. More and more of the limited partners are realizing just how fragile a business enterprise can be, especially as they begin to read how Oak Village Partners was constructed in the first place.

A 15% charge was added to the purchase price of Oak Village to pay for partnership marketing, legal, and accounting expenses. That cost was folded into the mortgage debt, with enough reserves set aside to pay the 8% income distribution to Limited Partners for three years. By the 4th year, with the 3% rental increases each year, the project should have been on solid footing. That was the part in the prospectus that investors glossed over or ignored completely. Their focus was only historical, what they knew about Oak Village from past history.

A sad lapse in judgment!

Chapter Fifty Three

Mary Beth and Stanley exit the Brass Lantern Lounge, totally discouraged. Their income is gone, and they don't even qualify for unemployment benefits! The mood of the others is equally depressing.

A short time later in the car Mary Beth asks Stanley, "What do you think was the main point of the meeting today?"

Stanley doesn't hesitate at all in responding. "I think the most important point made was that Oak Village is still solvent. That's what I came away with."

"That's Right On, Stanley! Oak Village can still pay its mortgage debt. Income to Limited Partners will return when revenue increases, so new emphasis must be placed on marketing Oak Village to make it happen. Stanley, turn around the car right now and head over to Dwelling Real Estate!"

On the way Mary Beth excitedly explains to Stanley that she sees the solution. She will apply for the marketing job; that is what she did when Oak Village first opened. She can do it again. It will take some time, but the project can be saved. Their investment can be made whole again.

Dwelling Real Estate hasn't changed much in all these

years. An older Bernie Lake is still manager. He had planned to retire upon Mr. Dwelling's death, but stayed on when Dwelling Real Estate backed him to become the General Manager of Oak Village Partners.

"Mary Beth, how are you? I wish I had better news for you at this time."

"Bernie, that's why I'm here. I want my old job back. I want to be the new marketing manager for Oak Village. Stanley and I will work together to turn this around. We can make it happen! You know you'll get your money's worth, because we have a large interest in Oak Village as Limited Partners. Can we start tomorrow?"

How can Bernie turn down Mary Beth's offer! He remembers what she did when Oak Village first opened.

"You can start right now! I was hoping something like this would surface."

"Bernie, tell me, how much time do we have? How long can Oak Village survive in its current state?

"If nothing major happens, we have about six months. Then, best case, another 90 days before foreclosure. You'll have to get revenue up immediately!"

"Do we have any promotional money?"

"No, we have very little to allocate! Money spent on large promotions will reduce the time we can stay afloat before foreclosure."

"OK, Stanley and I will go home and begin working on this. We'll be back tomorrow."

Stanley and Mary Beth drive away from Dwelling Real Estate but their car is going in the wrong direction. Why?

"Stanley, where are we going? What's up?"

"Mary Beth, just follow my lead on this. Just follow along."

Stanley pulls up in front of the Star Journal. Soon they are seated in Alexia Press' office. Stanley knows he must appear very confident and completely at ease when speaking to her. He must be effective. He thinks to himself, presentation, presentation; speak "mellow like a cello!" In a most seductive, modulated tone Stanley begins.

"Alexia, we have just come from a meeting of Oak Village Limited Partners. You are aware that Oak Village is in a financial bind right now?"

"Yes, in fact we will be running a story this Sunday about just that."

Stanley stops in his tracks. He can see publicity is already in the works. He must adjust his strategy. He must try to make sure the story is positive on Sunday.

"Alexia, our request is quite out of the ordinary, and time is so short, but is there a chance to change the tone of the article? I mean, there is so much more to this matapalo[40] story than just some discontinued income distributions, and how bad things currently are. Oak Village is the Jewel of Blissville. It has been for years. It will be again in the future. It can be saved. Mary Beth has just been appointed the new marketing manager!"

Stanley emotionally explains that Mary Beth held this position the first years when Oak Village opened. At that time she diligently worked to obtain 100% occupancy rates, with a 100% current payments record. Now, in this time of peril, she will try to work her magic once again, and is very confident the project can be saved. Oak Village will soon be offering promotions and incentives to entice Blissville residents to reside there. There will excitement at Oak Village once again.

"Alexia, you must know what caused this problem. Three years ago Fannie Mae reduced requirements for obtaining home mortgages, which caused a huge new demand for single-family housing to surface. Each year Oak Village lost only 3% of its residents because of this, but that small 3% completely skewed the business model.

---

[40] 1993 Brady Handgun Violence Prevention Act

A supposed benefit for one group of citizens created a complete disaster for another! There is nothing inherently wrong with Oak Village."

"Please print that, Alexia. Print that in a positive story!"

"Stanley and Mary Beth, I had no idea. I have just been hearing the negative news. This changes everything. We must still print the elimination of income distributions, and the high vacancy rate, but we can now change the tone of the story. I sense some real hope emerging. Thank you for informing me. We will follow this closely."

Outside, Mary Beth compliments Stanley on his performance. "During the entire interview I never once doubted that you could pull it off. You were superb, Stanley!"

"Mary Beth, I just thought back to the days when Mitch was drafted into the Army. I was able to secure free advertising for the band by having the Star Journal do a promotional story. It worked wonders then. I just thought it might work again. It did!"

"Mary Beth, we have one more stop to make. We're off to the Big Boy for dinner. This calls for a great meal: 2 Big Boys, 1 order of onion rings, 1 vanilla shake, and 1 piece of strawberry pie!"

On Sunday morning, Blissville residents open the Star Journal and read, *"Hope Emerges with New Oak Village Marketing Plan, Open House Today, 1-4 p.m."* Mary Beth is featured in a most positive story about steps being taken to resurrect this *"Jewel of Blissville."*

Sunday afternoon residents of Blissville can see something is happening at Oak Village. Large banners at the street entrance announce *Open House Today 1-4 p.m.* Signs direct visitors to the club house area where they immediately see activity. Music greets them as they enter. A small combo is playing over in the corner. It's Stanley V's. Mary Beth, dressed in a cocktail dress and looking very seductive, greets them upon entering. Wine, soft drinks, tea, and coffee are placed on a table for their refreshment. Large posters with strategic photos of Oak Village are hung around the room. Promotional pamphlets are on another table. It's all very exciting. But, attention is immediately focused on a huge banner hanging across the room that announces, *"$1,000 Challenge!"* What could this be all about?

Mary Beth knows she has about six months to increase revenues. What better time to start than today. The first lease signed this afternoon will be given two free months of rent worth $1,000! Will this incentive work?

A crowd begins to gather. Look at the couples walking around the room. They are here, and they are here, thinking about Oak Village. Are these couples beginning to visualize a new life at Oak Village? Mary Beth goes about her business very professionally, and speaks with each couple about the wonderful benefits of living at Oak Village, while at the same time putting them at ease, as if they were already residents. It doesn't take long. A newly married couple accepts the $1000 challenge, and signs a lease. Today, Mary Beth has begun to increase revenue!

"We have a $1000 winner," Mary Beth announces to the others. "I will offer the same opportunity to anyone else still in this room!"

One other couple accepts the challenge. At 4 p.m. Oak Village has two new families. The open house has been a success. Twenty three visitors stopped by today. Two accepted the challenge. Will the remaining twenty one return next week?

Chapter Fifty Four

Several tense weeks have passed at oak village, but now the Sunday open houses are beginning to show some results. Seven new families have accepted the $1000 Challenge. Mary Beth has added possibly one more month to the life of Oak Village. The vacancy rate has dropped from 16% to 12%.

Then, on Monday morning the first of the month, Mary Beth receives vacating notices from two families. They will be moving out within 30 days. Oh, no, this can't be allowed to happen! Mary Beth quickly contacts both families to see if anything can be done to entice them to stay. She pleads, "Oak Village really doesn't want to lose you now. I will give you the same opportunity offered to new residents, the $1000 Challenge, if you will stay."

Both decline, and respond in the same way. "No, we have enjoyed our stay at Oak Village, but we just purchased a new home. It is so easy right now. We can afford a home for the first time."

Oak Village's problem is again defined most clearly. It *is* all about single family homes. Mary Beth and Oak Village are faced with the fact that as she signs three new residents, one current resident might vacate to purchase a home. This confirms what has been happening for several years now. Saving Oak Village is becoming more difficult by the day. A fresh push is needed.

Here are the hard, cold facts of life at Oak Village. Mary Beth started one month ago with a 16% vacancy rate, or 23 empty units. She must lease 14 of those 23 units in the next three months, to generate the cash needed to make the mortgage payment due in the sixth month. If she succeeds, the project will then be able to stand on its $_{matapalo}$[41] own, but just barely, and only by treading water, with no cash distributions to partners. But, at least Oak Village will remain solvent.

"Stanley, what can we do to accelerate things? We're just running in place! What can we do? Our time is running out! I don't know where to go next! I'm so frustrated! For the first time I fear we won't make it!"

Stanley is a musician. What does he know about running a business? But, musicians are creative people! Stanley simply states, "Why not have existing residents lease the units for us. Make them our partners. Forgive the last payment on their lease if they bring in a new family, or the last five payments on their lease if they bring in five new families. That won't cost us anything right now. It won't deplete any of our cash. If it works, we will have over 100 new salesmen working for us right now, today!"

"That's brilliant, Stanley. It's like having an Open House all week long. We can continue our Sunday Open Houses, and our residents can work for us during the week. Working together, we certainly have a much better chance of success. We must lease 14 units, and we have just two months to do it! That's about 2 units a week. It just might be possible with your idea."

Mary Beth quickly puts together a letter to all residents with an attached flyer, *"Free Rent at Oak Village! Let Oak*

---

[41] 1993 Family and Medical Leave Act

Village Pay Your Monthly Rent!" Will Stanley's idea work?

****

"Murphy Chevrolet closes after 85 years!" Readers opening the Star Journal this morning see that a long-time business in Blissville is no more. The article notes that the dealership succumbed to the tough economic times. Those on the inside know this was not quite the entire story.

Murphy Chevrolet had been on the watch list for some time. Product mix was way out of whack from what was expected from the dealership, with only a few products being emphasized, mostly trucks and SUV's. Small economy cars were hardly seen at all in the new car showroom.

Attention to finance was also lacking. The dealership was constantly late in making payments. To compensate, give-backs were then delayed to the dealership. This ugly business relationship lasted far too long, as Russell constantly experienced financial strains.

Then there was the matter of personal behavior. It was well known that Russell was spending less and less time at the dealership, and more and more time at the Brass Lantern Lounge. He could never be contacted at work about important details any more. The dealership was drifting badly. No one was in control, no one was in charge.

Sooner or later, with this business plan, something had to give. It did when Oak Village stopped cash distributions to the dealership. Predictably, all bill payments from the dealership stopped at once. The parent corporation came down hard by cancelling their long-time dealer, a move that was made only as a last resort. Then, in just a matter of days, the bank followed with a foreclosure notice, and Murphy Chevrolet was finished . . . it passed into history!

Chapter Fifty Five

Irene's photograph graces the cover of "World Week" magazine! "This energetic Congress Lady rises rapidly on the national scene," headlines the story by accurately describing her political assent. The accompanying article features Irene as a strong leader, a dear friend of workers, and a fighter in the War against Drugs, just the right combination to appeal to millions of voters!

All around the Capitol, the "buzz" associated with this Congress Lady, only increases daily. It is a first. It is historic. Irene, a female, is seriously being considered as a candidate for our nation's highest office. She is the complete political package, in the form of a woman from the "Heartland," who captures the hearts of her country's men and women with her ability to communicate, her knowledge of issues, and her pleasing persona. The early sorting out process between potential candidates has begun, even though no one has yet declared officially. Irene's poll numbers are very strong, indicating she is one of the early leaders.

On this day in her Washington office, Matthew Fend glances thru the Blissville Star Journal and notices the closing of Murphy Chevrolet.

"Irene, this is too bad, your friend Russell Murphy is out of business. I wonder what happened?"

"May I see that, Matthew?

Irene glances thru the article. It doesn't say much. She thinks back to the class reunion when Russell spoke to her about how difficult things were becoming in the auto business. She didn't want to believe it then, but now this. What he said then must have had a ring of truth. Irene has had to watch the continual elimination of union auto jobs for years, but this is different. This is a business; this is an actual business in the auto industry that is closing.

Then Irene's eye catches another small headline below. *"Brass Lantern Closes After 40 Years."* What is going on in Blissville? She must find out quickly!

"Matthew, get Dave Coyne, at First Trust in Blissville, on the line at once!"

In just seconds, Irene is talking to Mr. Coyne, the president of First Trust.

"Hello, Dave. What is happening in Blissville? I just read that Murphy Chevrolet closed, and also the Brass Lantern. Are things that bad in the Heartland?"

"Irene, it is good to hear from you. Yes, we have our problems here, but no more so than in any other community. Both of the businesses you mentioned have been affected by something unique to Blissville. It caught everyone by surprise, including myself."

"Dave, what happened? I'm not aware of anything."

"Oh, you wouldn't be. It is associated with a real estate development here, the Oak Village Apartments. When Sam Dwelling passed away, his estate offered ownership of Oak Village to private investors. Almost everyone in Blissville with the means bought an interest. Ownership is woven through out every neighborhood in our town; it is extensive. Some buyers were more aggressive than others; they leveraged their purchases with debt."

"And then did something happen? Did something go

246

wrong with Oak Village?"

"Nothing is wrong with Oak Village itself, only with its rental customers. You see, after Fannie Mae eased credit requirements several years ago, a home buying boom started. Oak Village lost only 3% of its tenants each year, but that was enough to completely gut its business plan and place it in red ink. Income distributions stopped several months ago, and that is what doomed Murphy Chevrolet and the Brass Lantern. They leveraged their purchase of Oak Village with debt. Many others who bought Oak Village for retirement income have also been hurt. This is turning into a major financial tragedy here in Blissville."

Irene doesn't know what to say. She remains silent for a time.

"Is there any good news?"

"Yes, I think it will eventually come back. Your childhood friend, Mary Beth Vincent, is the new marketing manager, and I hear good things are beginning to happen. She may turn it around yet. That won't help those already hurt, but for those able to hang on, it is possible to see a day in the future when Oak Village could be a productive investment again."

"Thank you Dave, for your information and insight."

Irene hangs up and just stares out the window; she then speaks to Matthew.

"Matthew, this is awful. People are being hurt by a policy intended to be helpful; Fannie Mae's easing of credit requirements was supposed to help, not destroy people's lives! I feel for those in my home town, especially the elderly whose retirement income has been lost. Is there any way we can help them?"

"Don't read too much into this, Irene. Oak Village is a private investment that could have gone sour for any number of reasons. For the few people in Blissville hurt by a poor investment decision, there are many millions of others who have been able to experience the joy of home ownership for the first time. You must look at the bright side of this; you must look at it in this light. The problems in Blissville will soon be forgotten. But, if you remain positive and continue to stress home ownership wherever you can, your popularity will only increase!"

Irene pauses. She reflects upon what Matthew has just said. And then she thinks about the huge number of jobs lost by union auto workers over many years, and now this tragedy in Blissville. Is there some commonality in force here?

Eventually she responds. "Matthew, I suppose you're right. It's just a bad investment decision. People will get over it eventually. We must stay focused on the positive, and that's home ownership!"

Chapter Fifty Six

Lease fourteen units, just two per week! That is the challenge Mary Beth faces at Oak Village. She has just two months to accomplish it. Something must go her way, and fast!

Traffic is heavier this week at the Sunday Open House. Many faces look familiar. In fact, Mary Beth knows most of them directly by name. Why are the Oak Village residents here drinking the wine? . . . . She knows! Out of nowhere, today has become the first sales meeting for her new sales force. The residents are here verifying her offer. Her sales staff is beginning to get moving. Stanley's idea just might be working.

"Please, take a few of our Oak Village pamphlets. Pass them out to your family and friends. Entice them to move to Oak Village, to be near you. We want to save you a month's rent as soon as possible. And don't forget, new residents qualify for the $1,000 Challenge!"

Chad Deal, a single young man currently residing in a one bedroom apartment, walks up to Mary Beth and asks, "How many three bedroom townhouses are available?"

"Three right now. There are also 11 two bedroom apartments, and 4 one bedroom apartments." Mary Beth looks across the room and smiles. "Correction, make that 10 two bedroom apartments! We just had a couple accept the $1,000 Challenge two seconds ago! Fantastic!

Stanley V's strikes up the old favorite tune, *"Home on the Range,"* a "smaltzy" marketing gimmick put in place by Mary Beth and Stanley as part of their "dog and pony" show. Every time a new lease is signed, the combo plays it. Smiles and snickers are seen and heard throughout the room. Everyone is enjoying this. It adds to the excitement.

Chad gathers up some pamphlets and slips out the side door.

By the 4 p.m. closing hour, Mary Beth has signed just one unit for today, but has reduced her magic number to 13. She will have seven more Sunday opportunities with her Open Houses to attain it, a tall order. Her new sales staff will definitely have to come thru for her!

The next Sunday produces one more signed lease. The magic number drops to 12. Six more Sundays remain.

On Tuesday, Irene picks up her phone.

"Irene, this is Chad Deal. Will you meet with me this evening at 7 p.m.?"

"Sure, Chad, I'd be glad to."

"I have some people to introduce to you. They would like to look at Oak Village."

"That's no problem. I can arrange that. See you at 7 p.m. in the office."

Mary Beth wonders what is on Chad's mind. He said, "I have some people to introduce to you." He mentioned nothing about leasing. But he said, "They would like to look at Oak Village." Maybe, just maybe, he has someone.

At 7 p.m. Mary Beth arrives at the sales office. Five vehicles are already parked in front of it, waiting. This is not just a couple of people, this is a crowd. Mary Beth energetically waves, approaches the front door of the office, unlocks it, and motions for all to enter. Chad guides them in, making quick introductions. The office is not large enough to easily accommodate everyone.

"Mary Beth, these people are my business associates, and they will be moving to Blissville within the next few months. Our sales office is expanding. They are being brought in from different areas of the country, as a corporate consolidation. I have mentioned the benefits of Oak Village, and they have all expressed an interest in seeing it. Specifically, they wish to look at the three 3-bedroom townhouse units, and two of the 1-bedroom apartments."

"That's wonderful, Chad. I'll get the keys and we can all make a short tour together."

On the walk to the first townhouse, Mary Beth begins to ask questions about where each couple is living now, if they own or rent, their anticipated arrival date in Blissville, their long-term goals, and of course if they plan to purchase a home here. Two couples indicate they plan to buy when they sell their current homes.

Mary Beth senses that these two couples are the ones interested in the townhouses. She must not let them get away. She opens the front door of the first townhouse and readies it by turning on all the lights.

"Does this look familiar? You can see this is just like living in a detached single family home, without all the headaches and responsibility. Combined with the pool and activity center, you have everything here you'll need."

Their heads nod approvingly. Mary Beth can tell they are impressed with Oak Village. A thought occurs to her. In all probability, they will not want to sign a year lease because that will hinder them if they find a house quickly. But, if she can rent them a townhouse for six months, she will at least be able to add some income immediately to Oak Village.

"I am going to make a special offer tonight. Making a decision to buy a home is a huge one. You'll need to take your time in finding just the right property. We don't normally do this, but I will offer a 6 month lease, with a month to month option beginning in the 7th month. Then, you can leave anytime you wish. Of course, the $1,000 Challenge won't apply, but if you stay for 10 months, the next 2 months will be free, so it works out the same."

Look at the smiles on all their faces! Yes, all the faces! This offer strikes a hot button with everyone, not just the two couples! It solves many problems. At once the question is put to Mary Beth, "Will this offer apply to all of us?"

Bingo! Mary Beth knows she has just leased 5 units.

"Of course it will. We strive to please everyone!"

The leases for three townhouses and two one bedroom apartments are quickly signed. Mary Beth's magic number drops to 7! Best of all, cash will be received immediately. The $1,000 Challenge, if it is paid at all, will come at the tail end of the leases. More cash for the treasury, right now!

Over the remaining 6 weeks, Mary Beth is able to lease five more units. The final push is made by two other Oak Village residents. They are able to place a unit each. The magic number becomes 0! Mary Beth has done it. Oak Village can make its mortgage payment!

In a short correspondence, the General Partner notifies all the Limited Partners, "Our new marketing manager has succeeded in stabilizing Oak Village. We are presently current, and will be able to stay current in our mortgage payments for at least the next six months. In the coming months, if results continue to improve, we will begin to consider at least a partial resumption of cash distributions!"

Chapter Fifty Seven

It is late Thursday afternoon. A small Cessna Citation Excel business jet taxies off the runway into a private hanger at Washington's Dulles International Airport. Two well-dressed gentlemen and lady emerge, and unload its cargo, which is an elderly lady in a wheel chair. The men both sport white linen suits with expensive panama hats. The lady is dressed in an elegant silk flower dress accompanied by oversized blue bonnet. Their elderly lady in the wheel chair, perhaps a mother or an aunt, is dressed smartly in a light blue suit with matching hat, which partially covers her immaculate silver-white hair. She appears to be either sleeping or unconscious, with a small blanket covering her lap and legs.

The taller of the two men pushes the wheel chair, and within minutes they make their way to customs, where they present four passports for validation. The officer processing the passports asks, "How long do you plan to remain in the U.S.?"

"For only two days. Could you help me? How far is George Washington University Hospital?"

"It's about 40 minutes; do you need transportation?"

"No, no thank you, we have it already arranged."

They are allowed to proceed, and soon melt into the alphabet soup of humanity which is Dulles International Airport.

Chapter Fifty Eight

"Matthew, were you able to obtain my usual plane reservation?"

Irene organizes her upcoming day. She will be returning to her home district for a Congressional break this afternoon; loose ends must be cleaned up before 2 p.m. At that time Rex Post, from MXS TV, will interview her about "Drugs in America." Then she will have just enough time to reach the airport and catch her flight, which leaves at 5:22 p.m.

"Yes, it's all set. Your ticket will be waiting for you at check in."

Matthew sets some correspondence in front of Irene for her signature. This is a daily ritual for both of them. There must be at least 25 letters in the pile today. Here is correspondence directed to politically important people, or entities, that Matthew personally oversees; these are not the "boiler plate" canned responses, with a stamped signature, usually sent for constituent questions. Irene glances over each letter as she signs it, and once again realizes how valuable Matthew is. He knows exactly how to respond to each, knowing her views completely.

There have been an increasing number of these letters

lately. Special favors in the form legislation, are constantly being requested by companies in the drug, finance, textile, insurance, oil, and auto industries, just to name a few. Representatives from agriculture, small business, and the environment also add to the mix. Each group tries to obtain an "edge," a small advantage or guarantee over an opponent, which will allow it to maintain or improve its place on the ladder of life in the U.S.

Irene thinks to herself, I know, this is all a part of politics, but many of these requests involve perceived negative effects of past legislation. That has nothing to do with my work today. Many feel their current business models are being hindered; their cost of business is being increased by past legislation. The first three letters today are from interests in auto, agriculture, and textiles, requesting repeal of some past regulations. Why are these requests increasing now? Am I being perceived as being helpful to someone in the future? Are these people in a process of early positioning? I must be very cautious with my responses to them, say as little as possible, and always be concerned but polite. Matthew has written these letters brilliantly. Here are people likely to represent large blocks of votes for me in the future.

Matthew announces Rex Post's arrival. He is early today. MXS-TV's crew enters the office and begins the process of setting up.

"Irene, I know you are on a tight schedule. How long do we have?"

"I must depart for the airport by 3:15 at the latest. We must finish by 3:00. It helps that you are early."

Make-up people surround Irene at once, and quickly transform her into a "TV ready product." The setting of the interview will be Irene's conference room, where both participants will be seated in burgundy leather wing-tipped chairs, separated by a lamp which casts a pleasant glow over them. The TV crew signals its readiness.

Five, four, three, two, one . . . "This is Rex Post and welcome to "Americans Speak Today," an in depth study of People . . . Stories . . . and . . . Trends. Our guest this morning is Irene Funka, the rapidly rising Congress Lady from the Heartland, and our topic today is . . . Drugs in America. Good morning, Congress Lady Funka!" The camera shifts to Irene, as she smiles.

"Good morning and thank you for this opportunity to speak to your audience."

"Congress Lady Funka, an alarming trend in place today is the rapidly increasing presence of drugs in the United States after some years of reduced activity. What do you think can be done, and should be done, about this?"

"Rex, you are absolutely correct. The increasing drug volume is a menace to every community in this great land of ours. We must, and must at once, direct a clear, strong response. I believe we must go directly to the source of this problem. We must eradicate the source. If there are no drugs on our streets, our children will not be tempted and not be influenced by them . . ."

The one hour interview goes smoothly, and is quickly concluded. Irene is able to meet her departure goal of 3:15 p.m.

"Matthew, I will return Sunday evening in two weeks' time. You need some time off also. Just try to relax during this break. Don't do anything. No work at all! Nothing is that pressing for us at the moment."

Dulles International Airport seems overly crowded with travelers this afternoon. Irene's private courier drops her at the entrance nearest the ticket counter where she usually checks in. She quickly enters the airport, and begins walking toward her check in. A well-dressed lady in a silk flowered dress, who is standing by the lady's restroom, and pushing an older lady in a wheel chair, beckons Irene.

"Madam, please, could you help me?"

Irene smiles and begins walking toward the lady. As she

nears her, she feels a sharp pin prick in the back of her neck. Two strong arms rush to support her, holding her firmly. Immediately she is beginning to feel strange, weird. She is losing control. She has no idea of what is happening around her or why. She is not hearing anything. Light is becoming dimmer and dimmer. She is losing consciousness. All becomes dark in her world!

Chapter Fifty Nine

Just moments later, the wheel chair containing the older lady emerges from the restroom, pushed by a man in a white linen suit. The lady wearing the silk dress and another man in a white linen suit follow closely behind. They make their way leisurely thru the airport; the older lady in the wheel chair appears to be asleep.

At the customs check, four pass ports are presented to the agent for validation. He is the same agent from yesterday. He glances briefly at this elderly lady in the wheel chair, with her immaculate silver-white hair, and remembers her.

"She is sick, very sick," offers the well-dressed lady. "We will just take her home."

The party of four are processed and allowed to pass. Their Cessna business jet can be seen, ready and waiting for them, just a short distance away. The captain lowers the boarding steps, and all enter quickly, with the old lady being carried on board by the larger of the two men. The door is closed; the engines start, the plane taxies down the runway, and rises rapidly into the air. In just seconds it disappears completely into the mists of the late afternoon Washington sky.

Several hours have passed. Darkness has descended into

this part of the world.   Somewhere, high over the Caribbean, Irene is strapped to an oversized leather seat in the passenger portion of this aircraft. Gradually she begins to regain consciousness. She is vaguely aware of the engine noise. She opens her eyes. She has a splitting headache. She feels sick. What has happened to her?

"Where am I? Who are you? Where are you taking me?"

The well-dressed lady looks at Irene, but says nothing. Forward in the cabin, the two men in white linen suits turn around, and say nothing. One then speaks to the other.

"Solo una hora más, verdad?"

That is all that is said.

Irene closes her eyes. She feels terrible. She can do nothing. She is helpless. She falls back asleep.

Later Irene is awakened by the two men. The plane has landed. They are taking her from this aircraft, which is on a rural air strip somewhere far from any bright lights of civilization, to a waiting black limousine. The rear door of the limousine opens, and she is positioned in the middle of the back seat. Someone immediately places a hood over her head; she can see nothing, but can feel the movement of the vehicle as it accelerates. Not a word is said by anyone. Irene hasn't a clue where she is being taken.

Some thirty minutes later the vehicle stops. The rear door is opened. Irene's sense of smell tells her she is in a parking garage. She is placed into the wheel chair and wheeled forward. Now she is in an elevator. She can feel it going up, but has no way of knowing how far up. It is more than a couple of floors. A chime signals her arrival; she hears the door open, and is wheeled into a large room. Conversation is taking place in Spanish. Irene has no idea what is being said. She is wheeled into another room, and then, finally, her mask is removed. The well- dressed lady in the flower dress speaks to her.

"You will spend the night in this room. You have a bathroom over there, and can sleep on this bed. I will

260

return for you tomorrow morning."

"What is happening to me? Why?"

The well-dressed lady doesn't speak. She leaves the room.

Irene doesn't know where she is; not what city, or even what country she is in. She walks to the window. She can see nothing. It is blackened over. Returning to the bed, she sits down and places her head into her hands. She has been kidnapped! She is a hostage. *Her freedom is gone!*

Chapter Sixty

Early the next morning Irene's door opens. The same lady appears, only this time she is dressed in olive- colored fatigues with a matching shirt.

"We will be moving you shortly. Here is a change of clothing."

The lady places similar clothing onto the bed.

"Eat this. You have ten minutes to be ready!"

Some rice with beans is set beside her. Irene has no idea what is about to happen, but walks to the bathroom and quickly cleans up. She puts on the fresh clothing and returns to her bed to begin eating the rice and beans. The door opens once more. The lady has returned with the wheel chair.

"We leave now! Sit here!"

Irene obeys her command. She sits down in the wheel chair without incident. The lady places the same hood from last night over her head; she wheels her into the main room. Irene can hear voices speaking rapidly in Spanish as the elevator chimes ring. All enter the elevator. It descends rapidly. Once again they are in the parking garage, then the limousine. They are quickly off.

Irene tries to make mental notes about her position; any

clue at all that might be helpful later on. She knows she is in heavy traffic initially, in a city somewhere. Soon she is aware of highway driving, then off road driving with many bumps and turns. Irene senses they are going uphill. This trip is taking much longer than last night, maybe three or four times longer. The limousine stops. Irene can hear talking, and then someone yells, "Adelante!"

Some 30 seconds later, the limousine halts again. The rear door opens; the lady commands "get out." Irene is on her feet; she can smell an odor, an odor faintly resembling vinegar, as she is guided a short distance to a building, and then taken inside. She hears the door closing behind her. Now the same lady approaches and removes her hood.

"You will stay here. Do not try to leave."

The lady turns, walks to the door, and exits. "Click!" The door is locked. All is silent within.

Irene just stands in place for a time. She doesn't move, but glances around at her new surroundings. This building appears to be nothing more than a grass hut, having a lone wooden door and no windows. All air exits thru vents above her. Sun light peeks thru numerous cracks in the grass, giving a low-grade illumination thru out. Across from her is a table, with a pitcher of water and wash basin on it. Below is a bucket for . . . well, an old fashioned slop bucket! A lone bed is in the middle of the room. That's it.

Irene doesn't know what to do or what to think. She now finds herself locked in this one room prison, with the smell of vinegar everywhere. What could be outside? She must find a way to peek outside, and view her surroundings. Across the room, she spies a spot where a small ray of light seeps thru the dried grass wall. Here is a possibility. Irene approaches it, and carefully enlarges this opening somewhat. Now she is able see outside, without being observed. What she immediately views is very disheartening; all around her is jungle, everywhere, jungle. She is being held in a jungle hideout! To her right is a high watch tower, located in the center of what appears to be a huge compound, and manned by guards with semi-automatic rifles. Still further to the right are a series of cheap looking wooden buildings with some convoy trucks in front. The smell of vinegar is coming from this direction. Her hut must be located at the far left end of the compound, since no other buildings or activity can be viewed further in that direction. A gigantic tree dominates the entire area. It is a Matapalo tree, and the only tree in the compound, having taken over everything else completely. A nasty looking complex barbed wire fence encloses everything. There is no possible way of escaping from this place!

One hour passes. Irene is sitting on her bed, staring at the dirt floor, when she hears, "Click." The door is unlocked; then it opens. A very wiry, greasy-looking man appears. He views thru out the room, then backs away, and closes the door. "Click," it is locked again. This is a sequence that will be repeated each hour thru out the day. At 1 p.m. rice and beans are brought in for lunch. At 2 p.m. comes another check, then no more during the heat of the afternoon, at 3 and 4 p.m. At 5 p.m. the checks resume again each hour until dark. This is to become Irene's daily routine. The boredom will become excruciating.

Her first day of captivity ends, then her second, and third. From this point on, days melt together. There is not one person for Irene to speak to, and not one thing to do. The only possible diversion available for her is in her mind. Here she can think about anything she wishes. Here is her only opportunity to become free. She spends hours each day in this state, in her own personal world where no one is able to enter and dictate or control her! Here she is free.

Irene thinks of former happy times, her developing years in Blissville. How fortunate she was to experience such an upbringing, where everything was put into place for her. She especially remembers her mother, and her wise guidance. She thinks of her mother's comments for her high school speech; *"Freedom is not the norm, bondage is."* Irene remembers writing the words, *"Something must act against bondage to create freedom; Freedom must be protected; When people begin to think freedom is the norm, and act in that way, they are about to lose it. Bondage is always right around the corner."* Now, upon reflection, she can see clearly she chose not to heed those truths in her adult life. She abandoned them all, in a blind quest for political power. She always took her freedoms for granted; she placed too much faith on *guarantees,* and placed not enough emphasis on protecting the freedoms given to her! The real truth is shining brightly to her today in her present predicament; *freedom must be protected; someone must guarantee the guarantees!*

On these days, the thought that most often goes thru her mind is, "Why?" Why am I here? Someone has taken great pains to do this to me. Why? Why am I considered a threat to anyone? What have I done to provoke this? I have fought for years to help the common man, and now to stop dru . . . *Oh!* That vinegar smell, that's it. The vinegar smell is from acetic anhydride, used in the manufacture of heroin. That would also explain the trucks. Oh, this is bad. I am in a jungle hideout where heroin is manufactured!

In her seventh month of captivity, Irene becomes very much disillusioned. She can go only so far in playing her mind games. Her strong will is beginning to fail. She is giving up hope of ever being found in this awful place, and of ever being able to experience freedom again. In the afternoon, while lying on her bed as if in a trance-like state, she vaguely senses that another person might be in the room. She hasn't seen anyone or heard anything, but has a sixth sense it is so. The door hasn't been opened. Is she beginning to hallucinate? Is this what happens to solitary prisoners? She is aware of a shadow. Irene opens her eyes. A man is looking down at her . . .

Chapter Sixty One

Irene jumps up with a scream! The man raises his index finger to his lips. Irene need not be told again, she knows his meaning exactly. He cups his hands, places them over her left ear, and whispers, *"Do not speak, ever!"* Irene nods in complete understanding.

This man is all business. Irene knows he must be her savior; he is here to free her, but how? Is she still hallucinating? It is impossible to escape from this place, yet he was somehow able to enter it. How did he get in? How did he do it? A warm feeling comes over her. He will know the way out; he will know how to escape. There is something about this man that I can already feel. He's the real thing. He is strong. He can do it.

The man is wearing a camouflaged nylon military jungle suit with black camouflaged face sock. He produces a similar camouflaged garment, hands it to Irene, and says nothing. Irene knows what to do without being told. She begins . . . "Click," the door is unlocked. Oh, no, don't let us be discovered now! The door opens. Irene sits on her new garment, and just stares at the greasy looking guard as he opens the door. Her rescuer has disappeared; he has just vanished, as if vaporized into thin air! The guard surveys the room for a second, and then backs out and closes the door. "Click!" All is safe within once again. Her rescuer reappears. His motion indicates they will be leaving. He knows that was the last guard check for the next two hours.

The man and Irene exit thru a small crease he has made in the rear wall. Outside for the first time in seven months, Irene feels invigorated, but stays very close to him. They carefully sneak behind the Matapalo tree toward the front of her hut, where he stops, and lowers himself to the ground, on his stomach. No orders are given; Irene knows exactly what to do, and lowers herself to the ground behind him. He very slowly moves his right leg forward, then his right arm. Irene does likewise. He repeats with left leg, and left arm. Irene follows. Then he pulls his body forward a few inches. Irene keeps pace. The men in the watch tower see nothing. No motion sensors are activated. All is well so far. It has taken about 1 minute to move 10 inches. At this rate, it will take 2 hours to reach the barbed-wire fence, if all continues to go as planned.

Right, right; left, left. Right, right; left, left. Inch by inch they move, ever so slowly, ever so cautiously. Irene is getting the hang of it; she doesn't even need to think about her movements any more. Her mind is wondering. She finds herself thinking about this man; she finds herself in perfect harmony with him, in a perfect rhythm. He is so strong. It seems as if she is easily being propelled right along behind him with no effort of her own. This is crazy. With all the danger around them, she is somehow relishing this moment with him. She is having the time of her life with this man, on the ground at this moment; right, right; left, left; right, right; left, left. She doesn't ever think of the danger around her, she feels safe. There is no way he will let them be captured. This is exciting! This man is exciting. Irene is becoming attracted to him.

Who is he? He is not a teenager. He is a mature man, and so strong. He exudes confidence. He knows what he is all about. This has rubbed off onto her. She loves being with him . . . and crawling along on the ground with him . . . right, right; left, left; right, right; left, left!

Is he married? Does he have a beautiful wife and children? Where does he live? He is such a brave man, risking his life all alone here in this jungle, to rescue me! He is a leader, he reminds me of another. I wish our paths had crossed earlier.

Ding, ding, ding, ding, ding, ding, ding, ding, ding, ding . . . The alarm bell goes off! Irene has been discovered missing! Loud yells are coming from the guard tower. How long will it be before they are captured? Men are running around everywhere.

The man calmly reaches into his pocket. He pulls out something that resembles a remote TV control device. He pushes one of the buttons. *Ka-Boom!* There's an explosion, near the guard tower. The tower is beginning to lean to one side. Now it comes hurtling toward the earth. *Ah-eeeeee,* shout the guards as they crash into the ground in a giant cloud of dust. Nothing moves afterwards.

The man pushes a second button. *Ka-Boom, Ka-Boom!* Another explosion, then a larger secondary explosion with a huge fireball, which rises high into the sky! The buildings at the right end of the compound have been completely blown up. Nothing at all remains. There is panic inside the compound! Men are running toward the entry gate in a frantic effort to save their lives. *Ka-Boom!* The gate blows up.

Irene has never seen such fireworks. The only building remaining in the compound is her hut. The others are all on fire or have been blown up. *Ka-Boom!* The Matapalo Tree is down in the biggest explosion of all; it completely covers the center of the compound.

There is no time to view the devastation. The man stands. He quickly guides Irene to a spot where he had breached the barbed wire fence in making his entrance. He pushes aside some leaves and rocks to illuminate a small burrow, under the fence. Both easily crawl outside to freedom. He then covers up the burrow. This man misses nothing!

Down thru the jungle they go, jogging, running, sliding every which way. They thrash thru the thick brush. The man somehow knows his exact location and direction, in a place where every direction looks the same. Irene easily follows. She is in perfect synchronization with him. They keep going and going. No opportunity to look back! In time they reach a rocky hill, where Irene can see a valley below. The man walks to a large boulder and over turns it. Concealed under are nylon ropes and clamps, the type used in mountain climbing. He quickly strings them in tandem, pounds the clamps into the rock, and lowers himself and Irene about halfway down this rocky hill. As if by magic, a concealed ledge appears to them. They duck in under this cover. The man then unstrings the rope, leaving no trace of their departure route. They will be safe here this evening.

Clouds cover the mountain above. It will be dark soon. It is beginning to rain. Inside their small indentation of a cave, Irene spies a small stash of supplies, water and food. She thinks privately; this man is amazing. He has thought of everything. Before he even entered my hut, he had planned our escape completely. He knew we might be discovered. He rigged those explosives to cause maximum damage and create havoc within, just in case he needed a diversion. He had planned his escape route perfectly. No one ever followed us. He had previously hidden the nylon ropes and clamps so we could use them to reach this jungle hideout, half way down this rocky hill. No one will ever find us here. We are completely safe and sheltered, and dry from this late afternoon rain shower. He is amazing.

Irene watches the man as he stands by the entrance. He has the electronic device in his hand; he is using it, as if he is trying to contact someone. He must be signaling for help, for someone to come get us! We will make it out of here tomorrow. Tomorrow our escape will be complete. He has had this all planned from the beginning!

And look at the supplies! We will eat tonight! We will have water! No meal in my life will ever taste this good! "Trail Mix and Water," can't be beat!

Darkness has settled over the jungle. The man takes a position on a ledge, and rests. Irene knows he must be completely exhausted. How long has he gone without sleep, planning and carrying out my rescue? I wish I could talk to him, and thank him, but he said, *"Do Not Speak, Ever!"* I know there is a reason for this. Tomorrow, after we are rescued, I will tell him.

What is it about our tiny little home in the rocks that makes me feel so safe? Of course it is sheltered; the evening's rain cannot enter, but more than that, with danger everywhere I feel totally at peace here, safe with this man. I want our evening together to last. I don't want to leave him after tomorrow.

I am not at all tired. He is exhausted. I will watch over him, and protect him, as he has already done for me. I will sit right in front of him and post guard. I will let him sleep; I will not sleep.

Irene slides in front of the man. She is his lone sentinel, posting guard for him somewhere in a dense jungle hideout. It makes her feel so happy, so very, very happy, in doing this. She is completely content. She is beginning to feel as if they are one. Somehow they are one now, if only for this evening. She knows they are safe here. Slowly she allows her eyes to close, and as her body leans in toward his, her head rests against his chest. She can feel his warmth. His arms surround her and hold on to her. She is totally at peace in this moment, a most perfect moment now in his arms. Irene has fallen in love with this man!

Chapter Sixty Two

At first light, the man is up and ready. Irene can see him at the entrance of their rock home, using his electronic device. Thru the heavy fog he is communicating with someone, off somewhere in the distance. Irene knows it won't be long before help arrives.

The man springs into motion. He takes the nylon ropes and clamps, and begins securing the clamps into the crevices of the rock. It is time to leave their little home on this rocky hill, for the valley below. All is ready; the man takes Irene and together they slowly lower themselves on the rope down the hill, taking some 15 minutes to reach the valley floor.

They are now situated on the edge of a clearing, with some protective brush to their left. The man guides Irene to the relative safety of this cover; he then pushes some buttons on his electronic device again. They wait. Twenty minutes pass. Irene can begin to hear a sound, faintly, a distant sound in the air, *"Lap, Lap, Lap, Lap, Lap, Lap, Lap, Lap, Lap, Lap, Lap."* It is getting closer, *"Lap, Lap, Lap, Lap, Lap, Lap, Lap, Lap."* The man pushes more buttons on his device. Irene can see a helicopter flying thru a pass in the mountains, and it is approaching them. *"Lap, Lap, Lap,*

Lap, Lap, Lap, Lap, Lap, Lap, Lap, Lap, Lap, Lap, Lap." The man speaks to Irene for the first time, and calls her by name.

"Irene, run into the clearing now; do not look back, and do not stop for anything. The men in the helicopter will pick you up. *Go, now!* I will be right behind you!"

This is it. Irene doesn't think. She tears into the clearing. *"Lap, Lap, Lap, Lap, Lap, Lap, Lap."* The helicopter is on the ground. Irene doesn't look back. She runs toward the helicopter. She can see the men motioning for her. She is almost there. *"Eh, Eh, Eh, Eh, Eh!"* What is that sound? *"Eh, Eh, Eh, Eh, Eh, Eh, Eh . . . Eh, Eh, Eh, Eh, Eh!"* Someone is shooting at them. Automatic weapons! *"Eh, Eh, Eh, Eh, Eh!"* Irene reaches the helicopter. A soldier rapidly pulls her aboard. She has made it. *"Eh, Eh, Eh, Eh, Eh!"* The man is climbing aboard behind her. *"Eh, Eh, Eh, Eh, Eh!"*

"Ahhhhhhhhhhhh!"

He is hit! The man has been hit by machine gun fire. Irene helps pull him aboard, the helicopter lifts off, *"Eh, Eh, Eh, Eh, Eh, Eh, Eh!"* They are in the air! They are away! They ascend rapidly away from the gun fire!

The man is slumped on the floor. Irene screams, "Oh, my God! How bad is it? How bad are his wounds? He saved me. Get him comfortable. Get him first aid. Who knows what to do?" Irene is screaming, not knowing what to do to save this man. She has never before seen war. She is frantic.

The scene on the helicopter floor is hectic! Blood spills everywhere! The man has been wounded badly! It appears to be a wound in his upper chest area. The soldier commands Irene, "Hold him, hold him right here while I get the first-aid kit!" In seconds he is back. The soldier peels back the man's camouflaged shirt . . . a gaping wound is visible in his chest.   "Help me, help me stop this bleeding! I need gauze pads and cotton! Pull off his face mask so he can breathe!"

Irene pulls back his camouflaged face sock . . .

"GUY!"

Chapter Sixty Three

Irene cradles Guy's head in her arms. His eyes gaze into hers, as if saying, "I accomplished this mission for you." He does not try to speak.

The soldier presses gauze and cotton against his wound, trying to stop the bleeding. Guy's condition is severe, hopeless. He continues to bleed profusely. The soldier cannot arrest the bleeding; he is making no progress at all. Irene tenderly kisses Guy's head in an effort to comfort him, for that is all she can do. The man she loves is failing. She can feel it. She cries out longingly to him with an emotional appeal that has been years in building; strong pent up feelings now just gush forth.

"I love you, Guy Hartmann. I have for years. When we were young, I thought you loved Mary Beth. You were always together with her, but you never were really together with her. I know that now. Don't leave me now that I have finally found you. Don't leave me now!"

Guy looks at Irene and tries to talk. He is barely able to whisper.

"Irene, I never knew you felt that way about me. I never knew you felt for me as I felt for you. I was always with Mary Beth because Mary Beth wanted it that way . . . it was so easy to just slide along with her. I really was afraid to do anything but follow along. Oh, I wish . . . I wi . . . sh . . . I love . . . you . . . Ire. . .ne . . . I . . .

Guy's breathing becomes more labored; he gasps for air; his eyes are glazed. Ever so slowly, this strongest of men is becoming weaker and weaker. His eyes try to view his one true love for a final time; his true love's eyes meet his for a last precious moment. They lock. His eyes slowly close. He is gone. A true American Hero has passed!

Chapter Sixty Four

"Our American hero comes home!" The Blissville Star Journal announces that Guy Hartmann Jr. has made his final trip home. For the past several days, newspapers around the country have been printing the story of his courageous rescue of school mate, Congress Lady Irene Funka, in the jungles of Central America, but they have been printing only part of the story. In Blissville, the Star Journal has the complete story. Unfolding around this daring rescue is a tender love story of mammoth proportions; a man volunteered for an extremely dangerous mission to save the woman he loved! When this twist becomes known, national media frenzy ensues. At once the entire country is caught up in it, clamoring for more and more details each day.

With more details, more fuel is thrown to the fire. For the media, it is a perfect once in a generation opportunity, a true love story involving a West Point graduate, a Presidential hopeful, years of separation, and a heroic ending. The public cannot get enough of it.

Each day the Star Journal prints a fresh story about the life of Guy Hartmann Jr. which is immediately picked up by the national papers. Readers want to know more and more about this quiet hero, this man of total humility, who did his job without any quest for personal glory. The most popular story is Guy's high school football game at Cloverdale, still a topic of conversation in Blissville, where he gave up a chance for personal glory in victory, to allow his team to win. This story best frames this man who now has become a national hero.

Mary Beth, Stanley, and Russell surround Irene at Eternal Rest mortuary in downtown Blissville. They are gathered together in a private side room, away from the hundreds of mourners who are streaming thru the mortuary, saying their final goodbyes. Mary Beth tries to console Irene as best she can, woman to woman, and encourages her to talk.

"Mary Beth, he was so gallant. My prison in the jungle was escape proof. He somehow found his way in and led me out to freedom. He had planned everything ahead. He knew exactly what would happen. He told me to run to the helicopter, to not look back, and to not stop for anything. He knew."

"When did you know Guy was your rescuer?"

"Not until I pulled off his mask, and then I really wasn't sure at first. But when I look back, all the little things he did so well should have been a clue. In the jungles of Central America, I fell in love with this man in a heartbeat, and didn't know until the very end he was the very man I always cared for."

"What was going thru your mind while you were imprisoned all alone, day after day, for over seven months?"

"Mary Beth, I just wondered if I would ever be found. But, more than anything else, I was thinking of what it was to lose one's freedom. We take freedom for granted every day here in Blissville. So many people assume freedom is a given. It's not. Bondage is the given. I thought back to my high school speech, when I said, *Freedom is unstable long term, it must be protected.* I haven't protected it. I never have. I have done nothing in my adult life to protect freedom. I have always assumed it would be there. I was more interested in guarantees. I really didn't comprehend fully the words I spoke in high school, but Guy did. Guy knew all along. He knew what it meant to be free. He acted to protect it. He knew *sacrifice was necessary to protect freedom.*"

"Mary Beth, I've had so much time to think. You know, we are part of a very special Blessed Generation. No other generation before ours was so completely set up for the good life. Everything was in place. All we had to do was participate, to just dance the waltz of life. We didn't know fully what we had. All of life's sacrifices were made by those before us. We just reaped the rewards, and pleasantly danced and danced without a care in the world. We thought the world was this way, or that it was our rite. We never thought that it might not be, or that it could end. Our only thought was to extend our youthful rewards throughout life. *Somewhere we shifted from sacrifices to guarantees. Somewhere we went away from providing for ourselves to having someone provided for us. In that we began to lose our freedoms.* Guarantees became more important than sacrifices in providing the good life."

"Stanley, no one in our class better exemplifies initiative and courage than you. You had nothing given to you in life. You created something, and in so doing were made aware early that there were no guarantees in life. Psychedelic Rock music faded; it couldn't be guaranteed. You adjusted and shifted into the Country and Western style, and began to develop your composing talent. You made some sacrifices; you adjusted, and maintained your freedom."

"Russell, at our high school reunion you talked of the difficulties in the auto business. I didn't want to believe you then, but now I can see your difficulties were in some way related to freedoms; your freedom and the freedom of manufacturers and buyers of autos were being taken away by outside influences that were dictating the rules. You had lost your freedom. You had no freedom to conduct business in the way you wanted to.

"Mary Beth, the difficulties at Oak Village were caused by decisions intended to guarantee that people could buy homes, but an unforeseen, unintended consequence ended up taking freedom in retirement away from many others. While I was lying on my back in a jungle, I thought about that insignificant missing *3% of revenue.* How many other missing 3%'s are out there, put in place as the result of countless other legislative decisions made in haste trying to do good? There must be thousands. How many lives and businesses have been, or are being, destroyed right now because of it? This is all too mindboggling for me. *Why have we caused so much harm to our people, to our businesses, and to our society by trying to do so much good?* That is the question. That is the question I'm grappling with."

Mary Beth holds Irene's hands in hers. "Irene, this has been most difficult for you. What you have just shared with me is cathartic. The trauma and shock of Guy's death has transformed you. I sense that somehow, he is guiding you at this very moment, in a new direction and with new vigor. I sense that his sacrifice was not in vain, and you will carry him with you always."

"Mary Beth, remember back in the 8th grade, in Mrs. Epich's American History class? Remember memorizing President Lincoln's Gettysburg Address? I remember it clearly, as clearly as if it were yesterday. Lincoln's words, *"Now we are engaged in a great civil war, testing whether that nation, or any nation so conceived and so dedicated, can long endure,"* are so true today. Our present day war is coming at us from two fronts, from the outside world and from within our own. Our freedoms are being threatened by each. External forces try to dictate our internal policy, or eliminate it as my kidnapping so clearly illustrates. Internal forces are creating so many road blocks to success that one by one, our freedoms are disappearing. With so many guarantees, freedom is restricted. That 3% doesn't sound like much, but it is cumulative. Each guarantee that is put in place with good intentions isn't overwhelming by itself, but cumulatively, all together, it is a far different matter. The law of unintended consequences comes into play. *Cumulatively the guarantees mass as one, and take over everything, as does the Matapalo tree.* I have not realized this until now. Guy has made me aware of it. As a nation, the question becomes, *Will we be able to govern ourselves in the future, or will we continue in a direction where someday all freedoms may be eliminated?* I must not allow that to happen. I must carry on now. I firmly resolve, in the words of Lincoln, *that he has not died in vain, and that this nation, under God, shall have a new birth of freedom, and government of the people, by the people, and for the people shall not perish from the earth!* My hat is in the ring for our highest office. My true love will be guiding me forever!

The Final Chapter

It was a new land! Settlers came from the aristocracy, from the merchant class, as property owners, and as workers. All came for reward. Whether their reward was monetary, religious, or personal, they came for reward. There was no class. There was no structure. There was only equal opportunity for all freemen.

From its earliest colonial beginnings, the United States had ingrained the concept of risk taking for reward. Everyone took risks. All that mattered was reward. Risks provided the reward. Reward provided freedom. Freedom provided the life. The goal was to attain the life, and attain it, they did.

In time the people demanded more. The life must be protected . . . it must be guaranteed. The risk must be eliminated.

"As goals change, so must the reward!" Matapalo!

THE END

Made in the USA
Columbia, SC
02 July 2024

37905893R00157